A QUIET
LITTLE TOWN

A QUIET LITTLE TOWN

•A RED RYAN WESTERN•

WILLIAM W. JOHNSTONE

AND J. A. JOHNSTONE

P

PINNACLE BOOKS
Kensington Publishing Corp.
www.kensingtonbooks.com

PINNACLE BOOKS are published by

Kensington Publishing Corp.
119 West 40th Street
New York, NY 10018

PUBLISHER'S NOTE

Following the death of William W. Johnstone, the Johnstone family is working with a carefully selected writer to organize and complete Mr. Johnstone's outlines and many unfinished manuscripts to create additional novels in all of his series like The Last Gunfighter, Mountain Man, and Eagles, among others. This novel was inspired by Mr. Johnstone's superb storytelling.

ISBN-13: 978-0-7860-4438-2
ISBN-10: 0-7860-4438-1

First Pinnacle paperback printing: March 2021

10 9 8 7 6 5 4 3 2 1

Printed in the United States of America

Electronic edition:

ISBN-13: 978-0-7860-4439-9 (e-book)
ISBN-10: 0-7860-4439-X (e-book)

CHAPTER ONE

The moment tall Texan Burke Forester stepped off the steam packet *Manxman*'s gangway onto a London Harbor dock he became the most dangerous man in England . . . if not the entire British Empire.

Forester's welcoming committee was sleet driven by an icy wind that cut to the bone and, a cable length away, swept the deserted decks of three great ironclads anchored in a dredged deepwater channel awaiting their turn in drydock. A few tattered gulls braved the elements, flapped above the tall masts of the warships, and stridently yodeled their hunger.

Wearing a black, caped greatcoat and red woolen muffler against the cold, Forester made his way toward a labyrinth of warehouses, a sugar refinery, and a paper mill that marked the limit of the dock area and began the adjoining industrial district. He'd been the *Manxman*'s only passenger, and there was no one else around. He carried a large carpetbag that contained a change of clothing and a Colt revolver, and in his gloved left hand he held a sword cane with an elaborately carved ivory handle in the shape of a Chinese dragon with emerald eyes. The sword had a twenty-three-inch steel blade, razor-sharp, a gentleman's weapon and a deadly one.

Forester's thoughts were on the cab that presumably awaited him and thereafter a blazing fire and perhaps a glass of hot rum punch. On that particular Sunday morning in civilized London town, he gave little thought to the cane as a weapon, considering it more of a fashion accessory. In that, he was mistaken. The blade would very soon be called into use . . . with horrifyingly fatal results.

Forester wore the high-heeled boots and wide-brimmed Stetson of a Western man, and, head bent against the slashing sleet, he didn't see the dockworker stride toward him until the man was almost past, his eyes fixed steadily on a point ahead of him.

Out of the corner of his mouth, the worker said, "Be careful, guv."

And then he was gone, and Forester briefly wondered at his warning and then dismissed it. After all, the English were a polite breed, much given to strange greetings.

This was a little-used, hundred-year-old dock once trodden by Admiral Lord Nelson that was scheduled to be closed. After a couple of minutes of walking, Forester found himself on a deserted concrete pathway between the paper mill and a rust-colored, corrugated iron warehouse. The mill was silent, its pious owner observing the Sabbath, but a massive ship's boiler awaiting the scrap heap took up much of the space on the path, and a pile of empty tea chests had fallen over in the wind and were scattered everywhere. Huge Norwegian rats, afraid of nothing, ignored the approaching human and scuttled and scurried among the debris of ten thousand spilled cargoes.

Forester saw the cab ahead of him, waiting for his arrival as it had for the past six days, be his ship early or late. The top-hatted driver muffled in a greatcoat, a woolen scarf covering his face to the eyes, sat in a spring seat at the rear of the vehicle. Despite the biting, cartwheeling sleet, he seemed to be dozing, and the Texan was close enough that he heard the clang of the impatient horse's hoof as it pawed the wet cobbles.

Forester quickened his pace, desirous of the cab's meager shelter, but he stopped in his tracks as three men, tough-looking brutes wearing flat caps and rough, work-men's clothing, stepped into his path.

The biggest of the three was a ruffian with simian fea-tures and massive, stooped shoulders. His hands hung at his sides like ham hocks, the knuckles scarred from many a fistfight, and his thick lips were peeled back from de-cayed teeth in a snarl that passed for a grin. "'Ere, matey, I be Bill Hobson, a well-known name in old London Town, and what's a toff like you doing, a-walking around my turf like you owned it?" he said.

"He's a toff right enough, Bill," another man said. "Looks to me that he can pay his way . . . for a safe pas-sage, like."

The human gorilla named Bill widened his grin. "Truer words was never spoke, Johnny," he said. "Money for a safe passage it is, so give us your wallet and watch, your bag, and whatever other valuables you own." He bowed and waved in the direction of the street. "And then you can go in peace."

"And we'll be a-taking of your fancy cane," Johnny said.

Burke Forester was irritated at being forced to stop in

the middle of a sleet storm, but since his mind was on other, more pressing business, he was willing to let this matter go. After all, three impudent toughs were just a temporary inconvenience.

"You boys step aside," he said. "This is a public thorough-fare, and I have no money for you." He motioned with the cane. "Now, be on your way and give me the road."

Bill Hobson's gaze became more calculating, mea-suring the Yankee's height and the width of his shoulders. The man seemed capable, and that gave Bill pause, but more disturbing was the fact that he wasn't in the least bit scared . . . and he sure as heck should be. Did the dandy know that he was facing three of the toughest men from the violent, disease-ridden cesspit that was the East End of London? Did he realize he faced men who could kick him to death if the need arose? Bill smiled to him-self. Maybe the fool needed a harsh lesson . . .

For clarity's sake, it must be noted here that Burke Forester was a professional assassin and a noted *pistolero* who'd put the crawl on half a dozen named men, includ-ing Wes Hardin and the notoriously fast King Fisher. Historians disagree on the number of men Forester killed, and a man in his line of business didn't boast of it. For him, it sufficed that his reputation was known to the rich and powerful businessmen, industrialists, and cattle ranchers who mattered and who considered him an effi-cient, and above all, discreet, executioner. Let Forester's lowest estimated number of kills stand at sixty-three, fifty-eight by the Winchester rifle and Colt's gun, three by the bowie knife, and two by his ever-present sword cane. Those numbers are probably near to the truth.

In sum, Burke Forester was a sudden and dangerous killer and a man best left the hell alone . . . something that Bill Hobson and his two companions soon would learn the hard way.

Forester realized that the Englishman's talking was done when the man reached into the pocket of his ragged jacket and produced a lead-filled leather sap, a vicious, bone-breaking weapon ideal for a close-range fight against a large opponent. Hobson grinned and tapped his open palm with the sap. "Come and get it, fancy man," he said. Then he swung the blackjack at Forester's left temple, trying for a killing blow.

But the Texan had already moved.

He leaped to his right, dodged the sap, and with incredible speed and dexterity, drew his blade from the sheath. Off balance, Hobson stumbled and desperately tried to regain his footing, his face panicked. But not for long. An accomplished swordsman, Forester flung his left arm wide and at the same time turned from the waist and elegantly thrust with his blade, running Hobson through. Three feet of steel rammed into his guts will shock a man dreadfully, and Bill Hobson's scream was a shrieking mix of pain, fear, and despair. As the Englishman slowly sank to the sleet-soaked ground groaning, holding his belly with glistening, scarlet hands, one of his cohorts turned and scampered, but the third, the man Hobson had called Johnny, slipped a set of brass knuckles onto his right fist and came charging. Forester was surprised by this aggression and reluctantly recognized the ruffian as a fighting man. It took sand to take on a sword with nothing but a knuckleduster. As a mark of respect, the Texan decided there and then to spare Johnny the pain he'd inflicted on his gutted companion. He backed off a step, away from the man's clumsy swing, and his blade flickered like the tongue of an angry serpent, and the point sank into Johnny's throat just under his larynx. A quick thrust and the steel projected four inches from the back of the man's neck and then was withdrawn. Dying on his feet, Johnny stared at Forester in bewilderment for long seconds and then sank to the ground, his face in the black, liquid mud.

Savvy swordsmen never sheathe a bloody blade since it can corrode the steel. Forester ripped the cloth cap from Hobson's head and wiped the sword as clean as he could. He then took a silk handkerchief from his greatcoat pocket and finished the job. He slid the sword back into the cane as Hobson whispered, scarlet blood in his mouth, "You've killed me."

Forester nodded. "Seems like. You won't survive that wound, my man."

"Damn you. Damn you to Hades."

"Better men than you have told me that."

"I need a doctor," Hobson said. "Get me a doctor."

Foster smiled and shook his head. "No, my friend, you don't need a doctor, you need an undertaker."

"I've got a wife . . . four . . . four kids still alive," Hobson said.

"That's sad. So very tragic," Foster said. He glanced at the leaden sky. "Well, I can't tarry here talking any longer. *Tempus fugit,* as they say."

"Don't go, mister. Help me."

"You're beyond help, pardner," Forester said. "All you can do now is die. A *balestra* followed by a thrust to the belly is always fatal." The Texan nodded, as though agreeing with himself. "Ah yes," he said. Then, "Well, I'll be on my way."

Hobson, his throat thick with blood, called out something, but Forester wasn't listening. He made his way to the waiting cab, walking head bent through driving, icy sleet made even colder by a savage north wind.

Only the driver's pale blue eyes were visible under the brim of his top hat as he looked down at Forester, sizing him up as the American gent he was there to meet.

"Been waiting long?" Forester said.

"Six days long, yer worship," the driver said, by his accent a cockney from the London East End. "From dawn to dusk, me an' his 'ere 'orse."

"The ship was caught by a winter storm in the mid-Atlantic," Forester said. "We were driven back by the gale. That's why I'm late."

The driver's shaggy eyebrows were frosted with rime. He nodded and said, "I got no time for ships and oceans. I'm a landlubber, meself."

"Well, I hope they're paying you enough," Forester said. "It's no fun sitting out for hours in this vile weather."

"That they are," the cabbie said. "They're paying me handsomely." Then, to Forester's surprise, he added, "The one who ran away is Charlie Tompkins. He lives with a loose woman in the East End and hangs around the docks, thieving whatever he can. He won't snitch to the law, never fear. They'd love to get their 'ands on old Charlie, the coppers would."

Sleet gathered on the shoulders of Forester's greatcoat, and he was anxious to get inside. "Maybe he'll talk, maybe he won't, but he should be taken care of," he said.

"He will be, and the two dead men back there," the driver said. "Mr. Walzer don't leave no loose ends."

"Ernest Walzer is a careful man," Forester said.

"That he is," the driver said. "There's a flask of brandy and a box of cigars inside, 'elp yourself. It's an hour and a half's drive to Mr. Walzer's house and most of it over cobbles."

Forester settled in the cab's leather seat, glad to be out of the storm, though the air inside was still bitterly cold. His breath steamed as he poured a brandy from the flask into its silver cup and then lit a cigar. Back in Texas, his rancher client had paid him well for acting as a go-between, making sure that Ernest Walzer held up his end of the contract, and Forester decided that he deserved every cent . . . nobody had warned him about the lousy British weather.

Chapter Two

"Did you have a pleasant crossing, Mr. Forester?" said Ernest Walzer, a round-shouldered man of medium height, his intense black eyes dominating a sensitive, fine-boned Semitic face. He wore a ruby red smoking jacket and a round black hat with a tassel. He had Persian slippers on his feet, and Forester guessed him to be somewhere in his mid-sixties. But he could have been any age.

"Pleasant enough until halfway across the Atlantic, when we ran into a storm," Forester said. "Pushed us back toward New York for four days."

Walzer smiled. "I hope you're a good sailor."

"I'm not. I was as sick as a poisoned pup the whole time."

"Ah, well, you're on dry land now," Walzer said. "The sherry is to your taste?"

"It's just fine," Forester said.

"I'm distressed about your unfortunate encounter with low-class scoundrels," Walzer said. "On behalf of my country, I offer you an apology."

"A minor incident of no great account," Forester said.

He waved a careless hand, and the blue smoke from his cigar made curling patterns in the air.

"Nevertheless, the one called Tompkins will not live out the day," Walzer said. "You can be assured of that."

He and Walzer sat on each side of a blazing log fire in the mansion's study that was furnished very much in the current, upper-class style, crowded and ornate with well-polished wood, stuffed animals and birds under glass domes, and thick Persian rugs. A portrait of grim old Queen Victoria hung above the fireplace. The room was warm, cozy, hazy from cigar smoke, and spoke of great wealth.

Walzer studied the Texan for a few moments and then said, "It was Tom Watkins who told me about the difficulty you had at the St. Katherine Dock."

"The cabdriver?"

"Yes. I have a dozen cabbies on my payroll. They are my eyes and ears and keep me informed. Rich people are such fools, Mr. Forester. They pay the driver no heed and indulge in the most intimate conversations. Little do they know that the cabbie up there on his high seat sees and hears everything, and in turn, so do I."

"And what do you do with the information?" Forester asked.

Walzer shrugged. "Besides my other businesses, I dabble in blackmail and extortion. It's a profitable venture that requires little capital investment."

"There were three of them at the dock," Forester said.

"Yes. Dock rats, louts, ruffians, the poorest of the poor and of no account," Walzer said. "As I said, the one who ran away will be dead by nightfall and the two you . . . ah . . . terminated have already been dumped in an East

End alley. The authorities won't even investigate. Violent death in all its forms is a daily occurrence in the slums, and seldom do the police get involved. More sherry?"

Forester extended his glass. "Please."

Walzer refilled from the decanter and said, "You have questions?" An Eastern European accent shaded the man's English, but Forester didn't notice. To him, all limeys sounded alike.

"Tell me this," the Texan said. "How did my client know you were in this line of work?"

"What line of work?" Walzer said.

"Hiring assassins."

"Well, he didn't know, because hiring assassins is not part of my usual business." Then, frowning, Walzer said, "How much of this affair are you entitled to know?"

Forester said, "All of it." The frown didn't leave the older man's face, and the Texan added, "My client trusts me."

Walzer nodded. "I'm aware of your reputation and your client's faith in you. He made that clear in his letters. I must confess, I wonder why he didn't hire you for this undertaking. You seem the ideal man to get the job done."

Forester shook his head. "No. I'm too close. I've done gun work for my client in the past, and a clever lawman might draw the right conclusions. My client must have no direct connection whatever to the assassins, and I hope you didn't disclose his identity to the men you hired."

Walzer said, "Of course, I did not. They were told the mark, his location, and nothing else. Professionals need no further information than that. By this time, they're already in Texas, and when the undertaking is finished, they will scatter and make their separate ways back to London and then to . . . well, wherever they hail from."

Forester said, "Tell me this, how did my client . . ."

"Between ourselves, let us drop the pretense, Mr. Forester," Walzer said. "Your client's name is Gideon Stark, and he's a big rancher who wants to be bigger, an empire builder who dreams of founding a dynasty. You know this and I know this, and it's all that I know. But at least now our masks have been removed."

A few moments of silence stretched between the men. A log fell in the fire and sent up a cascade of scarlet sparks. Sleet battered at the parlor window, and the frost-rimed wind raged around the mansion like a ravenous gray wolf.

"All right, then, as you say, our masks are removed," Forester said. "How did Gideon Stark choose you to take care of this matter?"

"He didn't, at least not directly."

Forester made no answer.

"This is very much between us," Walzer said. "Due to the sensitive nature of what I'm about to tell you, we will deal only in suppositions, Mr. Forester, not in facts. Do you understand?"

The Texan drew on his cigar before he spoke. "I catch your drift."

Walzer nodded and said, "Good. Then let us suppose that there is a certain English gentleman rancher in West Texas, the youngest son of a belted earl, who is prospering mightily in the cattle business. His fond papa is a nobleman who quickly ran through his wife's inheritance and now the meager rents from the kilted tenants of his Scottish estates do not support his extravagances, namely gambling and expensive mistresses. The earl is always, as the sporting crowd says, down to his last chip and in the dumps. Let me refill your glass."

Walzer poured more sherry and then said, "Now, shall we surmise, and this is all supposition, mind, that the earl is a member of the British Foreign Office and desperate for money. Could it be that happenstance threw the wretched blue blood in my direction, and we at once entered into a business arrangement?"

"What kind of business arrangement?" Forester said.

"If such were the case, one must imagine that money lending would be the likely arrangement," Walzer said. "But then we must answer the question: Would a savvy businessman lend money to, as you Americans say, a deadbeat . . . a worthless, sponging, idler like the exalted earl?"

"I guess not," Forester said. "Sure doesn't sound like a sound investment."

"And you guess correctly," Walzer said. "But what if the nobleman had valuable information to sell because at one time or another his position in the Foreign Office put him in the front parlor of a score of tin-pot dictators and warlords in India, the Orient, and South and Central America? What do such despots need to stay in business, Mr. Forester?"

"Money?" the Texan said.

"High taxes usually provide more than enough of that. No, tyrants need arms, cannon, rifles, carbines, and sabers for their cavalry and a plentiful supply of ammunition," Walzer said.

"And you supply them," Forester said. He smiled. "Hey, here's a battery of cannon, no questions asked."

"I will not say yes, and I will not say no, but it is

always possible that I deal in arms of all kinds, and that I use the earl as my go-between in those transactions. If that were the case, and I don't say that it is, I would pay him handsomely and keep him in line with five-pound notes, threats of blackmail . . . and worse."

Forester smiled. "In other words, Mr. Walzer, you're a world-class gunrunner?"

"Gunrunner. Yes, that's another of those new crude and hurtful American terms and one I would never use," Walzer said, frowning. "If I engaged in such a business, I'd call myself a contraband weapons dealer."

Forester made no comment on that. He said, "Gideon Stark has all the weapons he needs. What he does need are men who can use them."

"And he has them, four of the best I could find," Walzer said.

Forester shook his head. "How did one of the biggest ranchers in Texas ever shove his branding iron into your fire, Walzer?"

The older man smiled. "His branding iron into my fire? Hah, that's a colorful way of putting it. But here's how it might have happened, the very nub of the matter you might say."

Walzer took time to pour more sherry, and Forester said, "You'll make me drunk."

"I doubt it," Walzer said. He sipped from his own glass, the crystal engraved with an elaborate coat of arms. Forester guessed it was Russian, judging by the double-headed eagle.

Walzer said, "Gideon Stark and the earl's son, the young rancher I told you about earlier, share a fence and are neighbors and close friends. Or do you already know that?"

"Stark told me only what I needed to know for this job," Forester said. "He's a tight, closemouthed man. He didn't mention an Englishman, neighbor or no."

"Ah, leaving no loose ends also applies to the hired help, huh?"

"I guess it's something like that," Forester said.

Walzer fell silent as a tall, thin, melancholy man dressed in butler black stepped into the room and added a log to the fire. He bowed slightly from the waist and said, "Will there be anything else, sir?"

Walzer shook his head. "No, Mr. Lewis, nothing more for today."

"Very well, sir," the butler said. "Mr. Forester's room has been prepared, and the fire is lit."

Walzer nodded and said, "I took the liberty of assuming you'd sleep here tonight, Mr. Forester. I told the cabbie to pick you up in the morning after breakfast. As you know, I'm very isolated here. One can't just step out of the front door and hail a passing cab."

"Suits me just fine," Forester said. He glanced out the window. "Is that sleet, snow, or rain?"

"All three," Walzer said. "And there might soon be thunder. British weather, you know." He turned his attention to Lewis. "You may take the rest of the day off to visit your ailing . . . sister . . . isn't it?"

"Yes, my sister Ethel, sir," the butler said. "She's down with female hysteria and a wandering womb, and her husband's at his wit's end."

"So sorry to hear that," Walzer said. "Your brother-in-law is in service?"

"Yes, sir, he's third footman to Lord Rancemere."

"Then take the pony trap, Mr. Lewis, and I'll see you tomorrow morning."

Lewis bowed. "Yes, sir. Thank you, sir."

The butler glided silently to the door, and Walzer called out after him. "And Mr. Lewis, for goodness sake wear your oilskins and stay dry."

The butler turned and managed a ghost of a smile. "Certainly, sir. It's very kind of you to be so concerned."

Walzer waved a dismissive hand. "Think nothing of it, Mr. Lewis."

The door closed noiselessly behind the butler, and Walzer said, as though the interruption had not occurred, "I wasn't there, of course, and this is all supposition, but I imagine Mr. Stark conversed with the earl's son and happened to mention that he was looking for some skilled men to carry out an enterprise for him."

Forester smiled, "Murder for him, you mean?"

"Yes, just that. But Mr. Stark likely stipulated that the assassins must be unknown to the American and Mexican authorities and that after hitting their target they'd disappear back into their holes. Of course, the earl's son would recommend me as a discreet man who can get things done."

"How would he know that?" Forester said.

Walzer shrugged. "I suspect the young man is privy to all his father's secret dealings. I gather from the earl's letters that his son is not a stickler for the law and has hanged or shot many a man without trial."

"Rustlers and nesters, probably," Forester said. "Plenty of those in West Texas."

"Just so," Walzer said. "Now let's be frank. It's time for some plain talk. Several months ago, Mr. Stark and myself entered into a correspondence during the course of which I agreed to help him by providing assassins. For a fee of course." Walzer spread his thin-fingered hands and smiled. "And now here you are, Mr. Forester."

"The money is in my bag," the Texan said. "Five thousand in gold."

"And . . ." Walzer prompted.

"You'll get the other five thousand when the job is done and an additional sum to pay the returning killers."

"Quite acceptable," Walzer said. "Judging by his correspondence, Gideon Stark is a hard, unbending man, but I judge him to be honest in his dealings. Is that not so. Mr. Forester?"

"He's hung and shot more than his share his ownself, but I'd say he's honest enough," Forester said.

The day was shading darker, and the light from the fire cast a crimson glow on the high bones of Walzer's cheeks and deepened the shadows in his eye sockets and temples. Momentarily, as he leaned over to poker a burning log, his face looked like a painted skull.

"Since we're plain talking," Forester said. "Who is the mark?"

"Yes, a plainly asked question that deserves a plain-spoken answer," Walzer said. "The man's name is Ben Bradford . . . *Doctor* Ben Bradford."

Forester was surprised. "A doctor? All this secrecy and fuss over a pill-roller? Heck, if Stark had asked me, I'd have put a bullet in him as a favor."

Ernest Walzer shook his head. "My dear Forester, in this affair there are wheels within wheels that you know nothing about. Stark wants the man dead, yes, but nothing, and I mean nothing, about the killing must be linked to him. He's got to come out of this . . ."

"As clean as a whistle," Forester said.

"Cleaner. Smelling of roses. No loose ends, Mr. Forester. Above all, no loose ends."

Burke Forester sat back in his chair. "Well, I did what Stark paid me to do, and now I'm out of it." His gaze moved to the darkening window where lightning glimmered on the wet panes, the flashy herald of the coming thunder, and then he said, "As a matter of interest . . ."

"Ah, another question," Walzer said. "I was always told that Americans question everything."

"Just as a matter of interest," Forester said. At Walzer's nod, he added, "Who are the assassins?"

"No one you would know. The names are obscure."

"Try me."

"Ah . . . this is so tedious," Walzer said. "I grow weary."

"Let me decide what's tedious," Forester said. "After all, I'm in the same profession. It's always wise to be aware of the competition."

"Yes, there's always that, I suppose," Walzer said. "Then let me see . . . Ah yes, the most dangerous of the four is the Russian, Kirill Kuznetsov. He is very much in demand in Eastern Europe, and his fee for a kill is around five thousand of your US dollars. He's said to be very strong and can kill with his hands, but he's also expert with a pistol, as they all are. Salman el-Salim is an Arab, and he boasted to me that he's carried out two hundred assassinations with the jambiya fighting knife. Sean O'Rourke is an Irishman, a disgraced British army officer, and a hired killer. He's said to be very efficient. And finally, the German Helmut Klemm, a crack shot with a rifle who often kills at a distance. He never leaves Europe but made an exception for Stark since it's such a big-money contract. He talked about retiring to his estate in Bavaria after this task is done."

Forester sighed, less than impressed. "Heck, Stark could've hired four guns in Texas to do the job, men who work cheap and know how to keep their traps shut."

Walzer shook his head. "Not, not that, never that. Mr. Stark has too much at stake, too much to lose, and I mean losing something . . . very precious to him. The assassins he's hired will return to Europe after they honor the contract and will never be heard from again. Your Texas gunmen may know how to keep quiet . . . until they get drunk and boast to a gossipy whore about all the men they've killed or suddenly get a taste for a little blackmail. No, the risk is too great to use homegrown gunmen." Walzer shook his head. "It's out of the question."

He clapped his hands and said, smiling, "Now, enough of business for tonight. Are you sharp set?"

"I had breakfast on the ship and nothing since," Forester said.

"Then, as an honored guest I must feed you," Walzer said. "Unfortunately, I gave cook and the maids the day off, idle tongues you know, but the scullery maid is here. She's a stupid, doltish girl, but she cooks plain fare quite well. I ordered a meal of roast beef, gravy, and potatoes if you'd care to make a trial of it."

"Suits me," Forester said. "I got my belt cinched to the last notch."

"On the bright side, I have a very fine Napoleon brandy you can have with your coffee."

"Does the scullery maid make good coffee?"

"No."

"Then thank God for Napoleon," Forester said.

CHAPTER THREE

"His was not an easy death, Mr. Walzer," Lewis the butler said, looking down at the twisted corpse on the floor.

"No, it was not, Mr. Lewis. Cyanide can be so unpredictable," Walzer said. "It took him five minutes to die. Too long, Mr. Lewis, too long. Indeed, it was a horrific, painful death. He said the brandy tasted bitter, and I think he knew. He was a strong man, and even when he was convulsing, he still tried to reach his carpetbag. Was there a firearm in there?"

"Yes, sir, a .45 caliber Colt revolver. I took the liberty of removing it before I pretended to leave the house," the butler said.

Thunder slammed, and then Walzer spoke into the following quiet. "Money? Was there money?"

"Yes, sir, a large manila envelope, folded, and filled with high-denomination dollar bills. I left it on your desk in the study."

"What about the scullery maid?" Walzer said. "Does she suspect anything?"

Lewis shook his head. "No, sir, not a thing."

"Are you sure, Mr. Lewis? If there's the slightest doubt we can dispose of her."

"Annie Griggs is a dull, empty-headed girl who reads modern novels of the trashiest kind and lives her life through their pages," the butler said. "We have nothing to fear."

Walzer seemed satisfied with that answer, but said, "Still, keep good watch on her. No gossip, Mr. Lewis. I want no gossip . . . no scullery maids tittle-tattling over their tea."

"Very good, sir," the butler said. "As you ordered, Tom Watkins the cabbie is here."

"Right on time, as usual," Walzer said. "Send him in."

Lewis bowed and left, and a few minutes later, Watkins stepped into the parlor, hat in hand, a powdering of sleet on his shoulders. The frayed ends of his muffler hung to his knees. He saw the body on the floor and said, "Poor American gentleman."

"It was necessary," Walzer said. "Business is business, after all."

"Whatever you say, guv," Tom Watkins said. "Necessity knows no law."

"I want you to get rid of the body," Walzer said. "There's a gold sovereign in it for you. And you can keep his watch and chain and boots but I'll hold onto the sword cane."

"Thank'ee, guv. The American gentleman will slip into the Thames at Limehouse nice as you please," Watkins said. "An' him being a stranger here an' all, nobody will ever be the wiser."

Walzer nodded and then toed Forester's corpse. "Good.

Now get rid of the damned thing. It's making me quite depressed."

After a struggle, the stocky cabbie managed to sling Forester's body over his shoulder. Panting, he said, "He's a heavy gentleman, Mr. Walzer. But for a couple of pence I can hire an orphan boy to help me with him at the river. There's plenty of ragamuffins sleeping in the streets around Limehouse and they're terrified of the law."

"Yes, yes, do what you must," Walzer said, his gaze turned away from Forester's dead face. He threw up his arms in a theatrical gesture and said, "Now, just . . . just . . . get him out of here."

"Right-o, guv," Watkins said. Then, smiling, "The gentleman is a long way from Texas, ain't he?"

"I rather fancy that right about now he's a long way from anywhere," Ernest Walzer said.

CHAPTER FOUR

Red Ryan and Patrick "Buttons" Muldoon were being read to from the book by a little banty rooster in high-heeled boots and a wide-brimmed hat.

"On the route to the Perdinales River there's to be no cussin', no drinkin', and no loose talk about fancy women," Abe Patterson said. "Keep a solemn countenance at all times and try to look like you've said a prayer at least once in your lives. Remember the good name of the Abe Patterson and Son Stage and Express Company is at stake."

"Heck, Mr. Patterson, we've had holy rollers as passengers before," Buttons said. "I never heard one of 'em complain." He thought about that for a moment and said, "Well, they done plenty of complaining, but I never heard one grumble about me and Red cussin' an' sich."

"These four ain't your regular sin busters," Patterson said. "They're bona fide monks, wear the robe and sandals and everything. They're headed for a mission north of the Perdinales about twenty miles due east of Fredericksburg, and that's where you'll take them."

"I don't recollect a mission in that part of the country," Buttons said. "What about you, Red?"

"It sure don't ring a bell with me," Red Ryan said. "There's a couple of big ranches in that neck of the woods, but I never heard tell of a mission."

"Only one of them monks speaks English, sounds like an Irishman to me," Patterson said. "He says he and his brothers—they ain't real brothers but that's what them monk fellers call each other—plan to start a mission and to start things off, they got a holy relic with them."

"What's a holy relic?" Red said.

Patterson shook his head. "Ryan, you're some kind of heathen, ain't you?'

"Buttons, you ever hear tell of a holy relic?" Red said.

"No, I never did," Buttons said. "I recollect one time an old mountain man calling himself a relic, but he wasn't holy or nothing like that."

"I declare, damned ungodly pagans, both of you," Patterson said. "A holy relic is something that belonged to a saint, like his skull or a lock of his hair or something. Well, one of the monks is a German, and he carries a long leather case with him and the Irishman claims it's the staff Moses carried when he led the chosen people across the desert to the Promised Land. Heck, it's all there in the Bible. Read about it sometime."

Abe Patterson's pale blue eyes went to the window of his office, his interest caught by a cavalry patrol out of Fort Concho that jangled past, eight black troopers and a beardless white officer who looked all of sixteen years old. The little man leaned forward in his chair and growled like a terrier that's just seen a rat. "Damned Apaches!" He turned to Buttons and Red. "You boys just arrived. Maybe you ain't heard that the Mescalero and Lipan are out."

"We heard, boss," Buttons said. "How many you figure?"

"Thirty or so, all young bucks, and they're playing hob," Patterson said. "They crossed the New Mexican border sometime in the past month and the army is already bringing in settlers, them that will come. I just heard that the savages murdered and scalped three tin pans down on the San Saba and there's talk of a burned ranch house at Rock Spring and a woman kidnapped. But I don't know if that's true or not."

"Them monk fellers aware of all this?" Buttons said.

"Yeah, they are," Patterson said. "But the Irishman said God will protect them."

"Maybe God's never met up with thirty Apache bucks on the prod afore," Red said.

"Well, it's a big country," Patterson said. "You probably won't even see an Apache."

"Seems like we've heard that before," Buttons said.

"A few times," Red said.

Patterson stabbed a forefinger at his shotgun guard. "Listen, Ryan, if you do meet up with them savages, just stand up in the coach, beat your chest, and say, 'I'm a representative of the Abe Patterson and Son Stage and Express Company.' That will send them high-tailing it pretty damned quick."

Buttons and Red exchanged glances, and Red said, "Boss, we'll surely keep that in mind."

"Then see you do," Patterson said. "I'm tired of giving you good advice that you don't follow. When you boys pull out at first light tomorrow morning, I think I can get you an army escort as far as the San Saba and maybe further. We'll see. In any case, our new station has opened at Kickapoo Springs, and I hired a man named Jim Moore to manage the place. He'll see you all right for a fresh team and grub."

"Here, is that the Fighting Jim Moore from down old Fort Leaton way?" Buttons said. "He's got a wife that keeps right poorly and two simple sons?"

"The same," Abe Patterson said. "Moore was a blacksmith for Charlie Goodnight and then became a Texas Ranger for a spell. He's the one that killed Arch Benson, the Sulphur River Kid, in Amarillo that time."

"I recollect being told about that fight," Buttons said. "I remember Moore as a big man, favors his left leg some."

"That's him," Patterson said. "He told me he caught a bullet in that leg during a shooting scrape in El Paso and has limped on it ever since."

"A hard, unforgiving man is Jim Moore," Buttons said.

"I know," Patterson said. "That's why I hired him."

The office door opened and a tall, lanky drink of water with a hard-boned face and quick black eyes stepped into the office. Pete Crane drove for Abe Patterson, and a sea of bad blood lay between him and Red Ryan. They went back a ways, and none of it was good.

Crane greeted Patterson and Buttons Muldoon and then nodded coldly at Red. "Howdy, Ryan," he said. "It's been a while."

"At least a six-month," Red said, tensing up little.

"Took that long for my face and all to heal up and them two broken ribs you gave me," Crane said.

"You picked the fight, Pete," Red said.

"Maybe so, but you should've told me you'd been a

professional booth fighter back in the day," Crane said. "Keeping that to yourself was underhand and low down."

"A man accused of dealing from the bottom of the deck who then gets hit by a sneaky punch don't have much time for polite conversation," Red said.

"If I'd knowed you'd been a professional bare-knuckle fighter I wouldn't have punched you," Crane said. "I was mad clean through that day in the saloon, but I wasn't stupid. You compre what I'm telling you, Ryan?"

Red smiled. "Sure I do. Next time I'll tell that I was a prizefighter afore I pound you into the sawdust again."

"I'd appreciate that," Crane said. "It's what's called in Texas a common courtesy."

"Well now, that's true blue of Ryan, ain't it, Pete?" Abe Patterson said. "I mean, he says that next time he'll tell you he made a living with his fists afore he cleans your clock. He spoke it right out like a white man, didn't he?"

Crane seemed unsure, but he said finally, "Yeah, I guess he did."

"Good. It's water under the bridge," Patterson said. "Let bygones be bygones, I always say, especially between two fellers who work for me."

"Truer words were never spoke," Buttons Muldoon said. "Here, Pete, did you see the monks in town? A mighty strange sight in San Angelo, huh?"

Crane mentally shrugged off Red's treachery for the moment and said, "Yeah, I saw them." He grinned. "And so did Stover Timms and Lem Harlan."

Abe Patterson's weathered face twisted into a scowl. "Here, is that damned border trash interfering with our passengers?"

Crane was surprised. "Our passengers instead of just

the passengers? Heck, the Patterson stage company is coming up in the world." The driver read the irritation in his boss's face and said, "Stover and Lem . . . the boys are just having a little fun with the padres about wearing them brown dresses an' all, say they look like kinda ugly womenfolk."

"Until they're delivered to their destination, the monks are under the protection of the Abe Patterson and Son Stage an Express Company," Patterson said. He jumped up from his chair and shoved his hat on his head. "Buttons, Red, come with me, you too, Pete, and we'll put an end to this tomfoolery."

"I'll sit this one out, boss," Crane said. "Timms and Harlan are friends of mine. Red, you step careful around them two. Stover is fast on the draw and shoot and Lem is faster. They call you, and you won't even come close."

"There will be no shooting," Patterson said as he headed for the door. "I'll see to it that any man who pulls the iron in my presence gets hung."

"Or gets shot," Red Ryan said, looking hard at Crane.

CHAPTER FIVE

Maybe, and the local *Concho Times* newspaper's account of the incident is not certain on this point, the teasing of the monks began as nothing more serious than some good-natured joshing. If that was indeed the case, the situation had escalated badly by the time Abe Patterson, Red Ryan, and Buttons Muldoon arrived on the scene. But one thing is certain, the blood-splashed horror that followed the occurrence, despite some claims of divine retribution, was directly a result of Stover Timms's and Lem Harlan's meanness and their desire to humiliate, hurt, and torment . . . and later their terrible deaths were not inflicted by the supernatural as some claimed, but by expert killers. At the time, the law wrote off their murders as the work of Apaches and only much later did Red Ryan and Buttons Muldoon learn the truth.

Timms and Harlan were known to the citizens and law of San Angelo as toughs who were suspects in a rash of unsolved robberies in the area and the recent murder of an unemployed laborer named either Reilly or Rollins who'd won two hundred and fifty dollars at the gaming tables the night he was killed. At a time in the West when diversions were welcomed, Timms and Harlan's antics drew a crowd, some amused, a few scandalized, and all entertained.

The monks stood with their backs against the front window of the Concho Valley Mercantile, a false-fronted building that stood on the corner of College and Randolph Streets next to the Real Note Saloon, a future haunt of Teddy Roosevelt.

Stover Timms was a bearded man of medium height, dressed in whatever cast-off clothing he could throw together. He looked shabby and dirty, and his eyes were snake-yellow and ugly. He brandished a Remington revolver and ordered the monks to hike up their robes and dance while Lem Harlan played a creditable rendition of *Turkey in the Straw* on his harmonica and some in the grinning crowd clapped in time to the music.

The four monks, heads bowed, faces shadowed by their hoods, stood stock still, carpetbags at their feet, refusing to react to their tormentors. That seemed to incense Timms, who thumbed off a couple of shots and splintered the boardwalk inches from their bare toes.

"Dance!" he yelled. "Damn you, cut a caper for the folks."

The monks stood in complete silence, motionless as mourners at a graveside, and a hush fell over the crowd as though they feared a killing.

Then a roar of anger shattered the quiet as Abe Patterson arrived on the scene like the wrath of God.

"Damn you, holster the iron, or I'll shoot you down like a mad dog," Patterson yelled.

Stover Timms turned on him, his face twisted, the Remington at waist level. But then his eyes registered the scene in front of him and his resolve faltered . . . fast . . .

Patterson, as salty as they come, had been a lawman for a spell and he'd shot and hung more than his fair share. His Colt was up, hammer back and ready. He'd shoot to kill and Timms knew it. But what gave the ruffian pause, and there were those in the crowd who later testified to this, was the fact that Patterson was flanked by Red Ryan and Buttons Muldoon, known men who were not to be trifled with. Timms was gun handy, but he was no fool. Ryan had a rep as a pistolero that few could match on the draw and shoot, and Muldoon was a stocky, square-shaped man who'd take his hits and keep on a-coming.

Timms found his voice right quick. And he sugared it over with a sickly smile.

"We was only havin' some fun, Mr. Patterson," he said. "Giving the padres a big ol' Texas welcome to San Angelo was what we was doing. No harm done."

"Shooting at a man's feet to make him dance is not a Texas welcome," Patterson said. "It's no kind of welcome at all. Those men are holy monks, given to doing all kinds of good works, but more importantly they're fare-paying passengers of the Abe Patterson and Son Stage and Express Company and under my personal protection." The little man flourished his revolver. "Now be off with you or do you want to get shot in the belly?" he said. "The choice is yours."

Timms hesitated, but Harlan was out of it, his arms raised so high at his sides he looked as though he was about to take off on a flight over the Concho River. Red

Ryan ignored Harlan, but said to Timms, "Mr. Patterson asked you a question. Do you want gut shot or not?"

Timms made up his mind and put on a show of holstering his gun. "It's getting to it that a man can't have any fun in San Angelo anymore."

Red nodded. "Civilization is catching up with you, Timms."

"Yeah, it is. And I don't like it. I don't like it one bit."

It was then that Red Ryan saw something strange, an occurrence so sinister that it gave him a chill. At precisely the same moment, the same instant, the four monks raised their heads and stared at Stover Timms. Red couldn't see the faces under the hoods, but he knew their eyes were on the badman . . . and so did Timms. A criminal with the instincts of a lobo wolf, as the monkish stares scalded him, his expression changed from defiance to one of unease.

"Lem, let's go drink whiskey," he said. "I don't like the company here."

"Feeling's mutual," Red Ryan said. "Timms, you do have a way of stinking up the place."

The man nodded. "I'll remember that, Ryan," he said. His snake grin was repulsive as he tapped the handle of his revolver. "And I remember things real good."

The monks shuffled away, their heads lowered, sandals slapping along the boardwalk.

Buttons Muldoon watched Simms and Harlan mount up and leave and said, "You've made an enemy, Red. You'll have to kill that ranny one day."

"Could be," Red said. His attention was not on Buttons

but on the beautiful, flame-haired woman with startling green eyes walking toward Abe Patterson.

She was tall, slim, and shapely, filling out her blue riding habit in all the right places, and over the dress she wore a light, canvas duster designed for travel. Her lustrous hair was piled up under a veiled top hat and, unusual for that time, a large leather bag closed with brass buckles hung by a wide strap from her left shoulder. As she walked, the swirl of her skirts revealed ankle-length, high-heeled boots. She looked to be in her late twenties, and the years had not been hard on her.

Red Ryan thought the woman was stunning. Ditto for Buttons Muldoon . . . but Abe Patterson saw only dollar signs, a way to help fill a stage that was booked for four paying passengers but could hold six and eight at a pinch.

"And what can I do for you, young lady?" he said, smiling, as the woman stopped in front of him.

"I take it that you are Mr. Patterson," the woman said. Her voice was light, melodious but oddly commanding. She was a little too angular, like a well-bred racehorse, to pass as a Texas belle, Red decided. Her accent was definitely Yankee with a very slight nasally tone, and she was almighty handsome in a high-cheekboned way, not pretty.

"And you've been told correctly, dear lady," Patterson said. "I am indeed Abe Patterson of the Abe Patterson and son Stage and Express Company."

The woman stuck out a gloved hand. "And I am Augusta Addington of the Philadelphia and New Orleans Addingtons. How do you do?"

"I'm doing just fine," Patterson said. "Now, what can I do for you?"

"I wish to book passage on the stage as far as Fredericksburg, where I am taking up a teaching post," Augusta said. "Do you have a vacancy?"

"By all means," Patterson said, bowing slightly. "I will make space just for you." He cast an experienced eye over the woman. Riding habit . . . expensive. Top hat . . . expensive. Ankle boots . . . expensive. Gloves . . . expensive. Leather bag . . . expensive. Overall impression . . . well-to-do, upper-class lady with money in the bank.

"That will be two hundred dollars for the one-way fare, dear lady," Patterson said. "But that includes grub, I mean meals, and, where needed, overnight stays at one of the luxurious Patterson stage stations. A comfortable journey is assured when you book with Patterson." He waved a hand. "This is your driver . . ."

A bow then, "Patrick Muldoon, ma'am, at your service."

"And your shotgun messenger to ensure a safe passage . . ."

Red touched the brim of his plug hat. "Red Ryan, ma'am, of the Cow Horn Creek and Brazos River Ryans."

Patterson angled Red a hard look and then beamed. "These are two of my most virtuous employees, church-going members of the stagecoaching fraternity. Whiskey ne'er touches their lips nor does a cussword ever linger on their tongues. They shy clear of fancy women and saloons and consider faro, poker, and chuck-a-luck to be the pastimes of the devil." He gave Buttons and Red a sidelong glance. "Ain't that right, boys?"

"Right as rain, boss," Buttons said. "Truer words was never spoke to a lady."

"My, my, I declare that I surely find myself in safe hands," Augusta said. "The propriety of your employees is most singular, Mr. Patterson."

"Indeed it is, dear lady. I don't expect my men to be paragons of virtue, but it helps if they are," Patterson said. He blinked. "Like these two."

Red said, "Miss Addington, are you aware that the Apaches are out?"

"Out?" The woman said. "Out where?"

Red waved a hand. "Out there on the long grass. Thirty young bucks. No women or children with them, always a bad sign."

"Ahem," Patterson said, staring at Red with dagger eyes. "You have nothing to fear, young lady. I assure you, the savages won't interfere with the stage. They've been burned too many times in the past."

A brewer's dray drawn by a matched pair of Percherons rumbled past, the beer barrels thumping, before Augusta spoke again. "Mr. Patterson, it is a matter of the greatest moment that I arrive in Fredericksburg within the week. I will not allow the Apaches to delay me."

"And nor shall you be delayed," Patterson said. Then, after another sidelong glance at Buttons and Red, "These two stalwarts will see to that."

"You'll reach your destination in good time, Miss Addington," Buttons said. "Never fear."

"Then my mind is at rest," Augusta said. "Now, if you gentlemen will excuse me, I feel the need for a little nap."

"We pull out at sunup," Red said.

"Sharp," Buttons said.

"He doesn't mean sharp, he means sharpish," Abe Patterson said. "No reason to rush, dear lady."

CHAPTER SIX

The railroad clock in the Gray Wolf Inn joined hands at midnight when saloon girl Addie Turnbull decided to take a stroll in the moonlight to walk off a pounding headache, the result of noise, smoke, constant pawing by the sporting crowd, and too much cheap champagne. She took Irving Street and headed toward the dark ribbon of the North Concho River, past the Rowdy Peacock Saloon and then the Silver Garter bawdy house. By the time Addie reached the lot where stood the timber framework of what would soon be a hardware store, her headache was what she later described to the law as "a sight better."

Then, her pale blue, myopic eyes popping, she saw what was hanging from a crossbeam of the construction and she screamed and screamed . . . and her headache suddenly got a heck of a sight worse.

Game for any distraction, people spilled out of the saloons and brothels, and a gaping crowd quickly gathered, among them Police Constable Boone Sturdy, who glanced at the mutilated bodies of the dangling men and promptly threw up all the whiskey he'd drank that night and then green bile. When he recovered enough to address the horrified throng he said only, "My God. Oh, my God in heaven."

One soused rooster who sobered up fast would later tell the San Angelo *Standard-Times* that what he saw "was a sight not meant to be seen by a Christian man and was like to burn out my eyeballs."

Abe Patterson, dressed only in a long gown and sleeping cap and in the highest state of agitation, ran along the hotel corridor and hammered on Red Ryan's room door and then roused Buttons Muldoon. "Don't you hear the screams and commotion?" he said. "I fear our monks may be in trouble again."

Buttons, wearing his hat and long johns, scratched his belly and said, "Where the heck are they?"

"The Irishman told me they were planning to spend the night in prayer at the Church of the Immaculate Conception," Patterson said. "We must ensure that they're safe."

"Why would they do something like that?" Red said.

"Because they're holy monks," Patterson said. "That's what monks do. Now get dressed. We're going to church."

When Red Ryan and the others stepped onto the street outside the hotel, a youngster riding north on Irving Street reined in his galloping horse. "Apaches!" he yelled.

"Where?" Abe Patterson said.

The towheaded kid jerked a thumb over his shoulder.

"That way," he said. "I'm going to Fort Concho for the soldiers."

"Wait!" Patterson yelled, but the kid was already gone, a cloud of dust trailing his gray nag. "Right," he said. "Ryan, you go see what the Apache trouble is. Buttons, you come to the church with me. We'll meet back at the hotel."

"You reckon the Apaches attacked the church?" Buttons said. "And maybe scalped them monks?"

"Paying passengers, you mean. I don't know, but I aim to find out," Patterson said. "Red, you be careful. Apache bucks on the prod can be a handful, and they'll fight in the dark if the notion takes them."

Red nodded. "I'm always careful around Apaches," he said.

Red Ryan saw the crowd first, a cross section of the temporary and permanent residents of San Angelo, cattlemen, cowboys, gamblers, painted saloon girls rubbing shoulders with respectable matrons, hawk-eyed gunmen, businessmen, merchants, and the usual collection of young men on the make. Then Red saw what hung, head-down, from a crossbeam of a framed-up building, and wished to God he hadn't.

Stover Timms and Lem Harlan had been stripped naked, gutted, and hung by their ankles from the beam. Pink and purple coiled entrails spilled onto the ground below their dangling arms, and their entire faces and bodies were scarlet with blood. When Red looked closer, he saw that both men had been gagged with pieces of sacking, probably to stifle their death screams.

Members of the local volunteer fire department, wearing brass helmets and black tunics, were tasked with cutting down the bodies, and a doctor and his nurse attended to hysterical women who'd swooned away in fright when they'd first beheld the scene or heard the subsequent dire warnings that bloodthirsty Apaches were playing hob in San Angelo and might be lurking anywhere.

Red waited until the bodies of the dead men had been cut down and the undertaker and his assistants had packed what was left of them into pine boxes, including the bits and pieces. He walked to the scene of the crime, now lit by several guttering oil lamps. To his surprise, a woman was already there, examining the ground as had been his intention. To his surprise, he recognized Augusta Addington in the gloom, her nightclothes covered by her canvas duster, pale green slippers on her feet. She saw Red looking at her and smiled and said, "Firemen's boots have tromped all over the place. There are no other tracks to be seen, Apache or otherwise."

Red said, "Miss Addington, do you always visit the scenes of killings, especially one like this?"

"No, not always," Augusta said. "But I do when there's ones like this."

She sounded a little breathless, as though she'd been caught in the act of doing something she shouldn't. Her thick auburn hair was tied back with a blue ribbon and her unfettered breasts were firm enough to mound the canvas of the duster, reinforcing Red's opinion that she was one fine-looking woman.

"So then, what are you doing here?" Red asked.

"I could ask you the same question," Augusta said.

"Abe Patterson was worried about the four monks," Red said. "They've never been around Apaches before."

"And where are my saintly fellow passengers?" Augusta said.

"In church, praying."

"An all-night vigil?"

"If vigil means saying prayers, then yeah, all night."

"Very devout of them," Augusta said. "Apaches didn't kill those two men."

"What makes you so sure?" Red said. For some reason he was irritated. What did Miss Augusta Addington of the Philadelphia and New Orleans Addingtons know about bronco Apaches?

"Apaches don't attack a town of this size with an army fort full of cavalry right on its doorstep," Augusta said. "And if it was just a quick raid, why take time to disembowel two men and string them up from a downtown rafter?" Her beautiful eyes searched Red's face. "That doesn't make any sense, don't you think, Mr. Ryan?"

Red recognized the woman's cool logic, but that only irritated him further.

"Then you know all about Apaches, huh?" he said.

"I know nothing about Apaches," Augusta said. "I've never even met one. But they're men, and I know a lot about men."

"If it wasn't Apaches, then who killed Stover Timms and Lem Harlan?" Red said. "They were tough men, quick on the draw and shoot and mean as curly wolves."

The woman smiled. "I guess they were unfortunate enough to run afoul of men who were a great deal meaner."

"Who were they?"

"I don't know."

"You never did answer my question, Miss Addington," Red said. "Why are you here?"

"Curiosity," Augusta said. "Nothing more."

"You know what they say, curiosity killed the cat."

The woman smiled. "Why would anyone want to kill me, Mr. Ryan?"

"Nobody that I know would," Red said. He also smiled.

"In any case, I can take care of myself," Augusta said. She reached into the pocket of the duster and produced a stubby, nickel-plated revolver with yellowed ivory grips. "This is a British Bulldog in .450 caliber, Mr. Ryan, a gift from my papa. I'm really quite proficient with it."

Red nodded. "I'm sure you are. It's late, and since you're a passenger of the Abe Patterson and Son Stage and Express Company and I'm its representative . . ."

"You'll walk me back to the hotel," Augusta said. "You are very gallant, Mr. Ryan. Now give me your arm."

When Buttons and Abe Patterson met Red Ryan at the hotel, the only report they had to make was that the monks had spent most of the day in prayer and planned to continue their pious devotions overnight. Meanwhile, the army called out two full companies of cavalry and patrolled the streets of San Angelo until just before dawn and concluded that the Apaches had snuck into town, killed two citizens, and then left. Patrols would be sent out to track down the savages, and an entire regiment would remain on high alert until the culprits who did the actual killings were severely punished and the rest returned to the San Carlos.

Red echoed the thoughts of Augusta Addington and said that he doubted Apaches had killed . . . he used the word slaughtered . . . Stover Timms and Lem Harlan. But nobody cared to listen.

CHAPTER SEVEN

Red Ryan and Buttons Muldoon rolled out of their beds before dawn and hitched up the six-horse team, including two young wheelers, the big, 1,250-pound horses next to the coach. They were the largest and most dependable of the team, but Buttons broke his customary morning silence to say that he'd be glad when he changed them. "Damn broncs are mean enough to kick me so high St. Peter could slap his brand on my ass."

Red shook his head. "Buttons, you can't say damn or ass in front of them holy monks. Remember what Abe Patterson told us."

Buttons said, "All right then," and aired out his lungs with a stream of profanity that lasted all of a full minute. He smiled. "There, all my best cusswords are out of my system."

Red was mightily impressed but said only, "I sure hope so. You just cussed enough to melt the ears off them monks and set fire to all the grass within ten yards of us."

"Damn right," Buttons said. He slapped a hand to his mouth. "Heck, I done it again."

Ribbons of scarlet and jade cloud crimsoned the sky when Buttons drove the stage to the front of the hotel where his passengers were already waiting, including Augusta Addington, who looked more beautiful than a woman had a right to look that early in the morning. She wore her blue riding habit and top hat, but Red thought she'd changed her shirt to a white one with a standup, lace-trimmed collar that perfectly suited her slender neck. But she still wore the duster, and the big leather bag hung from her shoulder. Red wondered if the British Bulldog was still in her pocket. Probably it was.

The monks each carried a carpetbag, except for one who toted the staff of Moses in its leather case, and, ladies first, they waited patiently for Augusta to board.

It was then that the eyes of Red and one of the monks clashed. A large bloodstain on the front of the monastic's robe had drawn his attention. The man pushed back his hood, revealing a florid, crimson-cheeked face, carroty, tonsured hair and a thick, fiery mustache and eyebrows. The face was lean, stretched tight over coarsely molded features, the pug nose broken, the result of being slammed by a British soldier's rifle butt in his native Ireland, and the mouth was wide, thin-lipped and expressive. It was not the face of an Irish poet, but of a pugnacious fighter. The initial impact of the son of Erin's strong features convinced Red Ryan that before he took the vows of poverty, chastity, and obedience, this man had been a heller.

The voice was soft, remarkably cultured. Whatever he'd once been, the monk was an educated man. "A bundle of willow rods applied to a man's back and chest can draw blood," the monk said in his lilting accent. "Hazel is better, much more painful, but there were none of those in these parts."

"Who beat you like that?" Red said. "Give me a name." Next to him, Buttons Muldoon listened intently and scowled.

The Irishman smiled. "I did it to myself in the chapel. We all did. We scourge ourselves to mortify the sinful flesh. In our order, mortification without blood spilled is no mortification at all." He raised his hood again, signaling that he was all though talking.

The monks followed Augusta into the stage and Buttons whispered into Red's ear, "Strange rannies, these holy monk fellers."

"Did you see any whips made from willow branches in the church?" Red said.

Buttons shook his head. "Whips? No, not as I recollect."

"How about blood?"

"Didn't see that, either."

"Odd, very odd," Red said.

"What is?"

"The Irish monk said he and the others had whipped themselves with willow rods until they drew blood," Red said. "But you saw no rods and no blood in the church."

Buttons had his eyes on his watch and his mind on his schedule. "Told you them boys were mighty peculiar," he said. His head snapped up. "Heck, now what?"

Red saw Abe Patterson, wearing his hat, boots, and gun, looking feisty, step out of the hotel door and walk purposefully toward he and Buttons. The little man said, "While you two was dilly-dallying around, I got you another passenger. His name is Archibald Weathers."

Buttons's gaze scanned the street. He saw a small crowd of late revelers who'd gathered to watch the stage showboat out of town, but nobody looked like a passenger. "Where is he, boss?" he said.

"He'll be here directly," Patterson said. "A couple of the local constables have gone to bring him from the hoosegow."

"Boss, he's an outlaw?" Buttons said, his jaw dropping.

"No, he ain't an outlaw. He don't even come close to be being an outlaw," Patterson said. "The chief lawman around here came to see me this morning before you two were out of bed and told me exactly what he was."

"And what is he exactly?" Buttons said.

"A damned nuisance, that's what he is. The lawman said Weathers was offered a choice . . . get hung or get lost."

"And he chose the latter."

This from a smiling Augusta Addington who'd been listening at the stage window.

"Indeed he did, Miss Addington," Patterson said, touching his hat brim. "The town is paying me two hundred dollars to get rid of him. He won't steal another chicken or grab a cooling apple pie off a San Angelo windowsill ever again. And his career as a saloon swamper is over."

"He sounds like a desperate character," Augusta said, smiling.

"Don't you worry your pretty head about that, Miss Addington," Patterson said, misinterpreting her amusement. "There's no need to get a fit of the womanly vapors. If Archibald Weathers even comes near you, Red Ryan will shoot him down like a dog. Won't you, Red?"

Red nodded. "Sure thing, Mr. Patterson." He made a

gun of his hand and dropped his thumb like a hammer. "I'll ventilate him quicker'n scat."

"Then my mind is now very much at rest," Augusta said. She decided to play Patterson's game. "Oh dear, I do declare that the ruffian will be uncomfortably close to me in the stage."

"Pshaw, that ain't going to happen," Patterson said. "Weathers's fare is being paid by the San Angelo city fathers, so he ain't a paying passenger himself, if'n you catch my drift. He'll ride on top where he'll be a nuisance to nobody."

"Except to me and Red," Buttons said.

"Once you're a hundred miles out of town, maybe as far as the San Saba River, you can dump him," Patterson said. "And good riddance."

A few minutes later two police constables showed up with Archibald Weathers walking between them. If Red and the others expected the man to look even a little like an outlaw, they were doomed to disappointment. Weathers could have hired himself out to a farmer as a living scare-crow. He was short, skinny as a rail, wearing a stained white collarless shirt several sizes too big for him and ragged pants that stopped above his ankles, his bare feet shoved into laceless army shoes that had once fitted a much larger man. His face was gray, badly bruised, and his dull, chocolate button eyes were downcast, as though he was completely uninterested in what was happening to him.

Worried about his schedule, Buttons Muldoon took charge. "You," he said to Weathers, "get onto the top of the stage and then stay put. Move and I'll shoot you off of there, compre?"

Weathers, pale and weakened by hunger, made a hard

job of it climbing onto the stage and he had to be assisted by Buttons and Red who manhandled him aloft as they would a mailsack. The little man finally sat upright, hugged his knees, and stared straight ahead, his face expressionless.

But Buttons wasn't done with him yet.

"You," he said. "See all them people standing around? They're waiting to see the Patterson stage showboat its way out of town, so you just hold on tight up there and keep your trap shut. Understand?"

Weathers looked down at Buttons and nodded, one quick jerk of the head, his face blank.

"Well, see you do," Buttons said, puzzled. What was wrong with that little man? He'd never met anyone so . . . lifeless.

Abe Patterson's farewells were said, another dire warning given about cussing within earshot of the holy monks, and then he slapped Buttons on the back and wished him, "Bon voyage."

The Patterson stage left Fredericksburg with a sound of rolling thunder. Buttons stood in the box like an old Norse god in his sailor's coat and sweeping mustache and cracked his whip to supply the lightning. Half-drunk voices raised in wild cheers as the stage's spinning yellow wheels kicked up clouds of dust as it hurtled across the city limits and then rocked headlong into the wilderness.

Up on the seat, Red sat with his shotgun across his knees and grinned, "You gave them a show, Buttons."

"Damn right, I gave them a show," Buttons said. "One ol' Abe and them drunks will never forget."

Behind him, a terrified Archibald Weathers clung on for dear life.

CHAPTER EIGHT

The Patterson stage headed southeast across rolling grassland interwoven with red, white, and yellow wild-flowers and stands of timber. Buttons Muldoon kept the Concho River well to his west, taking a trail first blazed by the army in 1869. The team performed well, including the green wheelers, and the horses seemed glad that they'd escaped the confines of the barn.

The stage was ten miles north of Kickapoo Springs on a good wagon road when Red Ryan saw riders ahead, coming on at a trot.

"Yeah, I see them," Buttons Muldoon said.

"Army?" Red said.

"Could be. They ain't Apaches. Too much shiny stuff on them."

"Road agents?"

"I don't know but keep the scattergun handy."

Buttons leaned over and yelled into the stage window, "Riders coming, but keep calm. Let me and Red do the talking." He straightened up, then said, "Archibald, you set still and behave yourself, an' you won't get shot."

Then Weathers surprised the heck out of him. "The

man on the paint is Smiler Thurmond," the little man said. "And that's Jonah Halton with him."

"How the heck can you see that far?" Buttons said.

"I got eyes like a hawk," Weathers said.

"An' that's why you're a chicken thief, huh?" Buttons said, grinning.

"One of the reasons," Weathers said.

Buttons shook his head. "Feller, there's nothing about you makes any sense," he said.

"Smiler never crosses the Brazos. Everybody knows that."

"It's him," Weathers said. "And he's got the Barnes brothers flanking him, Ollie and Harvey."

Now Red shifted uncomfortably in his seat and white-knuckled the Greener. "Would that be Crazy Ollie Barnes, the ranny that shot up the Fidgety Ferret brothel in Abilene that time?"

"None other," Weathers said. "He's as loco as a bedbug, but when it comes to gunfighting he's no pushover."

"Who the heck is he?" Buttons said.

Red said, "He's a drawfighter who should never drink whiskey, drives him crazy, and when he's crazy he's pure pizen. He cut loose and shot five men in the Fidgety Ferret that night. Shot a real likable whore by the name of Nanette de Vere too."

Buttons didn't take his eyes off the oncoming riders. "Why did he shoot the whore?"

"By mistake," Red said.

"How come you know all this?" Buttons said.

"I was there, drinking at the bar. I'd just won a booth fight and was celebrating."

"Heck, Red, lucky he didn't shoot you," Buttons said.

"Lucky I didn't shoot him, you mean. I'd given my gun to the bartender, and by the time I got it back, Ollie was gone. He killed Brent Walker that night, a friend of mine."

"Brent Walker, the Amarillo outlaw?"

"Yeah, Brent had been a lawman for a while, but then he took up the bank- and train-robbing profession and he was doing pretty well at it," Red said. "But like mine, his gun was behind the bar that night."

Buttons tore his eyes away from the riders and said, looking worried, "Red, don't try to get even today, not when we're carrying passengers, especially four holy monks and a woman."

"While I'm a representative of the Abe Patterson and Son Stage and Express Company I won't waste my employer's time settling old scores," Red said. "One day my path and Ollie's will cross again."

Buttons seemed relieved. "That's true blue of you, Red," he said. "You're a credit to the company."

"Damn right," Red said.

"Now, here they come," Buttons said. "Let's keep a weather eye on them rannies."

The four riders drew rein at pistol distance. A morose-looking man, his long, narrow face clean shaven, an oddity at that time in the West, sat his horse and addressed himself to Buttons. "Name's Smiler Thurmond," he said. "My old man give me that handle as a joke, on account of how I never smile. That is, until the day I bashed his brains out with a mattock. I smiled that day and I've never felt the need to repeat it since. Now you know all about me, so what about you? Are you carrying a strongbox? And shotgun guard, if I was you, I'd keep that Greener acrost my knees and the only movement I'd make is to blink."

Red opened his mouth to speak, but Buttons, afraid of what might come out of it, jumped in quick. "Right pleased to meet you, Mr. Thurmond," he said. "I've heard a lot about you, how it's a natural fact that you're the fastest hired gun around and that you ain't never been bested in the outlaw's calling."

"I asked you a question, mister," Thurmond said. "I won't ask it a second time."

"Well, Mr. Thurmond, I'm as disappointed as a bride left at the altar to tell you this, but, as you can see, I ain't carrying a strongbox. All I got is four holy monks an' a schoolmarm an' I don't reckon they could put together fifty cents between them. As for me an' Red, well, look at us . . . we own what we stand up in."

Thurmond turned his head. "Jonah, go take a look in the stage," he said.

The man called Jonah, small and mean and scowling, wearing a buckskin jacket and canvas pants tucked into fancy boots no cowhand could afford, swung out of the saddle, walked to the stage and looked inside. After a moment he said, "Yeah, four monks in robes and a woman." He broke into a grin. "And the woman can drink champagne in my bed anytime."

"Jonah, git back here," Thurmond said. "Leave that woman alone." He looked hard at Buttons and then said, "You got nothing worth robbing. You're a sore disappointment to me, driver."

"Told you so, and I'm right sorry."

"How come you don't have a strongbox?"

"The Abe Patterson and Son Stage and Express

Company cornered the mail and passenger trade," Buttons said. "You want strongboxes, Mr. Thurmond, your best bet would be Wells Fargo or the Barlow and Sanderson Company. They carry silver mining payrolls up Leadville, Colorado, way."

Thurmond shrugged. "I know. Robbed them both at one time or another, but never scored a big haul."

"Right sorry to hear that," Buttons said. "You must've hit them on bad days."

"Seems like," Thurmond said. Then, "The Apaches are out."

Buttons nodded. "Heard that at Fort Concho."

"We seen the talking smoke," a hard-faced man with ice-blue eyes that Red recognized as Ollie Barnes said.

"Where?" Red said, testing the man. Did he remember him from the Fidgety Ferret?

His question was answered when Barnes looked at him without recognition and waved a hand. "Thataway, to the northeast."

"How long ago?" Red said, feeling Barnes out again.

"An hour, maybe less," the man said. Barnes still did not appear to recall Red, but he seemed uneasy, edging close to being afraid. But afraid of what? Then Thurmond made it clear.

"Where are you headed, driver?" he said.

"Name's Muldoon," Buttons said. "We're headed for the Patterson stage station at Kickapoo Springs to feed the passengers and change horses."

"Then we'll tag along with you," Thurmond said. "I can't rest easy with Apaches this close." His eyes swung away from Buttons to Augusta, who had stepped down from the stage. "You best get back inside, lady," he said.

"There are Apaches about and not a two-hour ride away from here. We seen what they can do to a woman . . . and a man."

"Sodbusters?" Buttons said.

"Rancher and his wife," Thurmond said. He recalled what he'd seen, and his face showed strain. "Mom-and-pop outfit." He shook his head. "Tough people . . . took them way too long to die."

Augusta Addington played the nervous New Orleans belle again. "Oh dear, those dreadful Apaches." Then, more genuinely, "Did they suffer very much, the man and woman?"

"Do you really want me to answer that question, lady?" Thurmond said.

"No, I guess not," Augusta said. "Are you a road agent?"

"Not today," Thurmond said. "Today, I'm just a fellow traveler."

"On account of how you ain't got anything worth stealing," Jonah Halton said. "Unless it's a kiss or two."

Augusta shook her head. "I think that would be quite as unpleasant as a robbery," she said.

"No, it wouldn't," Halton grinned. "Not for me."

"Jonah, git back here, quit the chitchat, and mount up," Thurmond said. "The sooner we get to the stage station and have walls around us, the better I'll feel."

Halton swung into the saddle. "Never knowed you to be this boogered afore, Smiler," he said.

"Yeah, but then I never seen what Apaches do to a white person afore," Thurmond said.

"Hellfire," Ollie Barnes said suddenly. "I know you."

Red's head snapped up, but the man wasn't looking at

him. His eyes were fixed on Archibald Weathers. Barnes pointed. "Smiler, lookee. Ain't that Chris Mercer?"

Recognition dawned on Thurmond's face. "Yeah, that's him. What the heck happened to you, Chris? Where are your gambler's duds and them fancy Russian pistols?"

"I gave all that up, Smiler," Weathers said. "A long time ago."

"Heck, you ain't exactly prospered since, have you?" Thurmond said. He addressed himself to Buttons. "Where are you taking this man?"

"Taking him?" Buttons said. "Well, I'm taking him a hundred miles from here and dumping him. The law in San Angelo wanted to hang him for a damned nuisance but decided to give him the option of being banished from the city limits forever. He took the option."

"Buttons," Red Ryan said. "Chris Mercer . . . don't that ring a bell?"

Buttons seemed puzzled, then his face slowly cleared. "Yeah, now I recollect . . . the Salt Creek War up Colorado way a few years back. Heck, big Jim Milk, nowadays he drives for Wells Fargo, was a hired gun in that scrap . . ."

"And Chris Mercer was top gun," Thurmond said. "You'd killed eight white men by then, hadn't you, Mercer?"

"About that," the man now called Mercer said. "Somewhere along the way I lost count."

"That's enough talk, now get this stage rolling," Thurmond said. "The Apaches could be getting close. I think I can smell them in the wind."

"Hold on just a cotton-pickin' minute," Buttons said. He turned and looked at the man hunched over on the top of the stage. "Here you," he said. "Was you Chris Mercer at one time?"

The little man nodded. "Yeah, I was. At one time."

"How come you quit the gunfighting profession?"

"Because of a Gypsy woman."

"She left you?"

"No, I was in Denver when she told me my fortune."

"Heck, man, did she read your palm, the way they do?"

"No, she saw me in a crystal ball."

"And what did she say when she saw you in the crystal ball?"

"I'd killed twelve men in fair fight by then and she told me thirteen was my unlucky number. If I tried to kill a thirteenth man, he'd be the death of me."

"And that's it?" Buttons said. "You hung up your guns?"

"No, I didn't hang them up. I sold the Smith and Wessons and my duds and bought whiskey," the man called Chris Mercer said. "I've been buying whiskey ever since."

"Buttons shook his head. "Damned tragic," he said. "All that shooting skill gone to waste."

Red said, "Maybe the Gypsy woman was wrong. Ever think of that?"

Mercer shook his head. "She was old, and old Gypsy women are always right. Anyhow, I can't take a chance."

"Hey, Chris, want me to shoot you and put you out of your misery?" Jonah Halton said.

"Maybe later," Mercer said. "I'll let you know."

Halton grinned. "Jonah Halton, the man who killed Chris Mercer. I like the sound of that."

Mercer's only reaction was a disinterested shrug of his skinny shoulders, and Red wondered at the man. There was a time not so long before when Western men talking around the potbellied stove of a wintertime mentioned Chris Mercer in the same breath as John Wesley Hardin and Wild Bill Longley. Had a Gypsy woman's crystal ball really spooked him that badly, or was there something else? Time and future events might answer that question.

Buttons Muldoon hoorawed the team into motion, and an hour later drove the stage into the Patterson station at Kickapoo Springs.

CHAPTER NINE

As soon as she stepped from the stage, Augusta Addington took Buttons Muldoon aside and told him she thought she'd caught a glimpse of an Indian on a black horse watching them at a distance. But Buttons and Jim Moore, the station manager, were skeptical. Gertrude Moore, Jim's tall, bony and angular wife who seemed to live on nothing but prune juice and scripture, questioned Augusta closely and then reported that she put the Apache sighting down to female hysteria accompanied by a heaviness in the womb and a tendency to cause trouble.

Buttons and Moore accepted that explanation, but Red Ryan was not so sure. He recalled Augusta calmly standing under the disemboweled bodies of Stover Timms and Lem Harlan, a British Bulldog revolver in her pocket, and whatever else she might be, the woman was not a hysteric. If she said she saw an Apache, then she saw one . . . it was as simple as that.

Western outlaws took good care of their horses, and Smiler Thurmond and his men put theirs in the stable with hay and a scoop of oats before they returned to the cabin.

While Buttons and limping Jim Moore, a man with heavy features, black eyes, and graying hair showing under a frayed Confederate kepi, left to change the team, Red gave Augusta his arm and followed Thurmond and the others inside the station, a spacious log cabin with two small windows to the front that could be shuttered from the inside. Apart from the usual outbuildings, barn, and corral, Abe Patterson had built what he called a redoubt, a crude, sod wall enclosure about eight feet high with timber firing platforms and a single narrow gate. The structure covered about twenty-five hundred square feet of ground and when Apaches were in the area it was manned day and night by Moore's witless sons Danny and Donnie and a surly hired hand named McKenzie who'd killed a man in El Paso a couple of years before. According to Jim Moore, all three were crack shots with a Winchester, and fear didn't enter into their thinking, such as it was. Abe Patterson's plan was that in the event of an Indian attack, the occupants would leave the main cabin, man the redoubt, and run up the Patterson and Son Stage and Express Company flag, a green and gold quartered banner, the colors of his coat of arms.

So far, the plan had not been put to the test, and Jim Moore hoped it would remain that way.

When Red and Augusta stepped inside, the two long dining tables were occupied, the one to the left by the four monks, the other by Smiler Thurmond and his men. The monks sat in silence, hoods pulled over their faces, and Chris Mercer, small and insignificant, sat alone.

Beyond the tables, at the far wall, was a stone fireplace burning logs, fronted by wrought iron stands that held a variety of pots, fry pans, a kettle, and a large, sooty coffee-pot. Gertrude Moore busied herself frying bacon and stirring beans, and the biscuits cooking in a cast iron skillet smelled a little scorched.

"Hey, Ryan, bring the lady over here and sit with us," Thurmond said. He nodded in the direction of the four silent monks. "You won't get much conversation over there."

"Or there," Ollie Barnes said, his eyes moving to Mercer. Then he called out, "Hey, mister, don't I know you?"

Hayden McKenzie sat at the end of a table, forking beans into his mouth. "You don't know me," he said.

"I swear, I seen you afore somewhere," Barnes said.

"You ain't seen me anywhere," McKenzie said.

"Y'all sure about that?" Barnes said. "Didn't I have trouble with you one time?"

McKenzie's sullen expression didn't change, but he remained silent.

"Ollie, leave the man be," Thurmond said. "He doesn't know you." He stood for Augusta Addington and, with a certain amount of Southern charm, said, "Please be seated, ma'am and allow us to delight in your company. I'm sure you'll prove to be a sweet distraction."

"You are very gallant, sir," Augusta said. "Y'all hush now, you're making me blush. Mercy me, I almost feel that I'm back in New Orleans." She sat, her petticoats rustling, and watching her, Red Ryan marveled that she'd already spent three hours in a hot, dusty stage but still looked fresh and pretty and smelled of French perfume.

Mrs. Moore served up food, bacon, beans and slightly scorched on the bottom biscuits. A devout Catholic, she attended to the monks first and asked for their blessing, which, after some hesitation on the brothers' part, she duly received, four strong hands making signs of the cross in the air.

As a top-class hired gun, Smiler Thurmond had spent time around the rich and powerful, men and women with airs and manners above his station. He was a quick learner and so with some sophistication talked to Augusta about trivial things and told her stories that made her laugh, leaving Red to sit in silence, feeling like a tongue-tied rube.

Then a strange thing happened that shocked everyone.

For some reason that Western historians, and psychiatrists for that matter, have never been able to explain, Haydon McKenzie took exception to the attention Thurmond was paying to the woman. He rose to his feet, a Colt in his hand, and stepped toward the outlaw. Thurmond, his whole focus on Augusta Addington, didn't see him coming. Three years after these events, dime novelist James H. Patrick claimed that McKenzie said, "Here, that won't do. Get away from the woman, you damned scoundrel." That quote was never confirmed, but Patrick and all historians agree on what happened next. McKenzie's mouth was wide open as he yelled obscenities at Thurmond . . . until an Apache arrowhead that entered neatly between his upper and lower teeth closed it permanently. An Apache Osage wood bow had a draw weight of between forty and sixty pounds, enough to send its arrow shattering though a glass pane of the cabin window and into McKenzie's mouth. There has been some discussion on whether or not it was an aimed shot, but no Apache ever took credit for it, so we'll never know.

For a long moment time stood still as McKenzie froze in place, his eyes shocked as bright scarlet blood ran from his mouth over his neck and chin. The iron arrowhead was jammed in his throat and he could not scream.

"Down!" Red Ryan yelled.

Along with Augusta, Smiler Thurmond and his men hit the wood floor as bullets splintered through the windows and pinged off the stove, others thudding into the fireplace and wall.

Red saw the four monks move with amazing nimbleness as they tipped over their table, swung it broadside to the door and crouched behind it. Just in time, because a second or two later a couple of arrows thudded into the tabletop.

"Where the heck are they?" Thurmond yelled. He had his Colt in his hand.

"Out there, somewhere," Red said.

"Damned savages have us pinned down in here," Thurmond said.

"Seems like," Red said.

Beside him, Augusta had her British Bulldog revolver in her hand. "Finish the story about the Missouri midnight caller some other time, Mr. Thurmond," she said.

Thurmond managed a grin. "If we get out of this alive, I sure will, ma'am," he said.

From outside, rifles roared, fired again, and Red figured it was Moore's sons shooting from the redoubt. Where was Buttons? Had he been caught out in the open with the horses? Red didn't want to know the answer to that question. Then, a brown, painted face appeared at the cabin window. Red snapped off a shot, shattered glass, and the face disappeared.

"Ryan, did you get one?" Thurmond said.

"I don't know," Red said.

McKenzie made a terrible sound, like a man drowning in mud. He lay on his back, choking on his own blood, the arrow sticking out of his mouth an obscenity.

"Damn them!" Thurmond yelled. He raised his revolver and thumbed a couple of ineffective shots through the window. Red figured the outlaw was shooting to make noise or to cover up his fear. Or maybe he didn't want to hear McKenzie dying so hard.

Not a man to lie on the floor and let the danger come to him, Red got slowly to his feet and stepped to the window, his boots crunching on broken glass. He glanced out the shattered window, ducked back, looked again. Beyond the stage road stretched miles of rolling, open country, a few trees growing here and there. But there were no rocks, no thick stands of timber within killing range where an Apache could hide. And the hot day was silent, slumbering in starkly white sunshine that revealed every blade of grass and even the bees that bumbled around the wildflowers.

After the initial flurry of gunfire, the Winchesters of the Moore boys had fallen silent. The Apaches might be gone . . . or they might not. They were a notoriously notional people with the patience of the devil. Behind him, Red heard Thurmond and his boys get to their feet and then the thud-thud-thud of Augusta's high-heeled ankle boots on the wood floor as she walked toward him. Red herded her away from the window before she said, "See anything?"

"Nothing," Red said.

"Have the Apaches gone?"

Red shook his head. "I don't know."

Behind him, Thurmond said, "Hey, Mercer, get the dead man's gun. You may need it."

"Smiler, he ain't dead yet," Ollie Barnes said.

"True enough, he ain't," his brother Harvey said.

"He's dead," Thurmond said. "He just hasn't stopped breathing yet."

"I don't want his gun," Chris Mercer said. "His, or anybody else's."

"I said, pick it up," Thurmond said.

"You go to Hell," Mercer said.

Ollie Barnes said, "Your Gypsy woman didn't say nothing about Apaches."

"An Apache is a man," Mercer said.

"Yeah, but he ain't a white man," Thurmond said. "When it comes to gunfighting, only white men count."

Mercer shook his head, and Ollie Barnes said, "He ain't gonna do it, Smiler."

"Then damn you, Mercer, make yourself useful," Thurmond said.

Rawboned and strong, the big outlaw grabbed Mercer by the back of his shirt. He frog-marched him to the door, opened it wide, and shoved the little man through.

"Get out there and scout for Apaches," Thurmond said, slamming the door shut behind Mercer.

Red watched what had just happened. Had Mercer been a bona fide, fare-paying passenger of the Abe Patterson and Son Stage and Express Company, he would have intervened. But since Mercer's fare was paid by a third party, the little man didn't count, and Red let it go.

This much he did do . . .

Red moved closer to a broken windowpane and yelled at the top of his lungs, "Buttons! Are you dead?"

A pause, then, "Not yet."

"Where are you?"

"In the redoubt with Jim Moore and his sons."

"Anybody hurt?"

"No. You?"

"McKenzie is dying. Took an arrow."

A longer pause, then, "Jim says he's sorry to hear that, even though McKenzie was a disagreeable cuss."

"You see any Apaches?"

"None. But that don't mean they ain't here. You stay put, Red."

"Buttons, listen. Chris Mercer . . ."

"Who?"

"Archibald Weathers. The chicken thief."

"What about him?"

"He's out on a scout. Keep an eye out for him, huh?"

"I don't see him, Red."

"Well, he's out there somewhere."

"More fool him," Buttons said.

"Well, if you see him, bring him into the redoubt."

"I'll do that. Shoot if you catch sight of an Apache."

"I surely will, Buttons," Red said.

Thirty minutes dragged slowly by, half an hour of unrelenting heat in the stark white glare of the sun. Buzzards gathered overhead and glided in lazy circles over the station, instinctively attracted to what might yet become a place of mass death. Mrs. Moore brought tin cups of water to the men stationed at the windows and gave Augusta hers in a green glass goblet. At some time during the thirty minutes, Haydon McKenzie made a gurgling sound and died. Everybody heard it . . . everybody saw the man's body twitch and then lie still in death . . . and nobody much cared. The man was a stranger to them, and in this unforgiving, often merciless land, strangers died all the time.

The Apaches hit with the suddenness of a lightning bolt striking a tree.

Thirty mounted warriors thundered past the cabin, raising a tan-colored cloud of dust, and in the first, fleeting moment a painted face hurtling by, blue and brown headbands, and the flash of sunlight on gunmetal was all Red Ryan saw of them.

"They're going for the horses!" Red yelled.

He ran outside, and Thurmond and his men, aware of how serious the loss of their mounts could be, followed. The Apaches had come under fire from the redoubt and Red spotted a couple of riderless ponies as the warriors reached the corral. Red's shotgun and rifle were with the stage, but Thurmond and his men opened up on the Indians with Winchesters, joining in the fire from the redoubt. Because of dust it was impossible to say if any Apaches were hit, but it soon became obvious that they were mightily discouraged. Nine well-armed fighting men were now shooting at them, and no Apache ever liked that kind of odds. They were first-rate fighting men themselves and didn't lack courage, but they always sought the advantage in a brawl. The Apache warrior was a pragmatist. If the odds weren't stacked well in his favor, he had no compunction about running away and fighting another day when his prospects might be brighter.

Deciding that this was not a good day to die, the Indians streamed away from the corral and galloped into the prairie. They had not managed to steal a single horse, and behind them they left four dead warriors.

Chris Mercer emerged from behind the redoubt looking dazed but otherwise unhurt. Buttons immediately took him into custody and ordered him to remain in the barn until the stage left. "On account of how you still ain't a hundred miles from San Angelo," he said. Then, frowning, "How come you're still alive?"

"The Apaches didn't see me," Mercer said.

"Or you being such a scrawny little feller, maybe they figured you weren't worth their while," Buttons said.

"Maybe," Mercer said. "Next time I see one of those Apaches, I'll ask him."

Red and Buttons agreed to help Jim Moore and his sons bury the Apache dead. Since Haydon McKenzie was a white man, he was laid to rest in a separate grave, and Moore said he would set up a marker. And a few months later he did just that, a flat slab of limestone that gave McKenzie's name and the date of his death "at the Battle of Moore's Station."

CHAPTER TEN

Although it was almost four in the afternoon, Buttons Muldoon decided to make up time and hit the trail for the privately owned Cave Springs Station, where his passengers could be fed and the team changed again. The 1869 Army report on the first ten miles between Kickapoo Springs and Cave Springs was that the "the grass is good but available water is muddy." The remaining ten miles or so was described as "rocky, but the grass and water is good." There was nothing in the report to give Buttons pause, but the sky gave him fair warning of a gathering storm to the north.

When Red pointed this out, Buttons nodded and then said, "It's four hours to the station, but I reckon we can outrun them clouds."

Jim Moore cast a weather eye to the sky. "You got a good team there, Buttons," he said. "You'll be well on your way before the storm hits. What do you say, Red?"

Red smiled. "Don't ask me, I'm just the messenger."

"Well, you can trust me," Buttons said. "When it comes to storms, I'm never wrong."

That last didn't exactly inspire Red with confidence,

but he helped get the passengers loaded, and when Augusta Addington glanced at the northern sky and said, "It's going to storm, Mr. Ryan," he assured her that they'd be at Cave Springs Station before the bad weather hit.

"If the worst comes to the worst, we can shelter there overnight," Red said. "But I don't think that will happen."

"Good. As I told you, I'm most anxious to reach Fredericksburg," Augusta said. Then, for some reason she added, "It's a matter of life and death."

That last surprised Red. But he saw the woman close down, unwilling to add to that statement, and he said only, "You'll be there the day after tomorrow, because Buttons will want to push on." He smiled and tipped his plug hat to a rakish angle. "Day and night, fair weather and foul, the Patterson stage never stops."

"Except when it does," Augusta said.

Red nodded. "Yeah, well, now and again an act of God will slow us down some."

"Then let's hope there are none of those between here and Fredericksburg," Augusta said.

Buttons overheard that last part of the conversation and said, "Miss Addington, you've met Abe Patterson . . . God wouldn't dare." But God did dare . . . and would soon make Buttons Muldoon eat his words.

"Should we tell her?" Buttons Muldoon said, his gloved hands on the lines never still as he constantly made little adjustments that the team's experienced leaders understood.

"Tell who what?" Red said, the shotgun across his knees, his restless eyes scanning the vast rolling grassland ahead of him. To the south the sky was a uniform blue, but behind the stage the piled-up boulders of cloud were as black as coal.

"Tell Miss Addington about Honeysuckle Cairns. Prepare her for a shock, like."

"Do you reckon she'll be shocked?" Red said.

"Seeing a four-hundred pound, painted-up whore for the first time would shock anybody."

"Back a couple of years ago, it sure did me the first time," Buttons said. "And if seeing her wasn't bad enough, then I heard that little, squeaky voice of hers. A man would have to be pretty desperate to tackle that gal."

"And were you?" Red said. "Desperate, I mean."

"No sir, not hardly. But the feller with me, went by the name of Trinity River Turk Matheson, sure was. He was my new shotgun messenger then, after ol' Bill Simmons got hisself shot. Well, anyhoo, Turk had just spent two years panning for gold up Colorado way and when we arrived at Cave Springs, he hadn't seen a real, female woman in any shape or form in all that time."

Red watched a small flock of crows flap south, a worrisome sign, and then said, "And did he?"

"Did he what?"

"Did he indulge?"

"Indulge? He was flat broke after leaving Colorado, and Abe Patterson had advanced him a week's pay. Turk blew his entire roll on Honeysuckle at two dollars a turn. He was still there, trying to borry money from stage passengers, when I left." Buttons shook his head. "I never did find out what happened to ol' Turk Matheson. Maybe Honeysuckle Cairns was the death of him."

"Too much woman, I reckon," Red said.

"Too much woman for any man," Buttons said. "And Turk was just a little feller. He'd put you in mind of . . . what's his name?"

"Chris Mercer."

"Yeah, a scrawny little hombre like him."

"Sad story," Red said. "I mean, him running out of money like that."

"Yeah, ain't it though?" Buttons said. "So, do we tell her?"

"No, I don't think so. Let Augusta find out for herself," Red said. "I reckon she can handle anything life throws at her, including four-hundred-pound whores."

"Heck, what does Smiler want?" Buttons said. "Be ready with the scattergun, Red. I don't trust him."

Thurmond and his boys had been flanking the stage, and now the outlaw rode closer, looking worried as the day grew darker, and said, "Hey, Muldoon, do you see them clouds?"

"I see them."

"Do you hear the thunder?"

"I hear it."

"You know this road," Thurmond said. "Is there any-place we can find shelter?"

"Not until we reach Cave Springs, there ain't," Buttons said.

"I don't like this," Thurmond said. "There's lightning spiking all over the place, and me and the boys are the tallest things on the whole damn prairie."

"No, you're not, I am," Red said.

"Well, we're going to ride on ahead," Thurmond said.

"See if we can outrun the storm. We'll keep the coffee warming for you at Cave Springs."

"White of you, Smiler," Buttons said. "Good luck."

"Yeah, you too, Buttons. Good luck."

Smiler Thurmond and his boys were ten miles north of Cave Springs when the storm caught up with them. At first there was only a growing darkness. A dire warning. Then the tempest struck with terrible fury. A gigantic, roaring wall of wind and torrential rain accompanied by continuous thunder hurtled from the north like a landslide of monstrous boulders, stunning the senses and terrifying the horses. Suddenly, amid the deafening clamor of the storm came a more vicious noise, like the hiss of an angry snake, and a blinding flare of incandescent blue light followed by a rending crash.

A solitary cottonwood on the bank of a dry wash burst apart, rose several feet in the air, and then fell, great splinters of its white inner wood erupting into the air like shrapnel. A thin cry in extremis, and Jonah Halton, closest to the lightning bolt, went down with his horse in a tangle of kicking legs, reins, and saddle leather. Thunder bellowed, lightning cracked like a bullwhip, lashing across the plains and the air smelled of brimstone and charred wood and grass. Battered by wind and rain, Thurmond opened his mouth and yelled, a sound no one heard above the ear-splitting tumult. Fighting his rearing horse, the outlaw rode closer to Halton and swung from the saddle. Its reins trailing, his panicked mount immediately ran headlong into the prairie and disappeared into the storm. Thurmond never saw it again.

Halton's mount was standing head down, its left foreleg broken. The outlaw stripped the saddle and bridle and then put the animal out of its misery. He holstered his gun and kneeled beside Halton. Wind and rain hammered Thurmond and around him the roaring plains were dark, shot through with searing, blinding lightning flashes as though Heck had come to central Texas.

Thurmond gabbed Halton by the shoulders and yelled, "Jonah, wake up! Open your eyes!"

But the little outlaw did not respond, his face under its sunburn gray as ash. He did not seem to be breathing, and a thin trickle of bloody saliva ran down the corner of his mouth.

Ollie Barnes stood over Thurmond, his tall form shimmering in the flash of pulsating silver light and steel needles of rain. "He's a goner, Smiler," Barnes said. "The lightning done for him."

Thurmond shook his head. "I set store by Jonah. Why did he have to haul off and die on me?"

"Luck of the draw, I guess," Barnes said with considerable indifference. He'd never liked Halton much. He was always a finger looking for a trigger.

Now that it had done its worst, the storm passed. The darkness that had descended on the plains lifted, and the thunder now grumbled its way south, occasionally throwing out spiteful darts of lightning.

Smiler Thurmond and the Barnes brothers watched the Patterson stage, its sidelamps lit, slowly emerge from the gloom. When Buttons drew rein on the team, he looked down at the dead man and the dead horse and said, "You've been through it, Smiler."

"I reckon," Thurmond said. "Jonah Halton is dead, and I lost two good horses." He looked at the soaking-wet driver and guard and said, "You don't look so good yourselves."

Red's buckskin shirt was black with rain, and Buttons's blue sailor's coat hung on him like a wet sack. "Damned storm rained bullfrogs and heifer yearlings," Red said. "Sorry about Halton."

"I set store by him," Smiler said.

"Yeah, he was a right neighborly feller," Buttons said, straight-faced.

"What happened here?"

Augusta Addington, carrying her top hat after it was knocked off during the stage's violent charge through the storm, stepped toward Thurmond.

"Man killed by lightning," the outlaw said.

Augusta kneeled by Halton, peeled off a glove, and felt the right side of the man's neck. After ten seconds, she said, "How long has he been like this?"

"Quite a spell," Thurmond said.

"How long?"

Thurmond thought about and said, "Thirty minutes, maybe more."

Augusta nodded. "I can bring him back."

"How?" Thurmond said. "He's dead."

"Not yet. Not quite," the woman said. "I saw a Chinaman on the Barbary Coast over San Francisco way bring back a ship's carpenter who'd been struck by lightning." She laid aside her hat. "We have no time to waste."

Augusta forcibly opened Halton's mouth and carefully looked inside. Then she placed the heel of her right hand on the center of Jonah Halton's chest, put her other hand on top, and positioned herself so that her shoulders were above her hands. Using her body weight, she pressed down hard, and Buttons Muldoon would later say she almost flattened out Halton's chest before she stopped and let his breastbone return to normal. After a hundred of these compressions, she stopped to rest for a few moments and then started again. Augusta was breathing hard after her fifth round of compressions, but she kept at it. After another three, Halton showed signs of life. He coughed weakly and moved his head. Augusta paused for a moment and said, "He's coming around."

"He was spitting up blood," Thurmond said. "I saw it and figured he was dead for sure."

"No, I checked his mouth, and, as I suspected, he'd bitten his tongue when he fell from his horse," the woman said. "Here, help me sit him up."

Red and Buttons climbed down from the box, and the driver said, "Heck, lady, how did you do that? I mean, bring a man back from the dead."

"He wasn't quite dead, and I got to him just in time," Augusta said. "The Chinaman who taught me how to press on the chest that way told me it stimulates the lungs and the heart . . . something like that. He said that back in Shanghai he was a doctor."

"I reckon it takes a pretty good doctor to raise the dead," Buttons said.

Augusta smiled and let that go. Halton looked around and his eyes fixed on Thurmond. "Who shot me?" he said.

"You weren't shot, Jonah," Thurmond said. "You were hit by lightning. Your horse is dead."

"Damn," Halton said.

"The young lady, Miss Addington, saved your life. Brung you back from the dead."

Augusta said, "He wasn't . . ."

"Like Lazarus in the Bible," Halton said, interrupting. He turned his head and looked at Augusta. "Call me Lazarus."

"I prefer to call you Mr. Halton," Augusta said. "Now, let's get you to your feet. Mr. Muldoon, he'll have to ride in the coach."

Buttons shook his head. "No, he can't, not unless he has a hundred dollars, the fare from here to the Cave Springs station."

"I don't have a hundred dollars," Halton said.

Buttons nodded. "In that case, by the authority vested in me by the Abe Patterson and Son Stage and Express Company, you can ride on top, free of charge. Up there with the other drowned rat. Ain't that right, Archibald? Or whatever the heck your name is."

"I'll have to ride up there as well, Muldoon," Thurmond said. "My hoss is in the next county by this time." His hand edged closer to his gun. "Of course, I could just take over this stage, and you and Ryan can ride on top with the drowned rat."

When it came to rubbing shoulders with known outlaws, Red was a prudent man, and a mark of his caution was that he'd brought his shotgun down from the box with him. He lifted the barrel until the twin muzzles were in line with Thurmond's belt buckle.

"I can cut you in half from here, Smiler," he said. "This will be your only notification."

The outlaw dropped his hand. "A joke, just a joke," he said. "Damn it, I never did meet a shotgun messenger with a sense of humor."

"Having no sense of humor is a qualification for the job," Red said. "It's in the Patterson rule book."

"Damn right, and if it ain't, it should be," Buttons said. "Smiler, for once in your life are you gonna forget you're an outlaw and act true blue and straight up, or do we leave you here?"

"I'll ride on top with Jonah," Thurmond said. "Ollie and Harvey Barnes still got their nags."

"Crackerjack!" Buttons said. "Heck, Smiler, when we pull into Cave Springs, you'll be the first to catch sight of Honeysuckle Cairns."

"Oh yeah?" Thurmond said. "Who's she?"

"You'll find out," Buttons said.

CHAPTER ELEVEN

On all fours, Honeysuckle Cairns crawled out of the creek behind the stage station and came face-to-face with a red wolf. She got to her feet, stood firmly on vast, tree-trunk legs, and then pulled her cotton shift over her wet body, the white fabric clinging pinkly to her huge, pendulous breasts and belly. The wolf seemed more curious than aggressive—a massive, naked women climbing from an icy creek was not a sight the animal encountered every day. For her part, Honeysuckle looked over the wolf with a critical eye. He was big, and would probably dress out at around sixty or seventy pounds. His brick-colored coat was thick and free of scars or sores. She had her heart set on a wolfskin rug for the floor in front of her fireplace and he'd do. He'd do just fine.

The wolf stepped closer and watched Honeysuckle as she waddled to the gunbelt she'd left on top of the decayed stump of a long-ago felled cottonwood. She slid a self-cocking, .41 Colt Thunderer from the holster and a razor-sharp skinning knife from its sheath. Honeysuckle laid the knife carefully on the stump, raised the Colt, and neatly shot the wolf between the eyes. Aware of the old mountain man warning to never trust a wolf until it's been skun, she waited . . . but the wolf didn't move, undoubtedly as dead as the rotten cottonwood stump.

Honeysuckle had just finished skinning the animal and was standing beside the gut pile, bloody knife in hand, when the Patterson stage drove into the station.

Buttons Muldoon always claimed that the owner of the Cave Springs station, a sour, humorless Ohioan named Sam Young, had the longest Yankee face on him that he'd ever seen. "And I've seen more than my share."

Young, dressed like a preacher in a black, broadcloth suit, collarless shirt, and flat-brimmed hat with dome-shaped crown, stood outside the station cabin and watched the Patterson stage arrive.

Buttons reined to a creaking, swaying halt and said, "Howdy, Sam. It's been a while."

"A six month at least," Young said. "I was down with the rheumatisms all winter and lost my best hunting dog to a cougar. Missus took sick around Christmastime, and she ain't near yet recovered. My hired man got the croup and claimed it was because of me. He up and left, and now I'm single-handed."

Buttons put on his sympathetic face. "You've been through it, Sam."

"Heck, nobody cares, especially stage passengers. I need this and gimme that. It's enough to age a man. Well, I got a good team for you at least. Bacon and beans in the pot and coffee on the bile. I hear the Apaches are out."

"They sure are," Buttons said. "We had a run-in with them up at Kickapoo station."

"Lose any passengers?" Young said.

"No. But we done for four Apaches though."

"Is that a boast? Sounds like a boast to me."

"No. It's just a natural fact."

"Patterson drivers are big on the brag," Young said. "That's been my experience. Unload your passengers and let them stretch their legs and we'll get your team changed. You'll keep going, I take it."

"Got a schedule to keep, Sam."

"Both of them swings are sweated up and look mighty tuckered out," Young said.

"There's nothing wrong with the swings," Buttons said. "I know my horses, and they're just fine."

Red Ryan grinned. "Sam, you reckon you can charge Abe Patterson extry for replacing run-down horses? Seems like you've done that before."

"So long as Patterson puts two-bit nags in the traces, I'll keep on charging him extry," Young said. "When's an Apache gonna take that red hair of your'n, Ryan?"

"They'll have to catch me first, Sam," Red said.

"Maybe they will, this trip," Young said. His eyes moved to the top of the stage. "That's a desperate-looking bunch you got there."

"Two outlaws and a reformed gunslinger who took to drink," Buttons said. "There's a couple of other outlaws following on behind."

"I don't see them," Young said.

"Well, they're back yonder somewhere," Buttons said.

"Getting dark," Young said.

"Outlaws are used to riding the owlhoot," Buttons said. "They'll be here and hungry enough to eat your beans."

"More fool them," Young said.

His eyes were on the passengers and they grew bigger when he saw the tall, elegant, and beautiful Augusta Addington, and larger still when the four hooded monks filed silently into the cabin. Young looked up at Buttons, a question on his face, and was answered by a shrug and, "Holy men bound for the Perdinales River country. They plan to build a mission and convert the heathen cattlemen."

"Then I wish them good luck," Young said. "They're gonna need it. Gideon Stark is the cock of the walk down that way, and his Stark Cattle Company is the biggest ranch in Texas, or so they say. He's two shades meaner than the devil himself, and he can kill a man just by looking at him. Stark won't take kindly to monks building on his range."

Red noticed that Augusta hadn't yet gone into the cabin. She stood near the door and listened to the exchange between Buttons and Young about the rancher named Stark.

Buttons said, "I talked to a Ranger one time, and he told me it's a natural fact that Gideon Stark has hung more rustlers, road agents, and robbers than all the judges in Texas put together. And he's shot more than his share as well."

Augusta said, "He has sons?"

Young shook his head. "No ma'am, Gideon Stark has no sons, just one daughter. I've never seen her, but they say she's mighty pretty. He calls her Della, and half the young bucks in Texas would like to walk out with her, but don't."

"Why not?" Augusta said.

Young flashed a rare smile. "Because Stark is right handy with a bullwhip."

"A man to avoid," Augusta said.

"A hard, unforgiving man without a shred of mercy in him is Gideon Stark," Young said. "And you're right, young lady. He's an hombre best left alone." Young glanced around him, didn't see what he was looking for, and yelled, "Honeysuckle! Where the heck are you, girl?"

After the passage of a few moments, Honeysuckle Cairns waddled into sight, coming from the direction of the creek. Her damp shift was now stained with blood, as were her hands.

"What happened to you?" Young said.

"I skun a wolf," Honeysuckle said.

"Then get yourself cleaned up and put on your blue dress and feed the passengers," Young said. "We got four monks inside, so be on your best behavior. No cussin' or lewd talk, Honeysuckle, you hear?"

"I hear," the woman said. But she'd only half-listened, her eyes as round as coins, fixed on Augusta. After Young and Buttons left to change the horses, Honeysuckle stepped closer and reached out a blood-crusted hand, her finger-tips barely touching the skirt of Augusta's riding habit.

Augusta smiled and said, "It's silk. The jacket is velvet."

"The jacket is velvet," Honeysuckle repeated in a whisper. She lifted her baby-blue eyes to Augusta's face. "One time an army officer's wife stopped here. She was young and she wore a dress like yours, only hers was green. But she wouldn't let me touch it."

"Well, you can touch mine," Augusta said, smiled.

"She told me I was fat, the officer's wife did," Honeysuckle said. She sounded like a ten-year-old girl. "And she made a good joke. She said my ass looked like the south end of a northbound mule, and everybody laughed."

"That wasn't very funny," Augusta said.

"Would you have laughed?"

"No, I would not."

"You're too much of a lady."

"Yes, I suppose I am."

"An officer's wife is supposed to be a lady."

"Some women are not ladies, no matter what they're supposed to be," Augusta said. She smiled. "My, I'm getting hungry."

"Come inside, I'll fix you right up," Honeysuckle said. She waved at Red. "You too, shotgun man." Then, again to Augusta, "I'll wear my blue dress. You'll like it."

As Red ushered Augusta inside, he whispered, "You were nice to her."

"It doesn't cost anything to be civil," Augusta said.

"I imagine most people are not."

"I'm not most people."

"No, Augusta, you're pretty much one of a kind," Red said.

While Augusta and Honeysuckle Cairns were still talking outside, Chris Mercer had studied the monks who sat at one of three tables that took up most of the floor space in the cramped cabin. He was puzzled by what he saw. The monks had pushed back their loose sleeves, and their hands were visible as they sampled the heaping bowl of greasy corn dodgers, a specialty of the house, that crowned each table. During his time as a professional gunman, Mercer had trained himself to spot any quirks or mannerisms in an opponent that he might use to get the edge. One such man had been Ben Lawson, the Laredo drawfighter. Mercer had watched Lawson shade a wannabe in a Houston dance hall and noticed that just before he skinned the iron, he touched his tongue to his top lip. Mercer later killed Lawson in a dugout saloon in Kansas a split second after the man did his tongue thing. But what intrigued Mercer was the condition of the monks' hands. All four of them, without exception, had the slender hands of counting-house clerks, nails trimmed, well-cared-for mitts that had never seen a day's hard work. This was unusual, if not unknown, among monks who labored in monasteries at menial manual labor from dawn 'til dusk. These four were planning to build a mission? Mercer doubted if they could hammer a nail into a block of wood. His predatory instincts told them what they were . . . the question was . . . what the heck were they doing in this part of Texas disguised as monks?

Then the four spotted Chris Mercer. They saw the man, saw what was beneath.

An urgent whisper . . . and four faces turned in his direction, eyes glittering in the shadow of their cowls. Wolves in sheep's clothing, the foursome had instincts of their own, as finely tuned as Mercer's and much more savage. The casual observer saw Mercer as a small, undernourished nonentity whose lined, ashen face showed the ravages of alcohol. To the monks, and for now that's what we must call them, he was, or once had been, a gunman. The little man's brown eyes were intent, his gaze direct, calculating, summing them up, unafraid. The same eyes the monks saw when they looked in a mirror. But this was not a gun-handy lawman, a man who would have a much more challenging air. No, at some point in his life this little man had spent time around other gunmen as an equal. Now he was a drunken, washed-up nobody . . . but he had at least the potential to be dangerous.

One of the monks rose and walked toward Mercer, who by habit summarized him. No gun visible, but maybe carries a hideout. A smile on the man's face, slight, a killer's smile. The monk said, in an accent Mercer recognized as Irish, "A word of advice . . . use your breath to cool your soup. Nothing else."

Mercer nodded. "I'm over all that. My day is done."

"Then see it stays that way," the monk said.

When Red and Augusta followed by Smiler Thurmond and Jonah Halton stepped into the cabin, the monk took a corn dodger from the bowl on Mercer's table, held it up and said, "Thank you and God bless you, brother."

"You're welcome . . . brother," Mercer said.

CHAPTER TWELVE

Honeysuckle Cairns wore a tentlike blue floral dress that did a fair job of making her appear slightly less fat, though she still looked huge, something that attracted the attention of the monks. Red Ryan, watching, smiled to himself. The holy men had probably never seen the like of a four-hundred-pound whore serving up bacon, beans, and coffee.

Honeysuckle took extra care when she ladled beans onto Augusta's plate and beside the plate laid a round sugar cookie, slightly burned around the edges. "For you," she whispered. "I baked it myself."

"Thank you," Augusta said. "I'll enjoy this. I love sugar cookies."

"I'm glad I could give it to such a fine lady," Honeysuckle said.

Buttons Muldoon and Sam Young had changed the team, and Buttons declared that everyone had to eat their grub real fast since he was anxious to get back on the trail, "instanter."

But then something happened that ruined Buttons's

plans and spoiled everyone's appetite . . . two dead men thudded onto the cabin's doorstep.

Ollie and Harvey Barnes each had four arrows in their backs, and both outlaws had been scalped and their eyes gouged out. Since Apaches enjoyed a good joke, the men had been stripped and dressed in the colorful skirts of two unfortunate Mexican women, a sly comment on the dead men's worth as warriors. The Indians who'd dumped them from galloping horses were gone, but their dust cloud writhed in the darkness like a gray ghost.

Smiler Thurmond revealed his mortal fear of Apaches by lurching away from the bodies and promptly throwing up, his convulsive retching violent and prolonged. The others, stunned by the suddenness of this horror, stood in silence until Honeysuckle Cairns said in her whispery little girl voice, "Oh, those poor fellers . . ."

Thurmond, his eyes wild, returned to the front of the cabin and said, "Muldoon, take us back to Fort Concho. Now, before them damned savages kill us all."

"Heck, all they'll do is follow us," Buttons said. "There's another station at old Fort Mason and it's closer. We're headed for there."

"How far?" Thurmond said, his voice unsteady. Smiler had been up the trail a time or two and didn't want for bravery, but he was a frightened man that evening.

"How far? We'll get there before sunup," Buttons said. "After we ford the San Saba, the road is good all the way." Then, to sound reassuring, even to a man who was not a bona fide passenger, "We'll make good time, and there's a cow town nearby called Mason with some tough citizens and tougher lawmen. I don't think the Apaches will come anywhere near that burg."

"I reckon it's still safer here," Thurmond said. "I say we stay right where we're at until the army rounds up the hostiles."

"Mister, you got no say," Buttons said.

"Then ask the monks and Miss Addington," Thurmond said. "Well, ma'am, you've heard about what Apaches do to white people. Do we stay or go?"

"My vote is to push on," Augusta said. "I have urgent business in Fredericksburg."

"Well, ask the monks," Thurmond said. "What the savages did to Ollie and Harvey boogered them. You got four votes right there."

"There ain't gonna be no voting on this trip," Buttons said, his anger flaring. "As a representative of the Abe Patterson and Son Stage and Express Company, what I say goes. And I say we're heading for Fort Mason." He looked at Sam Young. "Sam, can you handle the burying?"

"Sure, me and Honeysuckle Cairns done it many a time afore," Young said.

"I'll help lay my boys to rest," Thurmond said. "I'm staying right here."

"And count me in, too, Smiler," Halton said.

"Suit yourselves," Buttons said. "Red, get the monks and Archibald Whatshisname in the stage. Miss Addington, please board when you're ready."

"I'm almost ready," Augusta said. "Just give me a minute."

Augusta stepped into the cabin and stood aside to let Red Ryan with the monks and Chris Mercer file past her on their way outside. She noticed that the monks didn't seem in the least "boogered" as Smiler Thurmond had claimed. She didn't think it strange.

Honeysuckle stood at a table scraping plates into a bucket. She still wore her blue floral dress and was barefoot. "Miss Cairns," Augusta said.

The woman turned her head and smiled. "No one's ever called me that before. Say it again, so I can hear it one more time."

"Miss Cairns," Augusta said. She reached into her pocket and produced a folded lady's handkerchief. Its scalloped edges had blue trim, and it was embroidered with blue wildflowers. "This is for you, a little memento of our meeting. I thought it would go nicely with your dress."

Honeysuckle wiped her hands on a rag and stepped to Augusta, her eyes wide. She stared down at the handkerchief and said, "A present? For me?"

"Yes, for you," Augusta said. "It's silk, and I bought it in New York a couple of years ago."

"It's so pretty and delicate, I daren't touch it," Honeysuckle said. She held up a hand and spread her fingers. "I've got big hands. They're not like yours."

"You won't damage it," Augusta said. "Here, take it. Something to remember me by."

The woman took the handkerchief and laid it against her plump, sunburned cheek. "It's so soft," she said. "I'll keep this forever and ever."

"You were kind to me, and I thought you should have it," Augusta said. She smiled. "People have not always been as kind to me."

Impulsively, Honeysuckle threw her huge arms around the other woman and hugged her close.

After a few moments of hesitation, Red Ryan stepped

through the open cabin door to tell Augusta that the stage was ready to leave. He stood still for a moment, struck by the contrast between the short, dumpy, straw-haired, and illiterate Honeysuckle Cairns and the tall, elegant, beautiful, and educated Augusta Addington. Two women whose lives were worlds apart . . . but sisters under the skin.

"Miss Addington, it's time to leave," Red said. He touched the brim of his plug hat. "Miss Cairns."

CHAPTER THIRTEEN

The side lamps of the Patterson stage glowed yellow in the gloom as it made its way south at a steady five miles an hour, trailing dust. The only sounds were the creak of the stage, the jangle of horse harnesses, and the fretful wind that moved the prairie grass as quietly as the rustle of a silk dress. The vast, shadowed land was barely visible under the light of the stars and a horned moon, lost in darkness, distance, and mystery. It was the midnight hour, a time for traveling men in Apache country to stay alert and watchful.

After a long spell of silence, Buttons Muldoon said, "Somebody's asleep."

"Snoring," Red Ryan said.

"Loud, like a ripsaw running through pine knots," Buttons said. "I bet it's one of them monks."

Red's restless eyes scanned the distances ahead and around him and said, "Why do you think it's a monk?"

"Well, listen to it," Buttons said. Then, "It ain't Miss Addington, and it ain't that little Whatshisname. He don't have the lungs for it."

"By the way, it was white of you to let Mercer travel inside," Red said.

"Yeah, I know," Buttons said. "But I'll dump him after we ford the San Saba. Good grass and plenty of water down that way."

"Buttons, he's a man, not a steer," Red said. "He can't survive on grass and water."

"Too bad," Button said. He thought about it for a while and said, "Yeah, that's just too bad." Then, after another pause, he said, "Yup, that's one of them monks snoring. It's a kind of holy snore that you hear in church."

"You've never been in a church," Red said.

"That's because I never lived for any length of time within the sound of church bells. And neither have you."

"That's true, but how come you know that god-awful snoring"—he hushed for a spell so that Buttons could hear it plain—"is a holy snore?"

"I just know, that's all," Buttons said, irritated. "Keep your eye on the trail, Red, and quit asking so many damn fool questions."

"It's an unholy snore, that's what is it," Red said.

"I don't want to talk about the snore any longer," Buttons said. "Just listening to it is bad enough."

Fording the San Saba was easier than Buttons Muldoon expected. He made the crossing at a bend in the river where there was a shallow, sandy bottom and no current.

When he reached the far bank, Buttons halted the team and gave the passengers ten minutes to stretch their legs and answer calls of nature. Even the monks availed themselves of a chance to leave the jolting, swaying and cramped misery of the stage and wandered off into the darkness.

Buttons took Chris Mercer aside and said, "If'n you want, Archibald . . ."

"My name is Chris. Chris Mercer."

Ignoring that, Buttons said, "If'n you want, I can drop you off here. I guess we're a good hunnerd miles from San Angelo. Just south of us is Rock Springs, where there's plenty of water. As I recollect, there's a bat cave down there somewhere that's a sight to see at sundown." Buttons slapped the little man on the back. "A young feller like you could make himself real comfortable at Rock Springs, providing he could catch jackrabbits an' wild turkeys an' sich for supper."

"Or he could starve to death, if he wasn't murdered by Apaches first." This from Augusta, who had overheard every word. "You're not leaving him here, Mr. Muldoon. That would be tantamount to murder."

"Tanta . . . tanta . . ." Buttons said. He looked confused.

"She means leaving Mercer here would be the same as murdering him, Buttons," Red said. "Why don't you put a bullet in his head and get it over with?"

Buttons snorted like one of his horses. "I'm not gonna . . . I mean, I'm not . . ."

"Leave him here to starve," Augusta said. "You can take him to the Fort Mason stage station, where perhaps he can find meaningful employment. And if not there, I'm sure he will find work in Fredericksburg."

"But it's a hunnerd-dollar fare from here to German Town," Buttons said. "Abe Patterson has that wrote down somewhere. And besides, all them square heads down there are farmers. Any way you cut it, lady, Archibald don't have the makings of a sodbuster."

"Then he can find something else that suits his talents," Augusta said.

"Damn it all, he only had one God-given talent . . . shooting people," Buttons said. "And he don't want to work at that profession any longer."

"I'm sure Mr. Mercer can find something," Augusta said. Then, frowning. "Mr. Muldoon, I repeat, you're not leaving him here."

Then Mercer said, "I'll stay here. I don't want to cause any trouble. Damn, I need a drink."

"You want a drink, you don't need a drink," Augusta said. "You're coming to Fredericksburg with the rest of us, and that's final."

The woman was a formidable opponent, and Buttons retreated a step. "What about the fare?"

"I'll pay the fare," Augusta said. "Mr. Mercer, you can repay me after you find gainful employment at any job you choose."

Red Ryan smiled. "Well, I'm glad that's over. Now, can we get back on the road?"

But, as the monks returned to the stage, Buttons wasn't quite finished. His conscience pricking him, he said, "For this once I'll forgo the fare, though Abe Patterson would fire me on the spot for saying that." A sudden scowl on his face, then, "But Archibald rides up top. I don't want him rubbing shoulders with the fare-paying passengers."

Augusta smiled, leaned forward and kissed Buttons on his stubbled cheek. "You're an angel, Mr. Muldoon," she said.

Buttons covered his embarrassment and obvious delight with bluster. "Archibald, get up top there and stop wasting everybody's time," he yelled.

He knew Red Ryan was grinning at him but didn't look in his direction.

CHAPTER FOURTEEN

The army had abandoned Fort Mason in 1871, and for years the nearby settlement of Mason had cannibalized the ruin for its own building projects until all that remained were the rock foundations of the headquarters building, the sutler's store, and a few other structures. The original stage station had been burned to the ground by Apaches two years before, and in its place, situated in what had been the parade ground, was a large tent with an adjoining corral.

When the Patterson stage arrived just before sunup, the place was in darkness.

Buttons booted the brake lever into place and said, "I'll go rouse them. The passengers need breakfast, and so does this driver."

But before he could climb down from the box, a party of horsemen emerged from the gloom, eight men carrying rifles across their saddle horns. The riders drew rein and one man kicked his mount forward. He was a stocky, gray-haired man with a tense face and lawman's star pinned to the lapel of his black frock coat.

"Identify yourselves," the man said.

Now Buttons was tired and hungry and in no mood to answer a damn fool question. "Heck, mister, who we are is written all over this here stage."

"Identify yourselves," the lawman said.

Buttons sighed. "I'm the driver, and my name is Patrick Muldoon of the Abe Patterson and Son Stage and Express Company. This here feller in the plug hat is Red Ryan, the shotgun messenger."

"Who is the man on top?" the lawman said. He looked severe, judgmental, like a hanging judge.

"He's a chicken thief by the name of Archibald . . . somebody," Buttons said. "We're taking him to Fredericksburg, where he can start a new life."

"Stealing chickens?" the lawman said.

"No. He's turned his back on that life and hopes to learn the farming profession."

"He don't look like he's got any farmer in him. Other passengers?"

"Four robed and holy monks and a young lady of good breeding."

The lawman was surprised. "Holy monks?"

Buttons shrugged and said, "Yeah. Are there any other kind?"

"See any Apaches?"

"Yeah, we saw them up close and personal at Kickapoo station."

"Jim Moore's place?"

"The very same."

"What happened?"

"The savages tried to steal horses and there was a shoot-out. They killed Jim's hired hand, a man by the name of

McKenzie, and lost four of their own. Killed Ollie and Harvey Barnes, too. They didn't get any horses."

"Then you done good," the lawman said. "My name is Frank Carson. I'm the law in Mason, and these fellers with me are members of the Mason mounted militia. We've been patrolling all night on the lookout for hostiles."

"See any?" Red Ryan said.

"Nary a one," Carson said. He looked a little disappointed. "Mr. Muldoon, you say you're headed for German Town, and I got bad news for you."

"Seems like I've had more than my share on this trip," Buttons said. "Let me hear it."

Its bit jangling, Carson's horse shook its head at a pesky fly as the lawman said, "Donny Bryson broke out of the Austin jail, killed two deputies, and then robbed the Drover's Bank on his way out of town on a stolen horse. The breed shot everybody inside the bank, five people, except for a pregnant woman he took with him, the wife of one of the deputies. That was a week ago, and she's probably dead by now or wishes she was."

"We ain't traveling as far as Austin," Buttons said.

"If you're anywhere near the Perdinales River country, you're far enough," Carson said. "The word is that Donny has kin there, blanket Apaches on his momma's side, and it's a lead-pipe cinch that's where he's headed."

Buttons and Red exchanged glances. Donny Bryson was bad news. A gun-handy madman, he killed for the love of killing, and the Texas Rangers, not prone to exaggeration, claimed that he'd murdered at least sixty white people, men, women, and children. He'd also played hob in Old Mexico. The number of peons he'd slaughtered in his forays over the border was unknown, but high enough that the alarmed Díaz government had placed a ten-thousand-dollar bounty on his head.

"We'll steer clear of ol' Donny," Buttons said. "I plan to drop off the four holy monks and then hightail it back to San Angelo."

Carson looked doubtful. "Well, between Apaches on the prod and a killer like Donny Bryson in the area, it promises to be an interesting trip." The lawman looked beyond Buttons, touched the brim of his hat, smiled, and said, "Ma'am."

Augusta Addington appeared from the side of the stage and dropped a little curtsey. "Good morning, Sheriff," she said. "My name is Augusta Addington of the Philadelphia and New Orleans Addingtons, and I'm bound for Fredericksburg to take up a tutoring post."

Carson's smile grew wider. "Ma'am, you are a sweet distraction for these old eyes."

"Why, thank you, Sheriff, what a singularly charming thing to say," Augusta said. "Are you familiar with the ranchers down there in the Perdinales River country?"

"Some of them, Ma'am. Some of them."

"Gideon Stark?"

"Ah, yes. His is a well-known name in that part of Texas, a rancher of immense wealth and influence."

"I am to meet his daughter Della in Fredericksburg on the eighth of this month at the Alpenrose Inn," Augusta said. "Our arrangement was made by wire a while ago, and I trust the Apache uprising has done nothing to change it."

"I believe I can set your mind at rest, Miss Addington," Carson said. "Mr. Stark would not allow his daughter to travel alone. I assure you, she'll have a strong escort of tough cowboys, enough to discourage the unwelcome attention of the savages or a murderous half-breed for that matter."

"Then I am content that our meeting will go ahead as planned," Augusta said. "Miss Stark is most anxious to learn French and improve her English-language skills." She trilled a laugh. "But I'm afraid I will teach her how French is spoken in New Orleans, not Paris."

"I'm sure your New Orleans French is perfect," Carson said.

To Red Ryan, the entire conversation sounded as false as a cracked bell. Buttons took it in stride, smiling in all the right places, but Red had the strong feeling that Augusta was lying through her teeth. She might be helping Della Stark, but not with her English. He asked himself the question . . . who the heck was Augusta Addington? And more to the point . . . what was she?

At that instant Augusta turned her head and locked eyes with Red. For long moments neither dropped their gaze, and at last Augusta, revealing finely tuned feminine intuition, said, "Red, speak to me in Fredericksburg."

She looked away and left Red Ryan with yet another question . . . speak to her about what?

The tent flap opened, and a big-bellied man, his cheeks scarlet with spider veins, stepped outside. His eyes went to Frank Carson and his riders and then to Buttons. "See any Apaches?" he said.

"We had a run-in," Buttons said.

He didn't elaborate, and the man didn't push it. "Name's Ora Pelton," he said. "I own this here palace. I got a good team in the corral and fried beef and sourdough bread for breakfast."

Buttons's eyes went to the corral. "Mostly grays. I ain't keen on them."

"Like the fried beef, it's all I got. Take the grays or leave them," Pelton said.

"When grays get hot, they smell," Buttons said.

"Still smell better than people," Pelton said.

Buttons stared at him without comment and then turned his head and said, "Archibald, you'll help change the team, earn your keep for a change." He leaned out of the box and yelled, "Passengers out."

Pelton held the tent flap open for Augusta and for the monks, a sight that raised his eyebrows. He looked up at Buttons and said, "On this job I've met all kinds of passengers coming and going, but the Patterson stage carries the strangest cargoes I ever did see."

"It's our specialty," Buttons said. "When it comes to freaks and crazies, we've cornered the market, present company excepted of course."

Pelton smiled. "Of course."

After a breakfast of tough beef and greasy fried bread, the Patterson passengers, now showing signs of exhaustion, once again boarded the stage and headed south under a bloodred morning sky. Superstitious men like Red Ryan and Buttons Muldoon should have considered such a sky ill-omened, but, irritated that Frank Carson and his militia had refused to escort them at least part of the way to Fredericksburg, they didn't give it a second thought. As events would soon reveal . . . they should have.

CHAPTER FIFTEEN

In later years, Buttons Muldoon would always say that his real troubles on the Fredericksburg trip began when he ran over the sombrero thirty miles out from the town. He claimed he didn't see the Mexican headgear until it was too late, and that was true. Tired like his passengers and drowsy, he might have nodded off when the incident happened.

It was Chris Mercer riding up top who saw the squashed sombrero flopping around in the stage's following dust cloud, and he casually remarked to Red Ryan that they'd just run over somebody's hat. He could not have imagined the reaction this statement would cause.

"Buttons!" Red yelled. "We just ran over the hat."

Buttons immediately reined in the team. "Oh, my God! Where?" he said, his face shocked.

"Just a little ways back," Mercer said. Puzzled, he looked from Red to Buttons and back again. "What's the trouble? It's only a hat . . ."

But he talked to Red's back . . . he and Buttons were already scrambling down from the box.

"It's the hat all right," Red said. As dust settled around

him, he stared down at the mangled sombrero and shook his head. "Buttons, this is bad. I mean, real bad."

"Yeah, I know it's bad," Buttons said. "You don't have to tell me it's bad. Did I move it?"

"Yeah, you moved it," Red said. "Ran over it and moved it."

"Damn it, Red, it shouldn't have been there," Buttons said. "It should've blown away in a big wind."

"But it didn't, did it?" Red said. "It was right there on the trail where it's been for years."

"Bad luck, Red," Buttons said. "For me and for you."

"Well, I don't know about that," Red said. "You were driving, not me."

"I told you to watch the trail ahead," Buttons said.

"It was still mostly dark," Red said. "How could I be expected to see a hat in the road?"

"A sombrero," Buttons said.

"A sombrero is a hat," Red said.

Augusta Addington stepped beside Buttons. The monks were stretching their legs and seemed uninterested. "What's wrong?" she said.

"Everything is wrong," Buttons said. "We ran over the hat. That's like . . . like breaking a mirror, a hundred years bad luck."

"Seven years bad luck," Augusta said.

"A whole heap of bad luck then," Buttons said.

"What's so special about an old hat?" Augusta said.

"I'll tell why it's so special," Red said. "As it was told to me by a puncher who worked for the Anderson Cattle Company, a ranch to the north of here. Well, it used to be north of here. It went out of business four years ago. A year before that, one of the Anderson vaqueros was right here, on this road, rounding up strays, when a sudden thunderstorm blew up."

Buttons said, "The vaquero, some say his name was Alonzo, others Alvarez, got struck by a bolt of lightning that killed him and his hoss stone dead. His sombrero flew off his head and landed in the middle of the road. And there it stayed for years. Cowboys are a superstitious bunch, and nobody would pick up the hat, because to touch it would bring bad luck. Some even rode a mile out of their way to avoid getting close to the dead man's sombrero."

"And now Buttons ran over it with the Patterson stage," Red said to Augusta.

"Red, I'd be obliged if you'd stop saying that," Buttons said.

"Sorry, old fellow, but that's what happened," Red said.

"And now all the bad luck is on me," Buttons said. Suddenly he looked crestfallen, as down in the dumps as a normally cheerful man could be. "A hundred years of bad luck."

"A good story, but it's all nonsense," Augusta said, frowning. She picked up the battered sombrero and held it up to the horrified Buttons and Red. "Look," she said. "It's just a dirty old hat that someone lost." The woman held the sombrero by the brim and then slung it away from her. The hat sailed away and landed in a patch of scrub, startling a covey of sleeping quail that exploded into the air like shrapnel.

"Now," Augusta said, "can we resume our journey that's beginning to seem endless?"

Buttons was stricken. "Miss Addington, you shouldn't ought to have done that," he said. "Now the hat's been throwed, the bad luck will be a sight worse."

Augusta smiled. "No, it won't, Mr. Muldoon. The story about the hat is just an old wives' tale. Don't let it trouble you in the least."

Buttons was unconvinced. "I hope to God you're right," he said.

An hour later . . . twenty-five miles out from Fredericksburg . . . they heard the thin cry of a woman in grievous distress . . .

"Yeah, I heard it," Red Ryan said.

"I heard it, too," Chris Mercer said.

"It's a woman's voice," Buttons said. He halted the team and pointed east. "Somewhere in that direction."

"Seems pretty close," Mercer said. "And it's definitely a woman."

"There's one way to find out. I'll go look," Red said. "Buttons, cover me. It could be an Apache trick."

He climbed down from the box, and Buttons handed him the shotgun. The driver had his own Winchester ready. "Red, step careful," Buttons said. Then, "You hear that?"

"Yeah, it's a woman calling for help," Red said.

"Out here?" Buttons said.

"Seems like," Red said.

The whereabouts of the mad killer Donny Bryson was uppermost in Red's mind. He'd kidnapped a woman, but why had he brought her here, a good thirty miles from his kinfolk on the Perdinales River? Maybe to shake the Rangers or a posse from Austin?

Red had no answer to those questions, but they troubled him as he left the stage and walked toward the area from where they'd heard the woman's cries. He was good with a gun, fast and smooth on the draw and shoot, but he dreaded coming up against Bryson, who might even now be lying in wait for him. The man was so fast, so accurate, so deadly with the iron that the rumor was he'd sold his soul to the devil in exchange for a lightning draw. Red figured the tale was a big windy, but a man never knew . . . Donny had killed a lot of people.

Beams of wakening sunlight fanned into the morning sky as Red crossed a low rise where a few stunted juniper shared the ground with a post oak and thin patches of bluestem grass. Walking at a half crouch, his shotgun at the ready, he encountered a sandy flat and running parallel to it a dry wash that ran straight for fifty yards and then angled abruptly to the west. It was from this bend he heard the woman's voice again, a frail cry for help, but filled with deep despair and pain.

Red closed the remaining distance at a run and then came to a dead stop, staring dumbstruck at what lay before him. He would always remember his first sight of the woman, not really a woman, just a teenaged girl. What did she look like that morning? Years later Red would tell a horrified reporter, "Imagine a rag doll after two large dogs had fought for an hour over its possession, and you'll then have a good idea what Mrs. Alice Russell, the widow of deputy Mark Russell, looked like. I tell you this, Donny Bryson didn't only use her for his pleasure . . . he tore her apart."

Traveling booth fighter, sometimes hired gun, shotgun messenger, nothing in Red Ryan's past had prepared him to succor the sick or tend the wounds of the injured, especially a pregnant woman. To his mortification, he realized he hadn't even brought water. The canteen was still with the coach. But he scrambled into the dry wash, determined to do his best. As soon as the woman saw Red, she shrank away from him, her eyes wild with fear.

Red stopped where he was and said, "Ma'am, no need to be afraid of me. My name is Red Ryan and I'm a representative of the Abe Patterson and Son Stage and Express Company. I mean you no harm, and you need help."

Some of the terror left the woman's face, and she whispered, "My baby. Save my baby."

"Yes, of course I will soon. I mean I will . . . I mean . . ." Red's tongue got so tangled, he lapsed into silence. He saw the woman's swollen belly, but she was so covered in blood, all over her plain gray dress, that he feared the baby might already be dead.

The woman grabbed the front of Red's buckskin shirt in a death grip and said, "Mister, save my baby . . ."

Feeling helpless, hopeless, Red murmured, "I'll go get help, Ma'am."

"Red, she's terrified. Move away from her."

Augusta Addington stood on the bank of the wash in her dusty riding outfit, her hair pulled back from her face. She looked tired, shadows under her eyes, a woman worn out from stage travel looking at another who'd gone through Hell. Augusta slid her way down the embankment and kneeled beside the woman. She'd brought the canteen.

"I don't know what happened to her . . ." Red said.

"You don't?" Augusta said, her eyebrows arching. Red said nothing.

"Well, I do," Augusta said. "I know exactly what happened to her."

Chris Mercer had followed Augusta from the stage,

and he spared Red the need to say anything further. "No tracks on this side of the wash," he said.

Red pointed east with his shotgun. "We'll scout in that direction."

As Augusta tended to the woman, Red and Mercer worked their way along the other side of the wash where there were more trees and brush. But the horse tracks were obvious. They came in from the north, and the rider had stopped long enough to throw the woman into the wash from his saddle. He'd then headed due east at a walk, taking his time, confident of not being seen in that empty, uninhabited wilderness.

"If it's Donny, he's headed for the Perdinales," Mercer said. "My God, I don't believe the things he did to that poor woman."

Red didn't care to follow up on that and said, "You ever come across him before? I mean back in your gunfighting days."

Mercer shook his head. "No, but one time when I hired out my gun to a rancher up where Catfish Bayou meets the Trinity River in Anderson County I saw Donny's handiwork. At the time, he was walking out with a fallen woman who cheated on him and he dragged her out of bed one night, shot the man who was with her, and carried her away. In places, both banks of the Catfish are heavily wooded and he crucified her on a hardwood tree. Used ropes to tie her arms to a couple of limbs but also used nails to fix her hands and feet in place, and then he did some knife work. I saw the body when she'd been taken down. The law up there reckoned it had taken the young lady three days to die."

"Well, I sure enough asked you the question, and now I'm sorry I did," Red said.

"It's hard to talk about Donny Bryson without mentioning death, blood, and torture," Mercer said. "The Mexicans say he's a demon spawned in Hades, and they may be right."

For a few moments Red's eyes searched into the rolling distances of the hill country and then he said, "Looks like he's long gone."

"And thank God for that," Mercer said. "I hope I never get this close to Donny Bryson ever again."

"That makes two of us," Red said. He turned. Augusta Addington, blood staining her hands, stood staring at him with wide, unblinking eyes. Red knew what it meant. Donny Bryson had claimed another victim . . . two victims.

"She's dead," Augusta said when Red and Mercer joined her. "I think the baby died before she did." And then after a long pause, "I'm not a doctor. There was nothing I could do."

"There's nothing a doctor could have done, either," Red said. "At least she didn't die alone."

"That would have been a terrible thing," Augusta said. She fought back a tear. "She held my hand until the end. Red, I helped her, didn't I? For God's sake tell me I helped her."

"Of course, you did," Red said. "You helped her more than I could . . . more than anybody could."

"We'll take her back to the stage," Augusta said. "I don't want to leave her . . . and the baby . . . out here."

"We'll take her to Fredericksburg and get the local

law to wire Austin," Red said. "If she has kin there, they'll want the body for a decent burial."

The monks stood apart as the woman's body was gently lifted into the stage. One of them, the one with the Irish accent, had a rosary in his hands, praying in a low murmur.

Augusta elected to ride with the dead woman, the monks taking up station behind the stage. Mercer took up his usual position up top.

Buttons slapped the reins and urged the horses forward at a walk. No one talked, and the only human sound was the whisper of the praying Irish monk.

CHAPTER SIXTEEN

"Red, we got a dead lady in the stage, four holy monks walking behind us slow as molasses in January, and one of my gray wheelers is coming up lame," Buttons Muldoon said. "It's the curse of the sombrero, I tell you. The bad luck is beginning."

Red said, "Buttons, the gray is young, and he's tiring and the dead woman has nothing to do with your luck and everything to do with the mad dog killer Donny Bryson."

"But I feel it," Buttons said. "Bad luck is in the air, like a black fog."

"When did you ever see a black fog?" Red said.

"All right, then, a gray fog," Buttons said. "But it's in the air. Keep your eyes skinned for Apaches, Red. Them savages can sense when a man's luck is running bad."

Red smiled. "Once we get to Fredericksburg, we'll drop the passengers at the stage depot and then head to the Munich Keller for good German beer and sausages. That will fix you right up, make you feel a sight better."

Buttons shook his head. "Nothing will make me feel better."

"Damn, it all, Buttons, I've never seen you so down in

the mouth before," Red said. "You ain't exactly good company."

"Yeah, well, I never ran over a cursed hat afore, either," Buttons said. "Put that in your pipe and smoke it."

"You'll get over it," Red said. Then, "Hey, there's that blonde waitress who works at the Munich Keller . . . what's her name?"

"Lilly."

"Yeah, Lilly. You like her."

"She won't even look at me," Buttons said. "Not with my luck."

"Oh, damn," Red said.

"Oh, damn, what?" Buttons said.

"That gray wheeler is limping," Red said.

The oil lamps were lit in Fredericksburg when the Patterson stage drove along the main street that was lined on each side with a large variety of stores and warehouses. Buttons Muldoon pulled up outside the depot with five horses in the traces, the sixth tethered behind the coach. The town was settled by German farmers, some of whom later branched into manufacturing, and it had none of the boisterous saloons and whorehouses of the Texas cattle towns, though its several beer gardens did a lively business. It was a clean, well-ordered settlement of stone and plaster houses, churches, and schools. The county seat of Gillespie County, Fredericksburg had a young sheriff named Herman Ritter who spoke both German and English and attended Lutheran services every Sunday. He was as tough as he had to be but had no gun reputation.

Fredericksburg was a straitlaced town, a civilized town, a peaceful town . . . but not a good town to bring a murdered lady with a dead baby inside her.

The Alpenrose Inn was a two-story hotel that doubled as the stage depot with a corral and barn out back and beyond that a fenced pasture where a dozen horses grazed. The animals looked fit and sleek, and Red figured that boded well for the final leg of the trip to the Perdinales River. Buttons had a deep-seated prejudice against grays, and happily there were none to be seen. Red hoped that might cheer him up, but it didn't.

Looking grumpy, Buttons said, "The monks have decided to stay here in Fredericksburg for a few days of quiet prayer and meditation, whatever the heck that means. I told them the Abe Patterson and Son Stage and Express Company, doesn't do refunds, even partial refunds, and that Abe doesn't even know the meaning of the word."

"What did they say?" Red said.

They stood on the hotel porch while the depot manager and his two helpers took care of the team and the lame gray.

"It didn't trouble them none," Buttons said. "The Irish feller told me they'd book rooms here at the inn." He shook his head. "I didn't know monks had the money for fancy hotels. I figured they'd pay a few cents a night to sleep at the Lange livery stable over yonder."

"Me too," Red said. "But then I don't know much about holy monks and their finances."

"Miss Addington has also booked a room here," Buttons said. "I don't know where Archibald is. He scampered down and vanished as soon as I stopped the stage."

The body of the dead woman had been carried into the foyer by Buttons and Red and covered with a sheet awaiting the undertaker. But the hotel manager, a small, harried-looking man named Watson, who was probably a nail-biter, was not entirely happy with the arrangement and had already sent a bellboy running for the sheriff.

"I have to think of my guests," Watson told Buttons. "A dead woman in the foyer is bad for business. Who gave you permission to dump her there?"

Now two things in that speech rubbed Buttons the wrong way. One was that, depressed as he was, the manager's whining grated on his ears. The second was the man's use of the word "dump." The woman was not dumped in the foyer, she was laid on the ground with all the respect and gentleness he and Red could muster. The upshot of all this was that Buttons drew his Remington, thumbed back the hammer, placed the muzzle between Watson's eyes, and said, "Are you trying to make trouble for me?"

Ninety-nine times out of a hundred, the business end of a gun barrel shoved into a man's mug will give him pause for thought . . . and Watson did pause . . . and then said in a rush, "No sir. No, not at all. Not me."

"Glad to hear it," Buttons said. He lifted the big revolver from Watson's face, lowered the hammer, and holstered the gun. "I can't abide a man who goes out of his way to cause vexing fuss and bother," he said.

Watson, fright ashen on his face, backed away a few steps and then turned and ran into the hotel and took refuge behind his front desk.

"A bit testy this evening, ain't we?" Red said.

"Heck, I didn't really plan on shooting him," Buttons said.

"You could've fooled me," Red said.

Buttons shrugged. "You're right, Red, maybe I would've plugged him if'n he'd given me sass and backtalk."

"Well, thank God we'll never know," Red said. "And just in time. Here comes the undertaker, and he's bringing the law with him."

"Ritter!" Buttons said. "He doesn't cotton to us. Remember the last time we were here with Hannah Huckabee?"

"I remember," Red said. "How could I forget."

CHAPTER SEVENTEEN

The undertaker, a little hopping crow of a man in a clawhammer broadcloth coat, stepped onto the shadowed porch lit only by the flickering oil lamps on each side of the inn door. With him was young Sheriff Herman Ritter . . . brown eyes, brown hair, and a serious, almost solemn demeanor. He wore a silver star on the front of his dark blue shirt, and a Colt revolver with an ivory handle was holstered at his waist.

"Mr. Muldoon," Ritter said. "What an unpleasant surprise."

Buttons said. "No matter what the hotel manager tells you, I wasn't really aiming to plug him. I was only funning . . . a right knee-slapper."

A confused looked flitted across Ritter's young face. "According to the messenger boy I spoke with, that was not the nature of Mr. Watson's complaint."

"He's a complaining kind of man," Buttons said.

"His complaint is that you dropped a woman's dead body in his foyer," Ritter said.

"We laid a murdered woman in his foyer," Buttons said. "We found her twenty miles north of here in a dry wash. She died shortly after my shotgun guard here discovered her."

"And you are?" Ritter said. "No, wait, I remember you . . . Red Ryan, isn't it?"

"Yeah, we met about a year ago," Red said. "The time Miss Hannah Huckabee . . ."

"A fare-paying passenger of the Abe Patterson and Son Stage and Express Company," Buttons interrupted.

" . . . shot the gunman Dave Winter," Red said.

"Yes, in the Munich Keller beer hall," Ritter said.

"The very same," Red said.

"Miss Huckabee is an adventuress, and at the time I was not impressed with her respectability, nor with yours, Herr Ryan and Herr Muldoon," Ritter said. "I'm still not."

Right there and then, an irritated Red decided to tattoo the lawman with the facts. "The dead woman was the widow of a deputy sheriff who was gunned down in Austin about a week ago. She was with child, and the killer kidnapped her for his own pleasure. The killer's name is Donny Bryson and we think he's still in this area."

Ritter's eyes widened. "Donny Bryson? Here in Fredericksburg?"

"Donny Bryson," Buttons said. "And he might be here or he could be anywhere."

"Oh, my God," Ritter said.

"Yeah, that's it. Get the good Lord on your side, Sheriff," Buttons said. "I think you're gonna need him."

A profound silence fell on the group into which the undertaker dropped words that fell like rocks onto a tin roof. "May I take a look at the dear departed now?"

Ritter nodded. "Yes, go right ahead. I'll join you."

A sweep of the undertaker's hand took in both Buttons and Red. "I take it that you gentlemen are the chief mourners?" He smiled, revealing teeth as large and yellow as old piano keys. "Oh, allow me to introduce myself. My name is Benjamin Bone, but you can call me Benny Bone. Everyone else does. I want us to be friends."

Buttons said, "Benny, we're no kind of mourners, and we don't want to be your friend. As I told the sheriff, we found the lady, and then she died." Then, "Kind of how our luck's been running."

"Ah, most unfortunate," Bone said. "Now, Sheriff, shall we take a look at the deceased? Burial fee at my usual rates, I trust?"

Ritter shook his head. "She's not the city's responsibility. The Patterson stage found the women, and the company should meet the cost of her interment."

"Sheriff, she's a murder victim," Red Ryan said. "And you're the law. It's time for you to hitch up your gunbelt and go get dirty."

"No, it's the Gillespie county sheriff's responsibility," Ritter said. "My authority ends at the city limits."

"So where's the county sheriff at?" Buttons said.

"Unfortunately, he developed a heart problem and is on extended leave," Ritter said. "He's convalescing with his wife's family in Dallas."

"Doesn't he have a deputy?" Buttons said.

"He did, but the man left to go gold prospecting, and the position hasn't yet been filled," Ritter said. "After all, the county sheriff left for Dallas only six weeks ago."

Augusta Addington, now wearing a white cotton day dress with long sleeves, had been standing at a distance listening to this conversation. Now, frowning, she marched to Ritter and confronted him. "What do you call yourself?" she demanded.

"I'm Sheriff Herman Ritter." The man seemed taken aback by Augusta's fierceness.

"I know what your name is, I meant, do you call yourself a lawman?"

"Of course, I do."

"Then you're living under false pretenses," Augusta said. "There's a dead woman lying in the hotel was who beaten and raped to death, her killer is still at large, and all you can talk about is who should bury her."

"But, I . . ."

"But . . . but . . . but . . . no buts," Augusta said. "Do your job, Sheriff. And if you can't do it, bring in lawmen who can, the Texas Rangers or the marshal from Austin. After all, the dead woman is one of his own." Augusta folded her arms, her beautiful eyes blazing. "Well," she said, "I'm waiting."

"Are you any kin to a woman by the name of Hannah Huckabee?" Ritter said, appearing to shrink.

"No, I am not. And I'm still waiting for your decision. Will you handle this matter or not?"

"Who are you, my *liebe Frau*?" Ritter said.

"I am Augusta Addington of the Philadelphia and New Orleans Addingtons, and I am not without influence. I am also a concerned citizen of these United States, and I demand action. Instanter!"

"Then I'll take a look at the body and we'll go from there," Ritter said.

"Be prepared, lawman," Buttons said. "It's not a pretty sight."

"*Danke, mein Herr,* but I'll be the judge of that," Ritter said.

"Oh, mein Gott! Oh, mein Gott!"

Sheriff Herman Ritter, turned away from the ravaged body, his face ashen. "What in God's name did he do? How could he . . ."

"Do you want me to explain it to you?" Augusta Addington said.

"No, I don't want you to explain it to me," Ritter said. "I saw for myself what happened to her."

To Augusta, Ritter looked too young to be a town sheriff or any other kind of lawman, and very vulnerable. "Sheriff, wire Austin and tell them what happened and ask them to send a lawman here," she said. "And the dead woman may have loved ones who would wish to take her body home."

"By Texas law, a body must be buried, embalmed, or placed in a sealed coffin within twenty-four hours, and the woman has already been dead for most of that time," Ritter said. "Austin is eighty miles away, and a relative would never get here in time. Besides, whoever it was would need to identify the body. Do you want a mother, a father, a sister, or a brother to go through that? She's so badly beaten, identification might be impossible."

"Alas, there's only so much repairing I can do," Benny Bone said. "As you say, Sheriff Ritter, identifying the deceased could be a most harrowing ordeal for the bereaved."

The young lawman's face hardened, signaling that he'd made a decision. "Mr. Bone, place the woman in a plain pine coffin. We'll bury her tomorrow morning in Der Stadt Friedhof."

"What the heck is that?" Buttons said.

"The City Cemetery," Benny Bone said. "It's a nice place. She'll be happy there."

"If the woman has kinfolk who want to take her to Austin, they can exhume the body," Ritter said.

"And what about Donny Bryson?" Augusta said.

"As I told you, out of my jurisdiction," Ritter said. "But I'm sure he's long gone from Gillespie County."

CHAPTER EIGHTEEN

Food and a soft bed for the night, preferably with a plump woman.

Donny Bryson figured his needs were few, and the isolated farmhouse a few miles east of Fredericksburg might just provide them.

He sat his horse in a patch of wild oak and studied the cabin. He was a tall, round-shouldered man in his early thirties with a great beak of a nose and the golden, predatory eyes of a hawk. He was dressed all in black: black shirt, black pants tucked into black boots, a black hat, black gunbelt with two holstered, black-handled Colts. And a black heart. A cautious, organized psychopath, Donny Bryson killed men for challenging him or simply getting in his way. But women were a different matter. He enjoyed using, abusing, and then murdering the female sex. When he was younger, his victims had been mostly whores and older woman. He'd gain their trust and then rape and torture them. As he grew older, Donny branched out, expanding the field of his endeavors to include respectable matrons he kidnapped, married women in isolated farms and ranches, and their daughters and any other women from runaway wives to stagecoach and train passengers that crossed his path. And all the time, the tally of men he killed grew, and Donny became a named man, acknowledged to be one of the West's premier shootists.

In the words of Texas Ranger and United States Marshal John Barclay Armstrong, "Donny Bryson was fast on the draw and shoot, but he was an evil off-scouring of society, filth so vile his very shadow polluted the earth he walked on."

Vicious beyond reason, a man without a conscience, Donny was a creature of darkness, and he melted into the night, man and murk becoming one.

The cabin didn't look like much, a rickety structure held together with baling wire and twine. The roof swayed badly, and the whole structure leaned to one side. There was no corral or any other building to be seen. Donny's hopes fell. There was little chance a desirable woman would live in such a place . . . or any kind of woman.

A soft bed for the night? Maybe.

There was only one window to the front of the shack, and it was roughly boarded over, but the orange glow of an oil lamp showed between the gaps of the timbers, and smoke rose straight as a string from the iron chimney, so there was somebody to home. Donny kneed his horse forward and moved like a wraith toward the cabin.

At that time in the West it was customary to announce oneself when approaching a stranger's dwelling. For politeness's sake, Donny should have sat his horse and called out, "Hello, the cabin!" But then, he was not a polite man. His method of entry was simple . . . kick the door in.

It took two swift boots to the door before it splintered free of its rawhide hinges and crashed flat inside. Then things happened very quickly. The old man standing at the stove inside had time to register a look of horror before he turned and made a play for the holstered old Walker Colt hanging in its holster from a nail in the far wall.

Donny knew he had to act fast . . . the eggs and bacon cooking in the frypan might burn. For the sake of speed, he shot the man in the back of his gray head and before he hit the ground, Donny grabbed the pan from the heat of the stove. Hallelujah! The bacon was sputtering and the edges of the egg whites were crispy black, but tonight's supper was safe.

Donny scouted around, found a spoon, and stepped outside with the frypan, away from the sweat and pipe smoke stench of the cabin's interior. He ate quickly, not wanting the eggs to get cold. To his surprise the food was good, pepper and salt, everything seasoned and nicely fried, the bacon just right. He turned his head and said, "You done good, old man."

But the dead have no voice, and there was no answer.

Donny finished eating, tossed the spoon and pan away, went back in the shack, and stepped over the sprawled body. There was a smelly, unmade bunk, a fireplace with an ashy, cold log and on the mantel a tintype of a scantily clad woman in a silver frame. She'd written on the picture, but the ink had faded, and all Donny could make out was, M . . . favori . . . wboy . . . Ellswor . . . 872 . . . Rox . . .

Donny took the tintype from the frame and stuck it in his pants pocket. A further search of the cabin turned up twenty-seven dollars in a rusty peach can, a nickel railroad watch, a Barlow folding knife, coffee, a small poke of sugar, and a plug of Star of Virginia chewing tobacco. Donny took it all and kicked the dead man in the ribs on his way out. "Not much to show for a life, you old skinflint," he said.

That night Donny Bryson spread his blankets under the stars, his newly acquired watch telling him the time was ten-thirty. No soft bed, no soft woman, but all in all it had been a successful evening. He'd made a profit of twenty-seven dollars, ate a good meal, and that made a man slumber peacefully o' nights. A night bird called in the distance, and insects made their small sound in the brush as he closed his eyes and let sleep take him.

CHAPTER NINETEEN

Red Ryan and Buttons Muldoon occupied two small, cramped rooms at the rear of the Alpenrose Inn that were reserved for stage drivers and shotgun messengers.

About the time Donny Bryson settled down for the night, Red Ryan awakened with a tap-tap-tap at his door. Thinking it might be another Buttons crisis, he rose, put on his hat, and opened the door, standing there in his long-handled underwear.

"Did I waken you?" Augusta Addington said. A slight smile tugged at her lips. She was fully dressed and held a brown manila envelope in her hand.

Red stammered his confusion and embarrassment. "Yes, I mean, no. I mean . . . let me get decent."

"You're decent enough," Augusta said. She elbowed Red aside and stepped into the room. "Exciting, huh?" she said as her smile grew.

"Of course, it's exciting. Do you always come to a man's room at this time of night looking as pretty as a field of bluebonnets?" Red said. He pulled the patchwork quilt from his cot and held it around him.

"No, not always," Augusta said. "Just when I need something."

Red opened his mouth and tried to speak but the words stuck in his throat. That night he thought the woman somewhat beyond beautiful, her face as delicate as bone china, dark eye makeup, full lips glossy pink, eminently kissable. Large breasts swelled against the thin stuff of her dress, and she smelled like . . . Red tried for a way to describe it . . . like a woman who'd just risen from a bed of musky wildflowers.

"What . . ." he swallowed hard . . . "do you need?"

"Your help," Augusta said.

"What . . . what kind of help?" Red said.

"The kind of help that saves lives," Augusta said. She read the disappointment on Red's face. "Not quite what you were expecting?"

"A woman shoves her way into a man's bedroom at night, what should he expect?" Red said.

"If he was a gentleman, he might expect that being a damsel in distress was her only reason."

"Like you?"

"Like me."

Red took a deep breath and said, "There's a chair. Why don't you sit and tell me what this is all about? Then I can simmer down and get back to bed."

Augusta sat and for a moment played with the springy coil of hair that had fallen over her forehead. Then, she dropped her hand and said, "I'm not a French and English tutor."

"And I'm not surprised to hear that. Go on."

"But I am a Pinkerton agent."

"You mean a detective, like they have in the dime novels?"

"Yes. I work for the Pinkerton Detective Agency."

"Huh. Now I am surprised."

"I was hired by Mr. Allan Pinkerton himself, and it was he who gave me this letter." Augusta opened the manila envelope and produced a single sheet of paper. "I'd like you to read it."

Red looked bewildered. "But why me?"

"Because I can't trust the law, but I believe I can trust you. Red. You're a shotgun messenger, and that means you're a brave and resolute man who's good with a gun and can care of himself."

"Lady, I'm only brave part of the time," Red said. "Maybe half the time."

"And the other half?"

"If the other half was melted down it couldn't be poured into a gunfight."

Augusta smiled. "Then I'll be happy to accept the help of even half a brave man."

"What's in the letter?" Red said.

"I think you should read it. Della Stark, the daughter of the rancher Gideon Stark, sent it to Allan Pinkerton. But Mr. Pinkerton was very sick from gangrene, so he handed over this investigation to me before he died."

"I don't think that the daughter of Gideon Stark, one of the richest men in Texas, needs to ask anybody for help," Red said.

"She does if she suspects her father or some other party could be scheming to murder the man she loves," Augusta said.

"Let me see the letter," Red said. "But I ain't making any promises."

Augusta passed the letter over. It was fairly short and to the point.

My dear Mr. Pinkerton,

My name is Miss Della Stark, the daughter of Gideon Stark, the Texas rancher and I am writing to you because I need your help on a matter of the greatest moment. To put matters in a nutshell, I am in love with a man, a physician, but my father demands that I wed another, like himself a wealthy rancher and a hidalgo in his native Old Mexico.

My father has recently informed me that if I meet with the doctor again, I will be locked in my room at the ranch until I agree to marry his choice of husband, ere it take years of imprisonment. By a most singular circumstance, one of my father's drovers let slip in my presence that my physician's life is now not worth "a plugged nickel."

Mr. Pinkerton, I fear a terrible murder is about to take place, and I beg you to do all in your power to prevent it.

> *Yours Respectfully,*
> *Della Stark*

Red passed the letter back to Augusta, who took it and said, "The letter was mailed from here, the Alpenrose Inn. Miss Stark reserves a room for overnight stays when she visits town."

"Where is the doctor?" Red said.

"I made some enquiries, and there are three doctors in Fredericksburg," Augusta said. "I'll know more when I speak with Miss Stark tomorrow."

Red smiled. "Do you really think a highly respected rancher like Gideon Stark is going to send some of his boys to punch the ticket of a small-town sawbones? For God's sake, he'd be looking at a noose or twenty-to-life in Huntsville."

"Red, the nineteenth century is quickly coming to a close, and the old ways are dying fast," Augusta said. "Men like Stark no longer do their own killing. He'll hire a professional so that the doctor's death can't be traced to him. I'm sure he doesn't want his daughter to know that he was responsible for the murder of her lover."

"I'm pretty sure she'd figure out that her old man was behind the killing," Red said.

"But she'd never know for sure," Augusta said. "And that alone would probably prevent her hating him for the rest of his life."

"Or she'd know, but couldn't prove it," Red said.

"Either way, Gideon Stark gets what he wants. The doctor is dead, his daughter marries a rich hidalgo, two enormous ranges are joined in holy matrimony, and Stark becomes one of the richest and most powerful men in the country. He's a big man who wants to be bigger, and such an alliance could take him all the way to the presidency of the United States."

"You sure credit ol' Gideon with a sight of ambition," Red said.

Augusta said, "From what I've heard and read about Stark, he gets what he wants, and he wants it all. He takes on all comers and makes the big operators toe the line and the small ones bunch up and eventually surrender. Some men lust after wealth, others after women, but Gideon Stark lusts after power. Not too long ago north of the Perdinales there were eight major ranches and a dozen smaller ones. Today, there's only one, the Stark Cattle Company. The rest were bought out, burned out, or just fled the country. The law turned a blind eye. They knew who and what they were dealing with, and no one wanted to take him on."

"Seems like the Texas Rangers would've shown an interest," Red said. "Maybe they still would."

"The Rangers had their hands full, first with Comanches and now with the Apaches," Augusta said. "Meanwhile Gideon Stark enforces his own brand of law in most of Central Texas, and the Rangers are happy to let him be. You don't bite the hand that helps feed you."

"Augusta, where is this going?" Red said. "You asked for my help, but I can't see that there's anything I can do for you."

"There's one thing you can do for me, Red. Make sure that Della Stark's doctor stays alive."

Red's spine stiffened. "Augusta"—he noticed she wore earrings, plain little gold hoops—"that ain't gonna happen. Me and Buttons will leave this burg as soon as we sign up passengers. Sooner, if Buttons decides we should just cannonball back to San Angelo empty."

"Speak to Buttons, Red. Give me a couple of days."

"Why? I mean, it could be weeks, months, before a hired gun shows up to shoot the doc," Red said. "Heck, even Sheriff Ritter can handle that."

"Red, I think the killers are already here," Augusta

said. "I believe the doctor doesn't have days or months. Right now, I think his life can be measured in hours."

"What do you want me to do? Hang around the doc's surgery with a Greener scattergun in my hands? His patients would love that, huh?"

"I want you to save a man's life, but I don't know how you should do it," Augusta said. "I'm pretty new to this detective business myself. In fact, this is my first case."

"Your first case." Red groaned. "And you plan to brace one of the most . . ."

"Powerful men in Texas. Yes, I know. But I won't stand idly by and see an innocent girl stampeded to further her father's ambitions."

"You said the killers are already here. Why do you think there's more than one? How many hired guns does it take to put a bullet in a pill-roller?"

"More than one if Gideon Stark wants his killing done right," Augusta said. "Nothing must tie him to the doctor's murder, so he's hired the best professionals he could find, men who do their job and leave no loose ends behind them."

"Who are these men?" Red said. "Heck, Augusta, if they're as good as you say, me and my Greener may not be enough."

"I have my suspicions, but I can't prove them, at least not yet," Augusta said. "And yes, Red, you may not be enough. Maybe a regiment of infantry wouldn't be enough."

"I can't bring the exact entry in the rule book to mind, but since you were a fare-paying passenger of the Abe Patterson and Son Stage and Express Company and may be again, I believe it's my duty to help you all I can," Red said. "I'll talk to Buttons about it."

"I hope he'll give you good advice," Augusta said.

"Well, I've never known Buttons Muldoon to say a foolish thing," Red said. "Of course, I've never known him to say a wise one, either. But maybe he'll come up with a solution to your problem."

Augusta rose to her feet. In her white dress, she looked like a column of fine marble. "One last thing, Red," she said. "If I don't make it . . ."

"What do you mean, if you don't make it?"

"If I'm killed, please tell the Pinkerton agency that I did my job. There are other female detectives, and I don't want to let them down."

"You won't get killed," Red said. "I'll see to that."

"You will tell them? Red, please, if it happens, I want you to tell them."

Red saw seriousness and a trace of fear in the woman's face, and he suddenly felt woefully inadequate. "I'll tell them," he said. It was all he could manage.

CHAPTER TWENTY

It was not the staff of Moses that had been removed from its case and laid on the hotel room table, but a Marlin-Ballard sporting rifle in .32-40 caliber fitted with a thirty-one-and-a-half-inch brass telescopic sight manufactured by the famous L. N. Mogg Company of Marcellus, New York. Now gleaming in the light of an oil lamp, the rifle had been custom made for Helmut Klemm, the German sniper assassin, famous for head shots at distance. The Marlin-Ballard had accounted for twenty-seven victims, including an Austrian crown prince, a rich British merchant banker, and an eighty-seven-year-old dowager French countess with a pile of money and an impatient heir who'd feared that the old bitch would never die.

Klemm, a blond, blue-eyed man of ice, realized he was slumming on the American frontier, but the money had been too good to refuse, and anyway, he planned to retire to his idyllic Bavarian estate once the job was done.

Speaking in the halting English that all three of his henchmen understood, though the Arab Salman el Salim claimed the hated tongue scalded his mouth, the Irishman

Sean O'Rourke said, "Ernest Walzer made it clear that we split the kill fee four ways, no matter who pulls the trigger. Does that still stand?" There was a murmur of agreement, and O'Rourke said, "The mark is an easy target, but afterward our getaway has to be clean. I mean spotless. After the doctor is dead, we'll head to Austin and then catch a train to Houston and from there to New Orleans, where we can take a ship for England."

"Can we trust Walzer?" the big Russian Kirill Kuznetsov said. He was a man prone to bouts of deep, Slavic depression and dangerous beyond belief when a black mood was on him. "The old Jew didn't need four of us."

"Yes, we can trust him. We're his insurance," Klemm said. "The client wants the kill done right. Where one may fail, four will not."

Kuznetsov tried a futile smile, his wide mouth stretching humorlessly, and said, "I can walk out of here now, break the doctor's neck with my bare hands, and return to hotel." He snapped his fingers. "Like that."

O'Rourke shook his head. "And risk bringing the law down on us. No, Kuznetsov, this is a quiet town, and the doctor must be killed at night when all its citizens are in bed. We'll have horses ready, and as soon as we nail the mark's skin to the wall, we'll ride out of here. Let them blame it on Apaches like they did in San Angelo after we took care of those two idiots."

Klemm smiled and said, "Stover Timms and Lem Harlan were their names, remember?"

"Squealed like pigs and begged for mercy," Kuznetsov said. He pretended to spit on the floor. "Pah, they were not men. Who is foolish enough to ask Kirill Kuznetsov for mercy?"

The Arab Salman el Salim spoke for the first time. "There are four of us, and all our hands must be bloodied. No one walks away from this without taking part in the kill."

"I agree with those words," Kuznetsov said. "The payment from Walzer will be shared, and so must the killing."

"Yes, but silently is the way," O'Rourke said. "Klemm, you are a rifleman, and I use the pistol." He took his revolver from the pocket of his monkish robe, an Adams Third Model in .450 caliber. O'Rourke had carried the pistol as a British army officer until he was drummed out of the Inniskilling Dragoons for embezzling mess funds. He'd managed to salvage his cavalry saber and sidearm, both private purchases. The sword was long gone, but he retained the Adams and had racked up twenty-five kills with the weapon, resisting all temptations to switch to a much superior Colt or Webley. "One thing these weapons share is that they go bang when we pull the trigger. It is for that reason we will kill with the knife."

"Easy," Kuznetsov said. "I have a knife, and on several occasions, I've used the blade before."

El Salim nodded. "The knife is as quiet as a viper's whisper." He drew a finger across his throat. "And as quick as its tongue."

"An effortless kill," Klemm said. "And the easiest money we'll ever make."

"When?" Kuznetsov said, looking at O'Rourke.

"Come the morn, we hire horses and tell the livery stable that we're riding out to look for a patch of land suitable for the building of a mission to house the holy staff of Moses," the Irishman said. "Then, for the next day or two we lie low . . ." he smiled . . . "spending our time in prayer, so people get used to having monks in town. On the chosen day we make the kill and leave the town again, but this time we never come back."

"It seems like a sound plan," Klemm said.

"And how is your poor belly, Brother Helmut?" O'Rourke said.

"Was is das? My belly doesn't hurt," Klemm said, scowling.

"It does. It hurts like heck and in the morning, you will let Dr. Ben Bradford treat you for it," O'Rourke said. "That way we do two things . . . we study the layout of his place and when you show up, groaning in pain, he won't suspect that we're there to kill him."

"That the Russian and the Arab are there to kill him," Kuznetsov said. "O'Rourke, when you and the German stick a knife into him, he'll already be dead."

"Ah, Brother Kirill, you're a lovely man," O'Rourke said, smiling. "Thanks for pointing that little detail out to us. So are we settled on the plan?"

The other three exchanged glances and then Klemm said, "Yes, now let's get it done and soon we'll become men again instead of monks."

The delivery of Mrs. Nancy Brownlee's baby was routine, but she'd spent ten hours in labor, and a crescent moon rode high in the sky by the time Dr. Ben Bradford returned to his home and surgery on Crockett Street and without lighting a lamp flopped into a chair, exhausted.

The doctor's parlor was small, cramped, two brown leather wingback chairs and a Queen Anne sofa taking up most of the room. A threadbare Persian rug lay diagonally across the wood floor. Against one wall stood a mahogany bookshelf crowded with medical volumes and a copy of Texas Laws on Wills, Trusts and Estates, and on another a print of Rembrandt's *Bathsheba at Her Bath*, a present from a horse trader whose tastes ran to Junoesque ladies. The only window was high and narrow, shaded by a ruby-red velvet curtain. It was a dark, masculine room that smelled of pipe tobacco, leather, and the sharp odor of carbolic acid leaking from the surgery. But Dr. Bradford thought there were times when the room was radiant with light . . . when Della Stark moved through it like a candle flame.

Ben Bradford was the masculine opposite of Della's dazzling beauty. He was a serious young man with intelligent and solemn brown eyes, an inch above average height and not at all handsome. But dressed in his physician's black garb, he presented a solid, respectable appearance that reassured his patients and made women think of him not as an ardent lover, but as a rock-steady husband who would support his wife and family and always provide a shoulder to cry on. Starry-eyed Della Stark adored him. But years later, Buttons Muldoon would recall Dr. Ben Bradford as "the most boring man in Texas" . . . and no one argued with him.

Bradford took off his elastic-sided boots and stood. He divested himself of his frock coat and carried it with him to his bedroom. Then the feeling hit him. Creepy. Full of malice. As though he was being watched by someone with cruel, hostile eyes . . . the eyes of a predator. But that was impossible. The house was dark, the curtains drawn, and no one could see inside. The doctor was not a particularly brave man, but neither was he a coward. He tossed his coat on the bed and stepped into the patients' waiting room where he kept a large rolltop desk. He retrieved a bunch of keys from his pocket, opened the desk, and then took a four-shot Colt Cloverleaf House Pistol in .41 caliber from a drawer. Bradford had bought the little revolver for protection when he made late-night calls but had never felt the need to carry it in a law-and-order town like Fredericksburg. He checked the loads and went back to the bedroom, pulled aside the curtain, and stared into the night. There was a small barn behind the house where Bradford kept his mare and buggy and beyond that a vacant lot with a FOR SALE sign. The thin moonlight did nothing to illuminate the scene, but everything seemed quiet. The doctor left the bedroom and went into the kitchen, where he opened the back door and stepped into darkness. The night was still. There was no breeze and nothing moved. A circuit of the house made with gun in hand revealed nothing except a tiny calico cat who watched the human with feigned disinterest as she passed.

Dr. Ben Bradford lowered his revolver and stared at the sky and its tumult of stars. He felt slightly ashamed for acting like an old maiden aunt who hears a rustle in every bush.

Yet . . .

The feeling of being watched, stalked, studied did not leave him. He felt like the deer who feels the presence of the wolf. An intelligent man, Bradford knew his imagination wasn't playing tricks on him . . . his instincts warned him that someone, somewhere, wished him harm.

He felt a sudden jolt of alarm.

My God, was Gideon Stark so enraged that he was seeing his daughter that the quick-tempered rancher had arrived in town with fire in his eyes and a shotgun in his hands?

Bradford immediately dismissed the thought. Gideon may disapprove of Della's choice of a beau, but the wild old days were long gone, and Gideon was more likely to send a cease-and-desist letter from his lawyer than stoop to violence.

The doctor shook his head, baffled. Then why did he fell this way . . . so threatened?

He had no answer for that question . . . and that night he tossed and turned in uneasy sleep, the Colt under his pillow.

CHAPTER TWENTY-ONE

"My daughter has a closet full of clothes, but she says she has nothing to wear," Gideon Stark said. "Manuel, you will see that Della talks only to dress-shop ladies. Do you understand?"

The gun vaquero nodded. *"Sí, señor."*

"No shooting the breeze with doctors and the like, understand?"

"Sí, señor."

"But no violence, Manuel. Keep the iron holstered."

"Sí, señor."

"Young Will Graham will drive the surrey," Stark said. "That set all right with you?"

Manuel Garcia nodded. "He'll do, señor."

"He's good with a gun."

"Fast, señor. Very fast."

"The Apaches are out, but my daughter doesn't care," Stark said. "I don't want to force her to stay home. At least not now."

"The Apaches are to the north of us," Garcia said. "We are not in any danger."

"I heard the army chased them all the way to the Colorado," Stark said.

The vaquero nodded. "Yes, señor. I have heard that very thing."

Stark's eyes moved from the vaquero to the window. Outside, Della waited by the surrey, a Morgan bay in the traces, lanky towhead Will Graham already at the reins.

Stark said, "Della is ready to leave. Take good care of her, Manuel."

"*Sí, señor.* Where the señorita goes, Manuel will go."

Gideon Stark watched the surrey leave until it was lost in the distance, the day already bright with the morning sun. He stood outside his sprawling ranch house for a long time, deep in thought, his racing mind centered on his daughter and the man she claimed to love . . . unfortunately not the rich hidalgo Don Miguel de Serra, but a landless, penniless pill-roller. If the Englishman Ernest Walzer was a man of his word . . . and why wouldn't he be? . . . the assassins must already be in Texas, and Ben Bradford was a walking dead man. The question was when would they gun him? Today? Tomorrow? Next week? Next month? He had to know.

Stark was a man of medium height dressed in well-worn range clothes. Big shoulders. Big hands. Iron-gray hair cropped short, compensated for by a sweeping dragoon mustache and heavy eyebrows. An almost brutal face, lean, wide-lipped, anchored by a steamship prow of a nose with curved, flaring nostrils. His eyes were steel gray and reflected the gamut of his emotions . . . anger . . . annoyance . . . greed . . . envy . . . fear . . . cruelty . . . but nothing of joy . . . tenderness . . . love . . . happiness . . . sentiments he'd never felt. Such emotions stand in the way of empire building. Gideon Stark was a tight, bitter, empty man, and ambition was the driving force in his life. Some apologist historians say Stark's love for his daughter was his saving grace. But wiser heads know that he didn't love Della. He was incapable of such love. His plan had always been to use her as a pawn in the marriage game to make himself richer and more powerful. Don Miguel owned several vast ranchos in south Texas and across the Rio Grande into Mexico, and when joined with Stark's own immense acres, such an alliance would create a nation within a nation and propel him to the highest office in the land . . . the presidency of the United States. In the face of such ambition, the fact that Don Miguel was a fifty-five-year-old lecher who was rumored to have taken the mercury cure for syphilis was neither here nor there. And a mere small-town doctor who had beguiled a silly, headstrong girl would not stand in Stark's way, either.

He walked back into the house that was aggressively masculine: leather, dark wood, gun racks, and portraits of bearded Confederate generals and bleak oil landscapes on the walls. The only feminine touch was a clay pot of now-wilted wildflowers that Della had placed in one of the front windows.

Stark stepped into his study that smelled of cigars, bourbon, and horse sweat and sat at his desk. He pulled out a piece of notepaper, dipped a pen in the inkwell, and wrote:

Come. Now.

He folded the paper in half and stuffed it into a long envelope and addressed it to

The Right Honorable Harold Fairfax

There were several punchers grouped around the corral, and Stark gave it to one of the smarter ones to deliver to the neighboring ranch with the warning, "He's the son of a belted earl, so watch your tongue."

The cowboy read the name on the envelope and said, "I know who he is, boss."

"Good, then see that he gets it," Stark said. "I want him here before sundown."

The puncher nodded and left for the barn.

"Saddle a fast horse," Stark called after him.

The man waved, and a few minutes later galloped away on a long-legged American stud.

The Fairfax ranch house stood right on the fence between the two spreads, a thing Stark would have taken as an affront had he not allied himself with Harold Fairfax. The earl's son had a small ranch that never ran more than a few hundred head, most of them longhorns, but he was a ruthless, vicious miscreant with good connections, and for those reasons he stood high in Stark's esteem.

Fairfax would know where the high-priced assassins were at . . . and when Dr. Ben Bradford would die.

Donny Bryson lay on a shallow brush-covered rise overlooking the main wagon road that led from one of the big spreads to his east. He'd been saddling his horse when he'd spotted the rising dust. Wary of a hemp-noose posse, he'd grabbed his telescope and scrambled up the hill to take a look-see. The spyglass to his eye, he felt relief that it was a surrey with an outrider kicking up the dust and then interest when he saw the passenger . . . a blonde woman wearing a blue dress. At that distance, he couldn't tell if she was pretty or not. Cursing the small telescope's low power, in the fleeting time that the surrey was in view he managed to ascertain that the woman was slim, and that pleased him. But the vaquero with the gun was troubling, as was the driver, who was certain to be armed. If he rode toward them, those boys would shoot first and ask questions later, especially a pistol vaquero, always a finger looking for a trigger. The surrey and the woman in it were not easy targets, and Donny thought it through and then let it go. Probably a rancher's wife or daughter heading into Fredericksburg to buy women's fixin's, she would come back this way, and next time he figured he'd be better prepared, or at least within shooting distance of the wagon road.

Reluctantly, Donny returned to his cold camp in a cluster of wild oak and juniper cut through by a shallow stream. He'd had it in mind to ride south to the river country where he had Apache kin, if they weren't already hung or in jail. There he'd lie low for a spell, at least until the Austin lawmen stopped hunting him.

But the blonde woman in the surrey had changed all that.

Sluggish thoughts seeped through the foul sewer of Donny's mind. The woman might return later that afternoon or evening, or she might stay overnight in town and head back to the ranch the next day. He determined to climb the rise again with his glass and canteen and keep unholy vigil.

He suddenly felt the need for the woman, and by God he'd have her.

* * *

"Set your mind at rest, Gideon," Harold Fairfax said. "My father has complete faith in Ernest Walzer. The man has never been known to fail. I assure you, the assassins are close and biding their time."

"I sent a man to England with half of Walzer's payment," Stark said. "He won't get the other half until the job is done and Ben Bradford is dead."

"Wasn't that a risk, trusting the man?" Fairfax said.

"I trust no one," Stark said. "Walzer was told to get rid of the courier after the money was paid."

"Then the man is already dead," Fairfax said. "My father tells me that Ernest Walzer is quite the expert with poisons." He smiled. "But my dear, Gideon, surely you trust me?"

"Of course, I trust you, Harold," Stark said. "You and your father are in this thing too deep to turn traitor."

"I'm your friend, Gideon," Fairfax said.

Stark's smile was an unpleasant grimace. "Harold, you're a snake, and you're nobody's friend except your own. If I wanted to, I could hang you."

Fairfax's face didn't change, but his pale blue eyes hardened as he rose from his chair. "Why would you do that?"

"I don't know. But I could find something that cocks my pistol. What happened to the nesters over to Rusty Stone Creek?"

"They're gone. You know that."

"I know you hung the pa and his three young sons from a cottonwood. What happened to the womenfolk?"

"They left . . . why are you asking me these questions?"

Stark said, "To make something clear, Harold."

"And that is?"

Stark rose to his feet. "We're not friends. You work for me. Get that through your head."

"I own my own spread," Fairfax said.

"Yes, you do, and I could take it from you tomorrow and hang you from same cottonwood that the nesters swung from."

Harold Fairfax hadn't expected that last, and he didn't know how to handle it. His weak-chinned, inbred face with its popping eyes was ashen. He'd never tanned under the Texas sun. His skin got redder and then peeled and flakes of dead skin constantly clung to his nose and cheekbones. Right then he was scared.

But Stark had made his point, and he was prepared to be magnanimous. He laid a hand on Fairfax's plump shoulder and grinned. "I'm just messing with you, Harold. We're partners you and me, compadres, and that's how it will be forever."

Fairfax was relieved, and he smiled. "You're always a joker, Gideon."

Stark nodded. "Yeah, I sure am, always a one for a good joke."

Fairfax became serious. "As I told you earlier, you've no need to worry about the assassins. I'm sure they're in Fredericksburg, and they'll get the job done. In fact, I'll go there myself and see it through."

"No, you won't," Stark said. "You're too close to me. Della can't suspect anything that ties me to the sawbones' death."

"Yes, I understand," Fairfax said, nodding, looking earnest.

Stark shook his head. His face changed from smile to

deadly seriousness. "No, you don't, Harold. It just dawned on me that you don't understand a damned thing."

"Gideon, it's pretty clear," Fairfax said.

"I'll tell you what's suddenly clear, at least to me, and I don't know why I didn't think about it sooner."

"What's that?"

"That after this is over and Ben Bradford is dead, you could hold it over me. Threaten me with it."

"Blackmail, you mean?"

"Blackmail, I mean. And see, it was already in your mind."

"No, Gideon, no," Fairfax said. "I'd never do such a thing."

Stark smiled. "Sorry, Harold. I can't take that chance."

A few days later, Harold Fairfax's death was carried in the Gillespie *Tattler* newspaper as a suicide. The story made page one and told how respected rancher Gideon Stark confronted Fairfax and accused him of lynching an entire family of nesters who'd squatted on his land. When Mr. Stark told Fairfax he planned to go to the law about the atrocity, the Englishman, in a paroxysm of guilt and unable to face the consequences, pulled his pistol and blew his brains out. The *Tattler* was moved to add, "Thus perished a man who did not hesitate to slaughter the innocents, men, women, and children, and then revealed his cowardice by his self-destruction. The *Tattler* says good riddance. Gillespie County, and indeed the great state of Texas, does not need men of Fairfax's stripe. We also raise three hearty cheers for rancher Stark, who risked his own life to confront the murderer. Well done, Sir Gideon, this country needs more knights in shining armor like you!"

* * *

In fact, the reality of the killing was considerably less heroic.

Harold Fairfax habitually wore a Colt .32-20 revolver in a cross-draw holster and in a single, catlike move Gideon Stark yanked it from the leather, took a step back and shot the Englishman in the left temple. Stone-cold dead and still on his feet, Fairfax stared at his killer for a long moment and then his legs collapsed under him and he sprawled on the floor. Stark shoved the Colt into the dead man's left hand and closed his fingers around the handle.

Big John Cooper, Stark's segundo, and half a dozen punchers pounded on the ranch house door then scrambled inside. Gideon was cool, calm, and collected. He'd braced Fairfax about the deaths of the poor nester family out by Rusty Stone Creek and rather than face the consequences for his vile deed, he shot himself. Not by nature a deep-thinking man, Cooper accepted the story at face value, as did the cowboys with him. Harold Fairfax was universally disliked, so nobody much cared that he'd punched his own ticket. No one noticed, or thought it worth mentioning, that he wore his cross-draw Colt on the left side. He was a right-handed man who'd shot himself with the wrong hand.

Ah well, if anyone had dared speak up, Gideon Stark would've said, "Shut your trap. I don't give a damn what hand the idiot shot himself with."

CHAPTER TWENTY-TWO

It was a few minutes after noon when Della Stark arrived in Fredericksburg. The sun was high in the sky, and the day was hot and gritty yellow dust hung in the streets like a mist.

After the surrey stopped outside the Alpenrose Inn, Della told Will Graham to take the carriage to the livery and see that the Morgan was fed a scoop of oats.

"But Miss Della, the boss said I had to stay close to you," Graham said. His pleasant young face showed concern.

"I'm meeting a lady friend inside," Della said. "Do you really want to sit in a hot hotel room and listen to a lot of women talk?"

"No, Miss Della, I surely don't," Graham said. "But your Pa . . ."

"My Pa worries too much," Della said, "I won't leave the hotel, so I'll be quite safe."

Manuel Garcia sat his horse beside the surrey, a slender, dark-eyed young man with a pearl-handled Colt on his right hip. "But Señor Stark said you were going to a dress shop," he said.

"Yes, later. But first I want to visit with my friend," Della said. She smiled. "Manuel, why don't you and Will find yourselves a nice shady beer garden? Come back here in two hours, and you can escort me to the dress shop."

"Miss Della, first I must meet your friend, I think," Garcia said.

The girl frowned. "Manuel, now you're starting to make me very cross."

The vaquero shrugged, a very Mexican gesture. "I follow the patron's orders."

Della let out a highly effected sigh. "Very well then. Bring in my bag and I'll meet you in the lobby."

"Manuel, I'll head for the livery and tend to the horse," Graham said.

"I'll see you there in a while," Garcia said. Both men were aware of the other's gun skill and had no problem splitting up and going their separate ways.

Garcia took Della's carpetbag from the surrey, looped his horse to the hitching rail, and followed her into the hotel. The lobby was dark and cool, and Della stood talking with the desk clerk. After a while the man left and walked upstairs.

"Ah, good, you've got my bag," Della said to Garcia. "The hotel is busy, and you and Will must share a room tonight."

"We both sleep in the same bunkhouse, so I'm used to his snoring," the vaquero said.

The girl smiled and then turned as Augusta Addington came down the stairs.

"Miss Stark?" Augusta said.

"Yes, and you must be Miss Addington."

"You can call me Augusta."

"Likewise. I'm Della."

The two women embraced like long-lost sisters, and then Della said, "Augusta, this is Manuel Garcia, one of my father's vaqueros."

Garcia bowed and said, "I am honored."

Augusta smiled and said, "I've heard of vaqueros, but never met one before. I must say, Mr. Garcia, you look splendid."

The vaquero, dressed in his best go-to-town outfit, seemed pleased and flustered at the same time, and Della came to his rescue. "Two hours, Manuel," she said. "Augusta and I will be quite safe in her room until then."

Garcia nodded. "*Sí,* Miss Della. I will return for you later, but until then I'll keep watch at a distance."

Two women sat on each side of a small, square table covered by a white tablecloth, blue china teapot, cups, saucers, and a plate of sugar cookies between them. Afternoon sunlight streamed through the hotel room window and made dust motes dance, and outside a brass oompah band played the Radetzky March in a nearby beer garden.

Augusta Addington, tall, elegant, and beautiful, rose to her feet, closed the window, and said, "I think we've heard quite enough of that."

Della Stark was her opposite. A petite girl with blonde ringlets, pretty, hazel-eyed, a small, heart-shaped mouth that smiled readily, she lifted the pot and said, "More tea, Augusta?"

"Please," Augusta said. She waited until Della poured

tea and then added milk and a sugar cube and stirred, and said, "As you fear, your young doctor's life is in the greatest danger, and I think his would-be assassins are already in Fredericksburg."

Della's hand flew to her throat. "Oh my God," she said, her eyes wide and frightened.

"Do you really think your father could be behind all this?" Augusta said.

"I don't know what to think," the girl said. "My father is a hard, unyielding man, but I . . . I just don't believe he'd stoop to murder."

"He wants you to marry . . ."

"Don Miguel de Serra."

"Yes," Augusta said. "Tell me about him."

Della looked distressed. "He's a pig, a rapist who preys on women. He brings whores and peasant girls into his hacienda just to torture and humiliate them in every way he can. Even my father admits that Don Miguel loves to abuse women."

"And prostitutes and peons are an easy target because no one cares what happens to them," Augusta said.

"He is said to have syphilis," Della said. "It's a loathsome, terrible disease that . . ."

"I know what syphilis is," Augusta said. "And Don Miguel, he is rich?"

"The richest man in Mexico, a great landowner with many cattle," Della said. "A puncher once told me that when Don Miguel moves a herd, dust blackens the sky and blots out the sun for half a day."

"And your father wishes you to wed him so that . . ."

"The ranches will be joined by marriage, and my father becomes the richest and most influential Americano in

Texas. And he makes no secret of the fact that he'd like to be president of the United States one day."

"And in return, Don Miguel gets a pretty young bride to use and abuse as he pleases."

Della shuddered. "That is Miguel's price. And it seems my father is willing to pay it."

Augusta sat in thought for long moments and then said, "Della, an ambitious man who would sell his own daughter to a depraved, diseased monster for his own gain would not hesitate to plan the murder of an obscure country doctor who could ruin his plans."

"My father . . . I just don't think he could be capable of . . . of cold-blooded murder," Della said.

"Yes, you do, and it nags at you. That's why you're here," Augusta said. She wore her hair piled up on her head in glossy waves, and the sunlight angling through the window was warm on the back of her neck.

Della's troubled gaze fluttered over the older woman's face and finally came to rest on the table in front of her. "What am I to do?" she whispered. "But, please, let's keep my father out of this. You're so wrong, Augusta. The more I think about it, the less I believe he would have Ben killed. My father once threatened to use a horse-whip on him, but that's all."

Augusta had listened in silence, her face expression-less, and now she said, "Della, I'm a Pinkerton agent, and the first thing you did was hire me to keep both you and your doctor safe," Augusta said.

"Of course," Della said. "That goes without saying. I have no one else to turn to." She bit her lip.

Augusta lifted her cup and sipped her tea. It was cold.

"Della, the clock is ticking. I believe an attempt on Dr. Ben Bradford's life will happen very soon."

A yelp of distress, and then Della said, "Oh my God, what do we do?"

"You do nothing until I tell you," Augusta said. "Let me take care of it."

"I can't go back to the ranch," Della said. "I know my father is not planning Ben's murder. I know it, I know it, I know it . . . but after all these terrible accusations, I don't think I could look him in the eye."

"You'll stay here at the hotel until this is all over," Augusta said. She had begun to doubt Della's intelligence, and her abject failure to accept the obvious was telling.

"And when will it be all over?" the girl said.

"A few days, no more than that. The vaquero and the other man, where do their loyalties lie?"

"Manuel and Will work for my father and they ride for the brand," Della said. "I can put my trust in them."

"Then tell them you're staying in town for a few more days," Augusta said. "They'll probably be glad to miss their ranch chores. Fredericksburg is a square-toed town, but it has its attractions."

"And what will you do, Augusta?" Della said. "Stay close to Ben? Do you have a gun?"

Augusta smiled. "Yes, I have fine revolver, and I'll keep an eye on Ben. And I'm trying to recruit some help."

"The sheriff?"

"Possibly, but right now I'm thinking of men of a rougher, tougher sort."

"Outlaws?"

"No, not outlaws," Augusta said. "But I have a feeling there are times when they come pretty close."

CHAPTER TWENTY-THREE

"Buttons, you ever considered becoming an outlaw, leaving the stagecoach life behind?" Red Ryan said. "I mean like Jesse and Frank James and them."

He sat with a depressed Buttons Muldoon in the Munich Keller, a shady beer garden set in a grove of ancient oaks on the edge of town.

"This is where Hannah Huckabee shot Dave Winter that time," Buttons said.

"Held her hat in front of her and shot him right through it, didn't she?" Red said.

"Something like that," Buttons said. He looked at Red with bleak eyes. "No, I never considered being an outlaw, and now my luck's turned bad, it's the last profession a cursed man should be in."

"You're not cursed," Red said, smiling, a rim of beer foam on his mustache.

"I ran over the hat," Buttons said. "It's all up for me." His voice took on a plaintive tone. "You can tell me, Red, as a friend . . . is it all up for me?"

"Heck, no," Red said. "You're in your prime, Buttons. You'll live to be a hundred. Maybe a hundred and one."

"No, I won't. I'll be lucky if I live long enough to dirty another shirt." He shook his head. "Me, Patrick Muldoon of the Abe Patterson and Son Stage and Express Company done in by a hat. It's hard to believe. Difficult to comprehend. Ain't that what educated folks say?"

Red was spared having to comment by the unexpected appearance of Chris Mercer. The little man stood behind Buttons rubbing his mouth, his eyes fixed on the foaming tankards of beer on the table. Buttons followed Red's gaze, turned his head, and said, "Damn you, Archibald. Don't stand behind me like that, makes me feel like Wild Bill holding aces and eights. What the heck are you doing? Come around and stand where I can see you like a man and not a damned chicken thief."

"I was passing, and I saw you gentlemen sitting there and thought I'd say hi," Mercer said.

"Well, you've said it, now git," Buttons said, his gloomy, bitter mood getting the better of him. He looked Mercer up and down from his ragged shirt and pants to the unlaced shoes on his feet. "You ever think of buying yourself a new suit?"

Red smiled. "Sit down, Mercer. I'll buy you a beer."

The small man sat down immediately, smiling. After the beer came and Mercer took a few grateful gulps, he said to Buttons, "I'm looking for work, but can't find any."

"And no wonder," Buttons said. "Who the Heck is gonna hire a drunken tramp like you? I wouldn't put the duds you're wearing on a scarecrow."

Mercer's eyes hardened. "Muldoon . . . there was a time . . ."

Buttons stiffened and his hand dropped to his gun,

hearing something in the little man's voice he didn't like, an echo from Mercer's violent past. In his present depressed state, Buttons was unpredictable, and Red headed off any possible trouble. "I can find you a job, maybe."

"Red, this man ain't working for the Abe Patterson and Son Stage and Express Company," Buttons said. "I won't allow it."

"Take it easy, Buttons, it's not that kind of job," Red said.

"I don't take gun work," Mercer said.

"Heck, you should be grateful for any kind of work," Buttons said, scowling.

Red said, "You'd be a watchman, Mercer. Keeping watch to make sure a man stays alive."

"Sounds like a strange kind of job," the little man said.

"Finish your beer and then come with me," Red said. "You'll find out just how strange it is."

"Is it dangerous?" Mercer said.

"Damn right it is," Red said.

And Buttons smiled.

"Red told me about your problem, Miss Addington," Buttons said. He grabbed Chris Mercer by the back of the neck and pushed him forward. "And here's the man that can solve it. You remember Archibald from the stage?"

Red angled a glare at Buttons and said, "May we come in, Augusta?"

The woman opened her hotel room door wider, smiled and said, "Of course you may." Directed at Red, she said, "Miss Stark has gone to her room to rest." Then to the others, "Please sit wherever you can."

"It's all right, we'll stand," Red said. "This won't take long. I told Mercer here you might have a job for him."

Augusta seemed confused, "A job? What kind of job?"

"Watchman," Red said. "He'll keep watch over Della Stark's doctor for you."

The woman looked at Mercer and seemed unimpressed and even more confused.

"Scrawny little runt, ain't he?" Buttons said. "But there was a time when Archibald here was one of the most feared gunmen on the frontier. Ain't that true, Archie?"

"My name is Chris Mercer, and yes, it's true. I wish to God it was not."

"He won't carry a gun," Red said.

"I'll carry one, but I won't use it," Mercer said.

Augusta let that last dangle in the air and said to Red, "Did you talk to Mr. Muldoon about you and him providing protection for Ben Bradford for a few days."

"Yes, he did," Buttons said. "And he told me you're a lady Pinkerton agent, the first one I've ever met. But the fact of the matter is that I'm trying to rustle up some passengers, and when I do, me and Red are out of here." He shook his head. "Miss Addington, I'm a man under a curse, and the way my luck's been running, I'd just be a hindrance to you. Heck, I had just gotten out of bed this morning when I stubbed my toe on the leg of the dresser. I think it's broke."

"The dresser?" Red said.

"No. My toe."

"You could let Dr. Bradford take a look at it," Augusta said.

"And then he'd be smitten by some of my bad luck, and get shot fer sure," Buttons said.

"Who wants this doctor dead, and why?" Mercer said. He suddenly looked alert and interested, like a man who'd just woke from a long sleep.

Using as few words as possible, Augusta told Mercer about the threat to Bradford's life and how Della Stark suspected that her father might be behind the murder plot.

"And I suspect the assassins are already here in Fredericksburg," Augusta said.

"Yes, the four monks who are not monks," Mercer said.

After that statement, Buttons Muldoon suddenly felt the need to sit, the bed squealing under his weight. "The holy monks?" he said. "I don't believe you said that."

"Did you see their hands?" Mercer said. "None of those boys has done a hard day's work in their lives. I've made a study of men, especially men with gun rank. Did you ever see the likes of Bill Longley or Wes Hardin walk into a room? No? Well, I have. The moment they step through the door, they fill the place. You take those monks now. Four men, silent, still, but significant. Watchful. Cool, confident men who sit and wait . . . and God help you if they decide to make a play because they'll come down on you like the hammer of God." Mercer smiled slightly. "Dangerous men are not loud and boastful. They're quiet, so quiet you can smell the odor of their dead silence."

"Heck, I always thought them holy monks smelled funny," Buttons said.

Red Ryan said, "Mercer, it seems like you should tell Sheriff Ritter what you just told us. He could arrest the four assassins and tell them he'll free them in exchange for the name of the man who hired them."

Mercer nodded. "Yes, the rube lawman could do that . . . and guarantee his place in the sweet by-and-by in time for supper. Besides, I've got no proof. If I walked into Ritter's office and accused four rosary-beaded monks of being hired gunmen, I reckon I'd need a bushel basket of it."

Augusta said, "Mr. Mercer . . ."

"Call me Chris. When I was somebody, *Mister* sat just fine with me. It doesn't any longer."

"Mr. Mercer," Augusta said, "will you take on the job of guarding Dr. Bradford until I can resolve this problem?"

"Miss Addington is a Pinkerton agent," Red said.

"I sure didn't peg you for a schoolmarm," Mercer said. "Yes, I'll look out for him. That is, if he'll have me."

"Why don't we go ask him," Augusta said.

"Ask him if he'll accept a ragamuffin as a watchman?" Button said. He shook his melancholy head. "I'll retire to a madhouse."

Mercer ignored that and said, "Miss Addington, I always demanded expenses when I took on a job. Do the Pinks pay them?"

"Reasonable expenses? Yes, they do."

"Then I need pants, a shirt, and a pair of shoes," Mercer said. "And a gun."

Augusta didn't hesitate. "I can provide the funds for clothing. As for the gun, I will loan you mine."

"And leave yourself unarmed, with four killers on the loose?" Red said.

"They haven't killed yet, Red," Augusta said. She smiled. "And I have you to protect me."

"Don't count on it, lady," Buttons said. "With or without

passengers, me and Red are leaving this burg. The way my luck is running, if I stay here, I'll end up the one that gets shot. And a word of warning, give Archibald money for duds and a gun, he'll sell them and buy whiskey."

"Will you do that, Mr. Mercer, spend the money I give you on whiskey?" Augusta said.

"Look at me. I'll buy a shirt, pants, and a pair of shoes," Mercer said.

Augusta opened her bag and brought out her revolver. "It's a British Bulldog in .450 caliber."

"Self-cocker, five rounds in the cylinder," Mercer said. He took the revolver, hefted it for balance and expertly spun it around his trigger finger before it slapped back into his palm. "Fine weapon. One time up Fort Worth way, Luke Short told me he set store by the Bulldog because it hides in the pocket so well."

"I have a box of ammunition to go with it," Augusta said.

"I only need five," Mercer said. "I don't plan on doing any shooting,"

"Then a great watchman you'll be," Buttons said, his face sour. "And I never did like Luke Short, strutting little banty rooster that he is."

Red said nothing . . . but he had to agree, not about the gunman Luke Short but about Mercer. A watchman who won't shoot was as useless as tits on a boar hog.

Chapter Twenty-Four

The heat of the noonday sun on his back convinced Donny Bryson that waiting for the blonde woman to return from Fredericksburg was backing a loser. He cursed under his breath. Heck, she might spend days in the dress and hat shops.

Donny had coffee on the boil and was about to leave the rise when he caught movement out of the corner of his eye. He bellied down again, raised his telescope, and trained it to the west, about half a mile on the far side of the wagon road. Yes, there it was again . . . two figures, only one of them riding, emerged from the heat shimmer and moved slowly in his direction.

The sun baked him, a dry breeze parched his skin, and his mouth was as dry as mummy dust. But as enduring and patient as an Apache, Donny remained still for a long fifteen minutes, the glass to his eye. Damn, there might be profit in this. Little by little, the two figures came into focus . . . a man riding a mule and walking beside him a boy, or maybe a small, slight woman.

A few more minutes passed and Donny let them come within hailing distance before he rose to his feet, his Winchester cradled in his arms. The man on the mule saw him and drew rein. He was a graybeard, roughly dressed, with the look of a tin pan about him, and the woman seemed to be very young, no more than fifteen years old, wearing a thin, tattered, knee-length dress, washed out by the sun to a pale green color. Donny smiled. Things were starting to look up.

The rider mopped his face with a large red bandana and then said, "I smell something. Is that coffee on the bile?"

"Yeah, it is, and you're welcome," Donny said. He waved behind him. "My camp's back yonder."

"Well, I could sure use a cup," the man said. He was chunky, white-haired, and looked to be about sixty. His eyes were bright blue, overhung by bushy brows, but his skin was as dark as a field hand's, roughened to scuffed brown leather by sun and wind. He urged his rangy mule forward and followed Donny off the rise to his camp.

Before he told the man to step down and set a spell, Donny nodded in the direction of the girl and said, "Who is she?"

"Nobody," the man said. "My name's Lucas Bell. On my way to San Antone."

Donny said to the girl, "What's your name?"

"She don't have a name," Bell said.

The girl looked at Donny with dull, lifeless brown eyes. She was plain-faced, stringy hair, small breasts and narrow hips under her dress, large feet flopping around inside a mismatched pair of male, cast-off shoes.

"Does she talk?" Donny said.

"I don't know," Bell said. "Maybe she does, but I've never asked her a question or spoke to her much."

"Where did you find her?" Donny said.

"I didn't find her. I bought her for five dollars from a hog farm up Buffalo Gap way. The feller in charge said she was too plain and lean flanked to ever be a whore, so he let her go cheap."

"What do you use her for?" Donny said.

Bell jerked back surprised. "What are you, some kind of preacher? What the heck do you think I use her for?"

"Just asking," Donny said, the Sharps .50-90 across Bell's saddle horn inclining him to be social.

"She ain't much, but when it's all a man has, then he makes do or does without," Bell said. "But I intend to sell her in San Antone first chance I get. Maybe somebody will offer me ten dollars for her. Now how about that coffee?"

Donny Bryson was a twisted, vicious, homicidal killer and rapist, but even he considered Lucas Bell a thoroughly unpleasant man. He had no conversation apart from brothels, dance halls, whores, and whiskey. He spoke about the daily beatings he gave the girl and how, no matter how hard he hit her, she refused to cry out. Then, worn and weary from the trail and the talk, he told Donny he'd stretch out under a tree and catch a nap.

He picked up his Sharps and said, "Mister, this here Big Fifty is both wife and child to me, and I keep her close." Then, scowling, "Keep that in mind."

Donny was a careful man. The only things of value Bell owned were the rifle and the mule. And the girl, of course. And she was worth five bucks, though he figured the tin pan could have gotten her for three dollars and fifty cents. He decided to let Bell rest unmolested. Nothing the man had was worth risking a bullet from the Sharps.

His rifle handy beside him, Bell found a shady spot, lay on his back, and within minutes was snoring.

Years after the event, a reporter for the Gillespie *Tattler* famously told Theodore Roosevelt, "Lucas Bell lay down for a nap and to this day has still not woke up."

Donny Bryson drank coffee and then built a cigarette, watching the girl, who sat with her back to the rise in the full glare of the sun. He felt no real desire for her. He liked his women clean and pretty, and the girl was neither. But maybe if he got desperate. But would he ever be that desperate? Donny could come up with no answer to the question.

The girl rose to her feet, found Bell's canteen, and drank loud and long. She corked the canteen, tossed it aside, and then slipped her feet out of her oversized shoes. She saw Donny watching her and smiled for the first time, a slight tugging at the corners of her mouth. "Hot, ain't it?" she said. "I don't always say *ain't*. I was raised by nuns, and I can talk proper when I want."

An Appalachian mountain accent. Kentucky, Donny guessed. "Some hot, I reckon," he said.

The girl nodded and walked toward the wild oaks and the snoring Bell. She was short, not as ungainly in bare feet. Like Bell she was very brown, strands of her dirty blonde hair bleached almost white by the sun. She stopped. "Y'all drank coffee without me."

"I didn't know you wanted any," Donny said.

"Don't I look like I need coffee?" the girl said.

"Well, you ain't looking too lively at that," Donny said.

"Then pour me a cup, will ya?"

"Where are you headed?"

"I got something to do. Pour me a cup. The stronger the better."

"Bell said you never talk," Donny said.

"Not to him. He didn't want to talk."

"What's your name?"

"I ain't got one."

"Everybody's got a name."

"I don't. The nuns never got around to giving me one. Pour the coffee. Fill the cup to the brim. I got something to do."

"What you got to do?" Donny said.

The girl didn't answer. She resumed her walk toward the wild oaks. The day was still, no breeze, Bell's steady snoring rasping in the silence. Donny poured coffee as black as coal into a cup, never taking his eyes off the girl. What the blazes was she up to?

On cat feet the girl stepped to Bell and stood beside him. She looked down at the man, taking her time, staring into his bearded face. And then . . . slow as molasses in January . . . she bent from the waist and put both hands on the Sharps. She remained in that position for long moments and then with infinite patience, inched the rifle toward her. Bell stirred, muttered something in his sleep, and the girl froze.

Donny Bryson watched, smiling slightly, fascinated.

After a few tense moments, the girl moved again. She grasped the Sharps and lifted.

Lucas Bell's eyes flew open.

The girl was small and slight, and she struggled to

bring the nine-and-a-half-pound rifle to bear. Bell sprang to his feet, knocked the Sharps from her hands, and then backhanded her across the face. Hit hard, the girl staggered back and fell. Bell drew a wicked-looking bowie knife from his belt, raised it aloft and screeched, "You hussy, I'll kill you."

Donny was no longer amused. He drew and fired and hit Bell on his right side. The bullet entered his chest just under the armpit, and exited through the man's left shoulder blade in a scarlet mist of blood and bone chips. It was a terrible wound, and Bell screamed in pain and rage. But he was thickset and strong, and he took the bullet and stayed on his feet. Bell made a dive for the Sharps as Donny fired again. Another hit. Snarling like a wounded animal, his face twisted in hate, the tin pan hefted the Sharps to his waist and got off a shot that cracked the air inches from Donny's head.

But Bell was done.

Donny fired again. A hit. Bell rode that third bullet into Hell.

In the ringing silence that followed, Donny Bryson and the girl stared at each other for a long time before the girl moved her gaze to the body and said, "He's bleeding out like a butchered pig. Blood all over the ground." She got to her feet and said, "You saved my life, mister."

Donny thumbed cartridges into his Colt and grinned. "What life?"

"The one I'm gonna have someday."

"Where?"

"I don't know. In a town."

"Fredericksburg is close. It's the only town around these parts."

"Then that will do for a start."

"*If* I let you live," Donny said. "I haven't made up my mind."

"You'll let me live," the girl said. A trickle of blood from her mouth reached her chin. She used a foot to turn Bell's head so that his open eyes looked blindly to his left. "I want him to watch," she said. She pulled her dress over her head and stood naked. Her arms and legs were brown, her torso white as bleached bone. The girl lay on her back, spread her legs wide, and said, "Come here."

Donny stared at her, hesitated a moment, then said, "I reckon I will let you live."

"I figured you would," the girl said.

CHAPTER TWENTY-FIVE

The next day, Augusta Addington watched Dr. Ben Bradford and Della Stark embrace amid a shaft of late-morning sunlight that streamed through a window. They then clung closely, as though drawing strength from each other. Finally, the young physician said, speaking over Della's shoulder, "Miss Addington, do you really think my life is in danger?"

"I know it is," Augusta said. "And I pray to God that I can prevent your murder."

Bradford and Della separated, and then the man said, "Gideon Stark?"

"He has the most to lose if you marry Della and the most to gain if you don't," Augusta said. "And I believe his hired killers are already in Fredericksburg."

"My father would never do such a vile thing," Della said, stepping away from Bradford before rounding on Augusta. "There must be someone else behind it."

Chris Mercer, uncomfortable in stiff new clothes and even stiffer shoes, said, "Have you any enemies, doc?"

"Not that I know of," Bradford said. "I said Gideon Stark only because he doesn't want me to marry his daughter. He has in mind a rich Mexican rancher for a son-in-law."

"Then he wants you dead," Mercer said. "I've sold my gun to men with less motivation."

"That's just not my father," Della said. "You just don't know how he is. Ben, if he wanted you killed, he'd do it himself."

"And have you hate him for the rest of your life," Augusta said. "That's a powerful reason for having a murder done that can't be tied to him. And you said your father is interested in politics. Having a daughter who constantly blames him for her lover's murder is hardly going to help the career of an ambitious statesman."

"No!" Della shook her head so violently her ringlets bounced. "I won't listen to this talk a moment longer. Augusta, find the real culprit. I'm willing to stay here in Fredericksburg until you do."

Della Stark barged out of the room and then out of the house, Ben Bradford running after her. When he returned, he looked crestfallen. "She didn't want to talk to me," he said.

"She'll get over it," Augusta said. "There are some home truths that are astoundingly difficult to accept. Dr. Bradford, are you agreeable to Mr. Mercer staying with you for a few days as a watchman as I suggest? He will be armed."

The doctor's brown eyes became serious. "Under normal circumstances I would say no, that I can take care of myself. But something happened, something strange, and I'm willing to admit that it scared me."

"Do you care to tell us about it?" Augusta said.

"There's really not much to tell, and it may sound

ridiculous, especially now in the light of day. It's just . . .
well it's just that I felt I was being watched. That out in
the darkness someone, something, was studying my every
move. It felt . . . I don't quite know how to phrase it . . .
evil, malignant, that it wanted to do me harm. I turned off
the lamps, jumped into bed, and pulled the covers over
my head." He looked at the faces in the room. "You could
say I was terrified. So yes, Mr. Mercer, if that strange
feeling returns, I'd like to have you here as a watchman."

Mercer smiled and patted the leather couch he sat on
and said. "I can make myself comfortable here."

Augusta smiled. "Not too comfortable, I hope. You
must stay alert, at least during the hours of darkness."

"I don't sleep much," Mercer said. "Years of listening
for a step in the hallway or a rustle in the bush teaches a
man to be on guard."

"I have a revolver," Bradford said.

Mercer said, "Good. Then if something disturbs us in
the night, grab your gun and make some noise. Just don't
shoot in my direction, huh?"

Red Ryan accompanied a subdued, worried Buttons
Muldoon to the corral at the back of the hotel to check on
the stage and his team. The man in charge was a scrawny,
limping, old-timer named Esau Pickles who'd been a
Union artilleryman. He'd lost a kneecap at Chickamauga
that left him with a stiff-legged walk and a bad attitude.

After inspecting his horses, Buttons remarked that he
noticed four more saddle mounts in the corral. "Getting
crowded, Esau," he said.

Pickles nodded. "I seen a thing. Four damned monks

led them rental horses here from the Lange Livery. Said they planned to go on the scout for a place to build a mission to hold the stick that Moses used to part the sea or some sich. I didn't like the look of them boys, all hooded and not showing their faces and only one of them talking, sounded like an Irishman. I seen things in my time, but I never seen nothing like that."

"There's them who don't think those boys are monks at all," Buttons said.

"What would they be, then?" Pickles said

"Hired gunmen," Buttons said.

Pickles lived-in face screwed up in thought, then he said, "Now, here's a thing. One of them monks stubbed his bare toe on the water trough over there and yelled, *Hurensohn*! Well that's the German you hear it all the time in Fredericksburg, but do you know what it means?"

Red and Buttons shook their heads.

"It means son of a whore," Pickles said. "I never thought to hear that come from the mouth of a friar." He saw that Buttons and Red were drawing a blank. "Heck, have you ever hear any kind of reverend say that?"

"Can't say as I have," Buttons said. Then, "Esau, you've been around fighting men . . ."

"Been around Wes Hardin a time or two," Pickles said. "And some mighty thorny Texas Rangers."

"Yeah, well, do them monks put you in mind of Hardin?" Buttons said.

The old timer shook his head. "Nope. They sure don't."

"Not even a little?" Red said.

"Nope."

"Texas Rangers?"

"Heck, no. They put me in mind of mighty strange monks who cuss from time to time. And that's all they are."

"How were they strange?" Buttons said.

"Heck, Buttons, all them sin busters are strange, one way or t'other. Now you take the Reverend Josiah Brown right here in Fredericksburg. He goes out in the prairie with a net and catches butterflies. No matter how hot it is, even at high noon, you'll see him jumping around out there with his net. Of course, this recent trouble with the Apaches has forced him to catch his butterflies around town." Pickles shook his head. "One day he's gonna get mistook fer an Indian and get hisself shot."

"Esau, you've been around a long while, so how do we find out if them monks are gunmen in disguise or not?" Buttons said.

"Ask them," Pickles said. He placed his rough, veined hand on Buttons shoulder. "Stagecoach man, the word around town is you're riding a bad luck streak that's like to kill ya. So what have you got to lose? Ask them, pardner. Ask them."

"And then what?" Buttons said.

Pickles rubbed his stubbled chin. "Well, then, pardners, one of two things will happen . . . they'll either bless you or shoot you. Either way, you'll have your answer."

Buttons shook his head. "I don't like the odds."

"Fifty-fifty, I'd say," Pickles said. "Less'n, you're a man whose luck is running muddy, and then the odds get a sight shorter."

"Well, I'll study on it," Buttons said.

"Buttons reckons there's a curse on him because he flattened a Mexican hat that's been lying on the trail for years," Red said.

"Yup, been there for years and years, that sombrero," Buttons said. "Belonged to a feller that was struck dead by lightning. Nobody would pick up the hat on account of how it was bad luck." He shook his head, looking woeful. "And then I ran over it with the Patterson stage."

"Smashed it," Red said.

"Ruined it," Buttons said.

"Pulverized it," Red said.

Buttons scowled. "That's enough, Red. I reckon Esau's got the idea."

"And now the curse of the hat is on you," Pickles said.

"Seems like it is," Red said.

"Well, lookee here, Buttons, maybe I got a solution to your problem," Pickles said, looking crafty. "How well do you get along with Indians?"

"I don't," Buttons said. "Especially Apaches."

"Comanches?" Pickles said.

"Never had any truck with Comanches."

"Well, maybe that's all to the good, because there's an old Comanche medicine man on the south side of town they call Mukwooru, means Spirit Talker in American."

"And . . ." Buttons said after the old man paused.

"And I hear tell he can lift curses. I know he can get rid of the evil eye quicker'n scat. All you got to do is cross his hand with silver."

"You know this Injun?" Buttons said.

"Sure do. Two years ago, he told me my rheumatisms was acting up because somebody had put the evil eye on me," Pickles said. "Well, sir, I crossed ol' Spirit Talker's hand with a silver dollar, and he got shed of the evil eye and the rheumatisms and from that day to this I've been fit as a fiddle."

"Did the Comanche tell you who put the evil eye on you?' Red said.

Pickles shook his head. "He wouldn't tell me. But my guess would be the widder Flowers. I'd been sparkin' Dora Flowers fer quite a spell but she didn't hold with my drinking and threw me out of the house. She surely held a grudge, did that widder woman."

"Then I reckon the hombre who owned the sombrero hat put the evil eye on me," Buttons said.

His voice hollow, Pickles said, "From beyond the grave . . ."

"Right, that settles it, Buttons," Red said. "We'll go see the old Comanche. Make big medicine and get you a cure for the curse. A curse cure is what it will be. Then you'll feel a sight better."

Buttons looked miserable. "Red, you really think it will work?"

"Of course, it will work. The Injun cured Esau's rheumatisms, didn't he?"

"All right, I'll see him," Buttons said. "And then we head back to San Angelo and let folks in Fredericksburg work out their own problems."

"That's fine by me. We'll leave Augusta Addington and them to their troubles," Red said.

He didn't mean a word of it.

Chapter Twenty-six

"I don't think this is necessary," Helmut Klemm said. "I say we just kill the doctor and leave his body to be found. By the time he's discovered, we'll be well on our way out of town."

Sean O'Rourke shook his head. "No, Klemm. After he treats you for your bellyache today, he'll be willing to let you inside tomorrow evening when the pain is so much worse. We kill him then and his body will lie in the house all night and when he's found in the morning, we'll be long gone."

"That makes sense," Salman el Salim said. "I will go with the German to the doctor."

"No, I want Kuznetsov to accompany Klemm," O'Rourke said. "To explain your accents, you will visit the good doctor as Polish monks sent by your monastery to help establish a mission."

"Will Herr Bradford believe that?" Klemm said.

"Of course, he will," O'Rourke said. "Who the heck knows or cares what monks do?"

The German shrugged. "I don't."

"Nobody does." O'Rourke crossed himself. "Except his Holiness, the Pope in Rome."

"I don't care about monks," el Salim said. "Damned, chanting crusaders. I spit on them."

"Monks . . . I like monks," Kuznetsov said. "When I was a boy growing up in the Ural Mountains, there was a monastery near our village. The monks made jam from pine cones and wild berries and they gathered willow herb to brew Epilobium tea, a drink that heals the sick. The tea cured my grandmother of her depression and she lived cheerfully to be ninety years old." The big Russian smiled. "Her name was Katina, and she always smelled like baking bread. Then came the day when the czar sent Cossacks to punish our village for refusing to pay taxes and they killed her. Murdered my mother and father, my seven brothers and three sisters. From that day forth I was hell on Cossacks. By the time I was eighteen I'd killed a score of them before I fled the empire and settled in France. In Marseilles, where foreign ships come and go, I learned that a man who knows how to kill skillfully is in much demand."

Klemm nodded. "Kirill, it is good that you killed the Cossacks. Murderous scum."

"And it is good that you lived close to monks," O'Rourke said. He smiled. "That is why you play one so well."

"And it's because I had a holy mother. She told me that when I was still in the womb, she was visited by the Apostle Andrew who preached in the eastern lands," Kuznetsov said. "He told her that one day I would be a warrior of great renown." As O'Rourke had done, he blessed himself, but in the Russian Orthodox fashion, then tears sprang into his eyes and he said, "My mother was a saint."

O'Rourke was alarmed. The last thing he needed now was a gigantic, melancholy Slav on his hands. "Yes, I'm sure she was," he said. "Now, let us carry out the first part of our plan. Klemm, how is your belly?"

The German pantomimed great pain. "It hurts like the devil."

"Kirill Kuznetsov, are you ready?" O'Rourke said.

The big man wiped away a tear and said, "Yes, I am ready. I will take Helmut to the doctor."

"You're Polish monks, remember, and you don't speak good English," O'Rourke said. "Talk to the doctor as little as possible."

"Yes, as little as possible," el Salim said, smiling, his eyes sly. "Don't tell him you'll be back tomorrow night to kill him."

Dr. Ben Bradford escorted the rotund hausefrau Magda Schreiber to his front door, assuring her that she did not have a wandering womb but acute anxiety brought on by her businessman husband's absence, complicated by a too tightly laced corset.

"When Herr Schreiber returns safely from San Antonio, you'll feel much better," Bradford said. "In the meantime, take one of the pills twice a day until the bottle is empty."

"Oh, thank you, Doctor," Frau Schreiber said, rattling the pill bottle. "Since the savages are running around murdering and scalping, I do worry about poor Hermann so. As you know, like me he is of a most delicate constitution."

"I'm sure he'll be quite safe," Bradford said. "The

Apaches have been chased away by the army, and once Herr Schreiber returns to Fredericksburg, he'll be as safe as the snuffbox in Grannie's apron."

Magda giggled, her several chins bobbing. She slapped the doctor lightly on the chest with her plump hand and said, "Oh, Dr. Bradford, you're such a card."

As the woman waddled away, Bradford looked beyond her to the two men in monk's robes walking toward him, the taller of the two supporting the other. "What have we here?" the doctor said.

Kuznetsov spoke up. "Brother Dominik has bellyache. Very bad."

"Bring him inside to my surgery," Bradford said.

"I am Brother Lubomir," the Russian said. "We are Polskie."

"Well, come inside, gentlemen," Bradford said.

Dr. Ben Bradford examined Helmut Klemm, who played his role as the ailing Brother Dominick with aplomb, groaning in pretend pain every time the physician pushed on his belly. Kirill Kuznetsov found himself a chair and held a string of black rosary beads in his hands.

But his eyes were on Chris Mercer.

Kuznetsov . . . was aware. He remembered Mercer from the stage station at Cave Springs.

A gun will always sense the presence of another gun. It's almost as though they can smell each other. Neither man had a weapon in sight, but both knew that what hung in the air between them was a warning . . . a potential for violence. As Dr. Bradford talked, and Klemm groaned, the two men locked eyes. They each didn't try to outstare the other, but their message was clear . . . step around me, brother. I am your death.

To this day, there are some who say that Chris Mercer was such an unimposing little runt that a large muscular man like Kirill Kuznetsov could not be intimidated by him. But that was not the case. William Bonney was small and slight, but a man underestimated him at his peril.

Kuznetsov never made that mistake. He recognized men like Mercer who bore the gunman's Mark of Cain and treated them accordingly.

"I believe you have an ulcer, Brother Dominick," Dr. Bradford said. "I'll give you a powder that you mix in water," he said. "Take a teaspoon twice a day, and it will help reduce the acid in your stomach and ease the pain."

Kuznetsov finally broke his belligerent bond with Mercer and said, "If pain gets worse?"

"Then come back and we'll try something else," the doctor said.

"We pay now," Kuznetsov said.

Bradford waved a dismissive hand. "No charge to the clergy."

Mercer smiled and indulged in a little mischief. "Even your kind of clergy, brothers."

In that moment Kuznetsov and Klemm drew a line and made an enemy.

The Russian smiled. "Enjoy your life, little man," he said. He made a show of blessing Mercer. "Your time is short."

"Mr. Mercer, I didn't understand all that," Dr. Ben Bradford said. "What did the monk mean?"

"When he told me my life is short?" Mercer said.

"Yes. He seemed very serious."

"I don't know," Mercer said. At the moment he saw little need to alarm the doctor further. "Let me ask you a question, Dr. Bradford . . . who has a more valuable life, a washed-up drunk or a young physician?"

"All life is precious, Mr. Mercer," Bradford said.

"You mean, in the eyes of God?"

"I mean that as a healer I never forget how precious it is to be alive. And for that reason, one life is no more valuable than any other." Bradford looked Mercer in the eye. "Mr. Mercer, it's never too late for a man to be what he wants to be."

He glanced at his pocket watch. "Eleven o'clock. Time for coffee, I think."

CHAPTER TWENTY-SEVEN

For Donny Bryson it was an easy kill and a profitable score.

It was the girl with her young eyes who first saw the wagon in the distance as it headed west into the cattle country.

"Could be a supply wagon," Donny said, telescope to his eye. "Worth taking a look-see."

They'd earlier broken camp, and the girl rode Lucas Bell's mule. The dead man's Sharps rifle was too heavy for her to carry, but his gunbelt and holstered Colt hung from her left shoulder and across her chest. "Two people up on the driver's seat. I think one of them is a woman."

"You can see that from here?" Donny said.

"I can see far," the girl said. "But up close, not so good."

Donny was skeptical. "Even with the glass I can't see two people. I don't put that much confidence in your eyesight."

"Suit yourself," the girl said.

They were in hilly country, and she and Donny sat their mounts in the dip of a shallow saddleback. Stretching away from them lay a seemingly endless wilderness of prairie, here and there dotted with stands of Texas oak, mesquite, and juniper and bright patches of blue, pink, and yellow wildflowers. Under the bowl of a cloudless sapphire sky, the afternoon smelled clean of long grass and the earth, of distant dust and remembered rain . . . but would all too soon reek of gunsmoke, blood, and violent death.

Donny Bryson kneed his horse forward, and the girl followed, cursing at her balky mule. As they drew closer to the wagon, the driver and his companion came into focus, a gray-haired man and a plump, motherly-looking woman wearing a flowered dress, a red shawl draped over her shoulders. A mouse-colored, swaybacked mustang with its ribs showing labored in the traces of a small, four-wheeled farm wagon with a canvas cover carrying a wooden sign that read:

SAM A. HEIDELBACH
PEDDLER TO THE GENTRY

When the peddler was within hailing distance, he drew rein and yelled, "Welcome! Welcome to the Heidelbach mercantile on wheels." Then when Donny and the girl drew closer, he smiled under his beard and said in his normal tone of voice, "Mister, I have a wide section of goods for your perusal. I got tobacco, cigars, nuts, beans, and nails. I got pails, lanterns, ropes, fabrics, and sewing notions including needles and bobbins of thread. I have combs, soap, medicines, candy, crockery and dishes, pans, cartridges, coffee, pickles, soda crackers, candles, boots and shoes, glasses, beads and ribbons. And, at cost, calico dresses for the young lady."

In the West of that era, Jewish peddlers seldom traveled with their spouses, and that made the murders of Sam and Frieda Heidelbach all the more poignant. Early twentieth century historians, unwilling to accept that "gunfighter" Donny Bryson was an insane psychopath, claimed that Sam, suddenly afraid, reached for a revolver concealed under his coat and that Donny drew and fired in self-defense.

It didn't happen that way.

Two events occurred that triggered the killings.

The first was that Donny looked over the contents of the Heidelbach wagon and coveted what he saw.

The second was the girl's screech of, "Ooh, Donny, get me a pretty dress."

The girl would later testify that Donny didn't even speak. He just shucked his Colt and shot Sam and Frieda Heidelbach dead. What the girl omitted to say was that after the murders, she bounced up and down on her mule's back and yelled, "Look for the dresses, Donny! Look for the dresses!"

Donny Bryson and the girl loaded up with stuff they could use or sell in Fredericksburg. In addition, Donny discovered eighty-seven dollars in a cash box and a gold ring he took from Frieda's finger. The girl was all got up in shoes, underwear, and a yellow dress she found in the wagon. She'd added a straw hat with an artificial pink flower on the brim, a white parasol, and a heart-shaped metal pendant inscribed with the word, Love. Donny found himself a new blue shirt with a small collar and a pair of canvas pants.

And after they'd finished plundering the wagon, Donny found a couple of cans of kerosene and set it on fire with the Heidelbachs inside. For some reason that's never been explained, he tore the sign off the canvas cover and tossed it aside. Later the sign would help Texas Rangers identify the murdered couple.

CHAPTER TWENTY-EIGHT

Red Ryan and Buttons Muldoon walked south on Main Street, spotted a landmark beer brewing company building, and then made a left onto Lincoln, past a few frame houses of local merchants and then onto an area of litter-strewn open ground, mostly grass but with some red yucca and a few oaks. A cone-shaped Sibley tent about twelve feet high and eighteen feet in diameter, designed by the army to sleep about a dozen soldiers, dominated the patch and adjoining the tent a small corral held a couple of paint mustangs.

"Is this the place?" Buttons said. "Doesn't look very Comanche to me."

"It's got to be," Red said. "Look at all the Indian signs painted on the canvas."

Buttons was down in the mouth. "Don't make any difference to me anyhow," he said. "There ain't no cure for a hat curse. That must be wrote in a book somewhere."

Red grabbed Buttons by the front of his shirt and pulled him toward the tent. "Hello, the house," he yelled.

"That ain't a house, it's a tent," Buttons said.

"It's the Comanche's tepee, so it's a house," Red said.

The tent flap opened, and an old man with gray braids hanging to his shoulders stepped outside. He wore a collarless shirt, a black frock coat, and pants shoved into knee-high moccasins. His face was wide, heavy cheek-bones, and his dark skin was incredibly wrinkled. He could've been a hundred years old. The flap opened again and a young woman emerged, smoothing her buckskin dress over her hips. She frowned, looking displeased.

The old Comanche said, "When white men come to my door, it always means trouble."

"No trouble," Red said. He jerked a thumb at Buttons. "He's under a curse. And we were told you can remove it."

The old Indian looked at Buttons. "What kind of curse?"

"A hat curse. Can you cure me?"

The old man sighed. "A child can ask questions that a wise man cannot answer, but I will try. The answer is, I don't know."

"Damn it, Red, I told you this was a waste of time," Buttons said.

"I'll pay you a dollar to lift the curse," Red said, desperation edging in his voice.

"Two dollars," the Comanche said.

"Two dollars it is," Red said.

The old man nodded. "I am Mukwooru, Spirit Talker in your tongue. I will end the hat curse." He held out his hand. "Pay me, fire head."

Red dug into his pants pocket, produced the required amount, and dropped the coins into the old man's palm.

Spirit Talker turned to the woman. "Return later," he said.

The girl gave Red a killer look and then walked away, her ample hips swaying.

"A good woman," the Indian said. "Wild though. It takes a warrior to tame her spirit."

Despite being burned for two dollars, Red decided to be amiable. "And you are that warrior," he said.

"Heck, no, I'm not," the Comanche said. "But she says I'll do until a real warrior comes along." He motioned with a hand. "Please enter my lodge."

The air inside the tent was hot and still and smelled of sweat and tobacco smoke. A firepit filled with gray ashes took up the middle of the floor space, and the rest was filled with a couple of ancient buffalo hides, trade blankets, and some metal pots and pans. An almost-full bottle of Old Crow stood upright by the cold fire.

Spirit Talker seated Red and Buttons on each side of the firepit and then squatted between them. To Buttons, he said, "Tell me about the curse. Not a white man tell-me that goes on forever and ever, but an Indian tell-me, short and sweet."

With an ill grace and using as few words as possible, Buttons told the story of his encounter with the cursed sombrero and the unfortunate events that occurred afterward.

After Buttons stopped talking, the old Comanche was silent for long moments. Then he said, "Truly, you've been cursed, as I am cursed with the gift to see things that are yet to happen . . . and now I see that I will lift the curse."

"Then get it done," Buttons said. "I'm dying here, Injun."

"I will contact the spirit world and talk to the one who

owned the hat," the old man said. "It is he who laid the curse and only he can lift it."

"Then talk with him," Buttons said, in a high state of agitation. "Tell him if I had him here, I'd put a bullet into his sorry hide and kill him all over again."

"That is not the way to speak to the dead," Spirit Talker said. "I will address him in only the friendliest of terms and convince him that I am pure of heart." He uncorked the bourbon, held it close to his mouth and said, "Nothing like whiskey to lay bare a man's soul." He took a swig, took another, and put the bottle aside.

Spirit Talker closed his eyes, rocked back and forth a few times, and then said, "Owner of the cursed hat, do you hear me?" He cocked his head to the side, listening. Then, after a few moments he said to Red, "More whiskey!"

Red passed the bottle, the old man took another long swig, his Adam's apple bobbing, and Buttons said, "Heck, all the Injun's doing is getting as drunk as a hoedown fiddler. Red, get our money back."

Red put up a silencing hand. "Wait. Let's see what happens."

"If he's pulling my leg, I'll plug him," Buttons said. "I swear I will."

The old Indian ignored that, closed his eyes again and said, "Spirit of the cursed squashed sombrero, do you hear me?"

Then something that made both Buttons and Red sit up in surprise.

In a strangely hollow, sepulchral voice, Spirit Talker said, "I hear you, señor . . ."

"It's him," Buttons said. "It's the dead vaquero son of a—!"

"Shh," Red said. "Let the man talk."

In his normal voice, Spirit Talker said, "I humbly ask that you remove your curse from this wretched man, the one who calls himself Buttons Muldoon."

After a moment, the old man's voice changed again, back to the funereal tone. "There is no curse . . . just bad luck to him who moved my hat."

Sprit Talker said, "It was a mistake. The loco wretch ran over your hat with the Patterson stage."

"I know," the strange voice said.

"Then will you end this man's run of bad luck?" Spirit Talker said.

"Yes, I will," the vaquero voice said. "The one you call Buttons Muldoon is a well-meaning idiot, and I will torment him no further."

"Thank you, spirit," the old Indian said.

"*Vaya con dios*, Indian," the dead man's voice said. "In life, my name was Juan Lopez, and you will hear from me no more."

For long moments, Spirit Talker sat where he was, his eyes shut. Then they flew open and he said, "Whiskey! A lot of whiskey!"

After he and Buttons stepped out of the tent, Red Ryan took Spirit Talker aside and said, "Thank you, Buttons is back to his old self again." Red grinned. "First time I've seen him smile since he squashed the sombrero. I believe he swallowed every word you said . . . hook, line, and sinker."

The old Comanche shook his head. "I don't remember any of it."

"You pretended to talk to the dead vaquero," Red said. "And Buttons fell for it."

"For white men, I drink whiskey, shake a rattle, and talk nonsense, and that seems to please them. I don't talk to the dead. I never talk to the dead, especially for a white man."

"But the vaquero . . ." Buttons said.

"I didn't speak with a vaquero," Spirit talker said. "How does a vaquero speak?"

"You mean, you didn't . . ."

"I drank whiskey and fell asleep," the Comanche said. "At my age that happens."

"The vaquero said his name in life was Juan Lopez," Red said.

"Never heard of him," Spirit Talker said. "You must go now. My woman wants me."

"I didn't like those white men," the Comanche girl said. "The one with the red hair was a gunman. I can tell."

Mukwooru smiled. "It is good to play games of the mind with white men. Now the one with the big buttons on his coat thinks I spoke with a dead Mexican."

"And did you?" the girl said.

"I drank whiskey and it helped me speak in a ghost voice," the old man said. "Like this," he said, using the funereal tone.

The girl laughed. "Mukwooru, you are a wise one."

The Comanche nodded and smiled. "Wise enough to take the white man's two dollars."

* * *

"Red, I'm cured, fit as a fiddle," Buttons Muldoon said. "Since the old medicine man lifted the curse, I feel that there's a whole weight off my shoulders."

"The vaquero said it wasn't a curse, just bad luck," Red said.

"Same thing," Buttons said.

"You know, I never seen or heard the like," Red said, grinning. "The old Comanche really can raise up the spirits of the dead."

"That's why they call him Sprit Talker," Buttons said. "He's right neighborly with dead folks on a stony lonesome."

"The vaquero said that when he was alive, his name was Juan Lopez," Red said. "But he didn't mention being lonesome or getting struck and killed by lightning or anything like that."

"Doesn't surprise me none," Buttons said. "Lifting my curse was more important, so he didn't want to go into details."

He and Red sat a table shaded by oaks in the nearly deserted Munich Keller beer garden. The waitress was blonde and buxom, and her name was Lilly, and Red liked her just fine. He reckoned that looking at her was one of life's great pleasures, something that Buttons noticed.

"You thinking of sparking that gal?" he said.

"Yeah, thinking about it," Red said.

"Forget it," Buttons said.

"How come?"

"Heck, you're a stage coach messenger. Stick to your own kind."

"Buttons, there ain't any female stagecoach messengers," Red said.

"I know. Pity about that. But she might make courting time fer a driver." He smiled at Lilly who stood at the bar and smiled back, twisting one of her pigtails around her forefinger.

Irritated, Red said, "Stick to your own kind, Buttons."

"That rule don't apply to me. Drivers are a good catch, and the ladies know it."

The cuss that Red threw in Buttons's direction was drowned out by the roar of a six-gun.

"The doc!" Buttons said, jumping to his feet.

Red said one word. "Augusta!"

CHAPTER TWENTY-NINE

A man's body lay facedown in the street at the corner of Main Street and North Adams and by the time Red and Buttons reached there, a crowd had already gathered.

Buttons, stocky and strong, elbowed his way to the body and asked a young man, who looked like a respectable clerk of some kind, "Who is he?"

The man shook his head. "I've no idea. I've never seen him before today." He looked closely at the body, then turned to Buttons again and said, "I don't think he's from around these parts."

"Make way there! Make way!"

Sheriff Herman Ritter pushed his way through the crowd and examined the man.

"Is . . . is he dead?" a woman asked, nervously twisting the lace handkerchief in her hands.

"As he's ever gonna be," Buttons said. "He's been shot through and through."

The woman shrieked, and Red said, "Nice going, Buttons."

"What?" Buttons said, surprised.

Red was spared answering as Ritter said to the crowd, "Did anyone see what happened?"

"I did," the respectable-looking clerk said. "I was walking out of Doan's general store when I heard two shots and saw the man fall."

"Did you see the shooter?" Ritter said.

"I caught a glimpse of him as he ran into the alley across there on the far side of Adams," the young man said. "He's wearing a dark blue shirt and brown pants. That's all I saw."

Ritter, a man without deputies, looked around the crowd and spotted Buttons and Red. "Ryan, check out the alley. Muldoon, you stay here with me. The murderer might have accomplices."

It occurred to Red that Ritter was being a tad high and mighty with his orders, but he recalled that he owed the sheriff a favor or two dating back to the time of the adventuress Hannah Huckabee's visit to Fredericksburg, and he merely nodded and angled across the street to the alley.

A three-story brick warehouse with barred windows and big, shapeless bushes pushing up at its foundations stood to Red's right as he entered the alleyway. On his left, the rear of a general store, opened packing cases, and wisps of straw littered around its back door. Ahead of him more stores and another large warehouse with a parked freight wagon against its wall along with some empty wooden barrels. Red drew his Colt and walked deeper into the alley, hot and windless, the only sound the crunch of his boots on sandy gravel. A high, merciless sun bore down through a haze of dust, and the still air smelled vaguely of beer and boiled cabbage and outhouses. His eyes never at rest, Red stepped carefully and warily, his palm sweaty on the handle of his cocked revolver.

A narrow space ran between the warehouses, and he approached the gap carefully, annoyed that he could hear his own quick gasps of breath as he cautiously put one foot in front of the other. Suddenly he felt it . . . the nearness of another human being . . . as palpable as footsteps in a fog.

As tense as he was, Red almost jumped out of his skin. He brought up the Colt and yelled in the direction of the passageway between the warehouses and yelled, "Come out of there with your hands high or I'll drill ya."

"Don't shoot!"

A woman's voice, high-pitched and nervous.

"Walk on out, slowly," Red said. "I'm with six marshals here, all well-armed and determined men."

"Don't shoot. I'm coming out."

A plain-faced girl wearing a yellow dress, holding an open parasol over her head, stepped out of the gap. She smiled at Red and said, "Did I scare you?"

Red thumbed down the hammer of his Colt and asserted his manhood. "I've been scared by experts in my time, usually road agents or Apaches," he said. "But girls don't scare me." Then, frowning, "Did you see a man wearing a blue shirt run down this alley?"

The girl nodded. "Yes, I did, right after I heard a gunshot." She pointed in the other direction. "He was headed that way."

Red looked down the alley, but it was empty. "Seems like he got away," he said. "What are you doing out here by yourself?"

The girl hesitated a moment and then said, "My brother and me are visiting Fredericksburg for the first time, and I decided to take a stroll and see the sights."

"In an alley?"

"I got lost."

"You staying at the Alpenrose Inn?" Red said.

"No. We're further down Main Street at the Palace."

"Well, let me escort you home," Red said. "There's a killer on the loose."

The girl took Red's arm and said, "You are very kind."

As they walked, Red said, "Name's Red Ryan. I'm a shotgun messenger for the Abe Patterson and Son Stage and Express Company."

"You must be very brave," the girl said. After another moment's hesitation, she said, "My name is Effie . . . Effie Bell."

"Right glad to make your acquaintance, Miss Bell," Red said.

"Who was shot, Mr. Ryan?" the girl said.

"Some feller," Red said. "I don't know who."

"For a moment back there I was very afraid," the girl said. "I was gently raised, and I'm not used to shooting and killing."

Red smiled. "Well, don't be scared. You're safe with me."

The girl squeezed his arm. "Mr. Ryan, you're my knight in shining armor," she said.

* * *

"He's a shotgun messenger and he walked me to the hotel," the girl said. "He chased after you, and I met him in the alley."

"Did anyone recognize me?" Donny Bryson said. "Did he say?"

"No. He told me he was looking for a man wearing a blue shirt. That was all."

Donny unbuttoned the shirt and tossed it into a corner. "I won't wear that again in Fredericksburg," he said. "I'm sure the man I killed in the street recognized me."

"Who was he, Donny?" the girl said.

"I don't know. But if I had to guess I'd say he was a lawman from Austin. Damn devil looked at me strange."

"What will we do now?" the girl said. "Maybe we should get out of this town."

"Heck, no, we won't. At least not now. There could be something big brewing."

"What have you heard, Donny?"

"Right now, there are four monks in Fredericksburg who could make us rich if we play the cards right."

"What's a monk?" the girl said.

"A kind of holy man. He wears a robe and sich and lives in a place called a monastery where he says prayers all day long."

"So what are four monks doing here?"

"It's supposed to be a secret, but the desk clerk says the whole town knows."

"Knows what?"

"That the monks are here to build a mission out in the prairie around a holy relic."

"What's a holy relic?" the girl said.

"Well, this one is the staff of Moses . . . and don't ask me who Moses was. I'll tell you later," Donny said. "The thing is, the staff is supposed to be as tall as a man, made from solid gold and studded with jewels . . . diamonds and rubies and the like. It's valuable enough to keep a man in luxury for the rest of his life."

"Is that true? I mean, solid gold with jewels?"

"Yeah, back in them olden Bible days folks had all kinds of gold and jewelry lying around."

"When you said luxury, did you mean big house and horse and carriage luxury?"

"Yeah. That kind of luxury. Servants, private railroad cars, the whole enchilada."

The girl seemed eager. "How do we get the staff?"

Donny smiled. "The way we usually get things we want, kill the monks and take it. A golden staff will be of more use to us than them."

"Do you have a plan?" the girl said.

"Not yet, but I'm working on it," Donny said. "The clerk says the monks are staying at the Alpenrose Inn. We'll keep an eye on them."

The girl sat down hard on the bed, her face aglow. "Oh, Donny, I'm so excited," she said. "A big house, servants . . . I can't believe my luck." A pause, then, "Donny, will you call me Effie? Now I'm going to be rich, I need a name of my own."

"Sure," Donny said. "I'll call you whatever the heck name you want."

CHAPTER THIRTY

"Ryan, where the heck have you been?" Sheriff Herman Ritter said. "I thought you'd been shot for sure."

"You would've heard the bang," Red Ryan said. "I met a young lady in the alley and escorted to her hotel, there being a killer on the loose an' all."

"Was she wearing a blue shirt?" Ritter said.

"No. A yellow dress and she was carrying a parasol."

Buttons Muldoon smiled. "Was she pretty?"

"No, kinda plain. But nice." Red glanced at the body, now being attended to by undertaker Benny Bone and his unmerry men. "You any idea who he is?" he asked the sheriff.

A big-bellied man with cropped fair hair and piercing blue eyes, wearing a gold watch chain as thick as an iron-clad's anchor hawser over his brocade vest, answered for the lawman. "His name is, or was, Nathaniel Foxworthy. He's a drummer out of Chicago for Anderson and Lawson whiskey, came into my saloon often, but never drank. Look in his wallet and you'll see a tintype of his wife and six young'uns. He was always mighty proud of that photo and showed it around."

"He have any enemies in Fredericksburg?" Red said.

"I already answered that question for the sheriff," the big saloon owner said. "And I'll tell you what I told him . . . whiskey salesmen have no enemies." He turned his head and started intently at a saloon named the Frederick Haus and said, "Sheriff, I have to get back to work or those verdammt bartenders of mine will rob me blind."

After the man left, Benny Bone hopped to Ritter's side, cocked his head like an inquisitive raven and said, "Sheriff Ritter, will you contact the bereaved?"

"I can reach them through Foxworthy's company in Chicago," the lawman said.

"Yes, I saw you speaking with Gert Sperling," Bone said. "I'm sure he's done business with all the whiskey distillers." Then, after some hesitation, "Ah . . . does the deceased have enough money in his wallet to cover his embalming and burial?"

"I don't know," Ritter said. He juggled the dead man's wallet, wedding ring, silver cigar case, and watch and chain and said finally to Red, "Here, take the wallet and see how much cash is in there. Maybe I can wire some of it to his wife."

"A hundred and sixty-five dollars," Red said, handing the wallet back. "But maybe some of that's his company's money."

"Sheriff, I can cover the deceased for forty dollars," Bone said.

"Forty dollars?" Buttons said. "You could plant a whole tribe of people for that."

"It's the embalming that's expensive," Bone said. "Like the young Austin lady, loved ones may wish to claim the body."

"By the way, Mr. Muldoon, Austin wired me back and now the young lady has a name," Ritter said. "She was the wife of a deputy marshal called Mark Russell. Her name was Alice, and she was twenty-three years old."

"Damn, I hope I live long enough to see Donny Bryson hang," Buttons said.

"And I hope I'm the one who hangs him," Ritter said. The sheriff took forty dollars from the wallet. "Bury Foxworthy decent, Benny," he said. "We may have to send the body back to Chicago."

Bone nodded. "I'll do a nice embalming job, Sheriff. Depend on it."

"Sheriff, have you studied on the wanted dodgers in your office for any that have a likeness of Bryson?" Red Ryan said.

"No, I haven't," Ritter said. "But it's a good idea, because he might come this way. Today, I'll be kind of busy, but do you want to go through the dodgers, Ryan? I have a stack of them on my desk. Help yourself."

"Sure," Red said. "I might have some old friends in there that I haven't seen in a spell."

"Mr. Muldoon, until I find Foxworthy's murderer, how do you feel about signing on as my temporary deputy?" Ritter said. "I can pay a dollar-fifty a day."

To Red's surprise, Buttons didn't hesitate. "Normally, I'd say no," he said. "But two things happened that changed my mind. One is that a curse has been lifted from me, and I'm headed for a run of good luck. The other is that I want to see Donny Bryson hang. Oh, and there's a third . . . I haven't yet picked up any fares headed up San Angelo way or points north."

"Very well then, raise your right hand. Do you swear

to uphold the laws of Texas?" Ritter said. Buttons nodded, and the sheriff said, "Good. Then you're hired."

Red said, "Maybe I should explain about Deputy Muldoon's curse . . . an old Indian by the name of Spirit Talker squared him with a dead vaquero holding a grudge."

"Spirit Talker . . . you mean Mukwooru, the Comanche, is back in town?" Ritter said.

"That's the very feller," Red said.

"Well, if that don't beat all," Ritter said. He shook his head. "I thought he'd been hung years ago." Now he addressed Buttons. "We'll find the killer of Foxworthy, but we'll draw a blank on Bryson, Deputy Muldoon. I really don't think he'll venture into Fredericksburg." Ritter looked beyond Buttons, frowned and said, "Ach du lieber Himmel! What on earth is that woman doing?"

Red followed the sheriff's stare. Augusta Addington stood at the spot where Foxworthy's body had just been carried away by the undertakers, her head bent, eyes fixed on the ground. To his surprise, Della Stark, looking cross and out of sorts, stood at the entrance to the alley.

"Yes, Della, right there is where the killer stood," Augusta said. "And judging by the tracks, his victim walked toward him a few steps before he was shot."

"It's hot," Della said. "Are we finished?"

"Yes, we're finished," Augusta said. "Why don't you get inside and have a nice cool drink?"

"About time," Della said.

The girl crossed the street and stepped onto the Alpenrose Inn porch, and without slowing her pace, her high-heeled boots thudding on the timbers, passed Red and Buttons with her eyes averted, nose in the air as though she somehow blamed them for all her troubles, and walked into the hotel lobby.

Augusta followed, smiling, and said, "Good afternoon, gentlemen."

She wore her white day dress, formfitting with a minimal bustle, and a straw boater hat.

Red thought she looked wonderful, but Sheriff Ritter was less impressed.

"What were you doing out there in the street, Miss Addington?" he said.

Augusta waited until a dusty Buffalo soldier sergeant and four even dustier troopers, exhausted Apache hunters by the look of them, jangled past before she spoke. "Sheriff Ritter, I was merely honing my investigatory skills," she said.

"Why?" Ritter said. "The murder of Nathaniel Foxworthy is my investigation, not yours. And since when do *junge Damen* of obviously good breeding get involved in murder?"

Augusta smiled. "Since I became a Pinkerton agent."

"No!" Ritter said. "There are no female Pinkerton agents."

"There are now, Sheriff Ritter," Augusta said. "Like it or not." Before the young sheriff could respond, she said, "The victim was crossing the street when someone called out to him from the alley where Miss Stark was standing. He stopped, turned, and took several steps in the direction of his attacker before he was shot."

"I'm aware of all that," Ritter said, irritation pinking his cheekbones.

"The question is, did Foxworthy know his attacker, or was this a random attack? I think neither," Augusta said.

"Dismiss the obvious, and what's left is usually the truth . . . that the shooter thought Foxworthy recognized him and for that reason killed him."

"Then who is the killer?" Ritter said, his annoyance revealed by his aggressive, fist-clenched stance.

"I don't know," Augusta said.

"I don't know, either," Ritter said. "But I intend to find out. Why are you here. Miss Addington? Pinkerton work?"

"At this time, I'd rather not say," Augusta said. Then a moment of inspiration. "Miss Stark and I are friends, and I'm visiting for a while."

Ritter took the explanation at face value. "Then enjoy your stay, but keep out of my investigation," he said. Then to Red, "I don't want another problem like I had with Hannah Huckabee . . . I mean dealing with the ways of wild women. Do I make myself clear?"

"I'd say you have," Red said.

"Good, then we understand each other," Ritter said. "Deputy Muldoon, come with me. We will start with the alley"—he angled a glare at Red—"that's still to be properly searched, and then we'll inspect the hotel registers, see what strangers are in town."

Buttons seemed less than enthusiastic. "Seems a bit boring to me, Sheriff," he said.

"Maybe, but that's what routine police work is, Deputy Muldoon, boring. But it produces results."

CHAPTER THIRTY-ONE

A knock came at Della Stark's hotel room door, and she called out, "Who is it?"

The reply was immediate. "Manuel Garcia and Will Graham, Miss Della. We're kinda worried about you."

"Maybe it's time to head back home, Miss Della," Graham said.

Della opened the door, and said, "Come in."

Hats in hand, the two spurred drovers walked into the room, filling it. Both wore Colts and knew how to use them, especially the fast, accurate Garcia, who was ranked among some of the best and had been a top gun in the Mason County War back in '75.

"Sit where you can," Della said. "I want to ask you both a question."

Graham sat on a chair by the window, but Garcia remained standing, his back to the door, and Della didn't push the matter. She remained in the middle of the floor, a normally lively, vivacious girl who now seemed subdued, her blue eyes troubled. It seemed that she had some trouble framing her question, and Garcia prompted her. "You have something to ask us, Miss Della?" he said.

"Yes, and this is just between us three," Della said.

"Sets just fine with me," Graham said.

Garcia nodded. "Just between us."

Della took a deep breath and then said, "Do you think my father is capable of murdering the man I love?"

The question came at the drovers like a cannonballing express, and for a moment they were stunned into silence. Garcia recovered first and said, "Would this man be a doctor?"

"Yes, Dr. Ben Bradford. He is here in Fredericksburg," Della said.

Graham, younger and less considerate of Della's feelings than Garcia, said, "The story going around is that the boss wants you to marry another man."

"Yes, Don Miguel de Serra."

Graham grinned. "Heck, he's a Mex and he's fat and ugly."

"And very rich," Della said.

"And you don't want to marry him," Garcia said.

"No, I don't. I wish to marry Dr. Bradford . . . Ben."

"So you think your father wants to get the doc out of the way by murdering him," Garcia said.

"I refuse to think that, but others do," Della said. "I was told the assassins are already here in town."

Garcia said, "Miss Della, I'm a vaquero and I know cattle, but that's not why your father hired me." He tapped on his holstered Colt. "This gun is why." His clenched jaw relaxed and he conjured up a smile. "If your father wanted the doctor dead, he would've sent me to kill him."

"Then who?" Graham said. Both Della and Garcia looked at him with blank faces, and he said, "If the boss doesn't want Doc Bradford dead, then who does?"

"I don't know," Della said. "Maybe another doctor who doesn't like competition."

"Another doctor would invite him in for a drink and put poison in his glass," Graham said. "He wouldn't hire assassins to kill him. You have to admit that it seems unlikely."

"Can you think of anyone beside your pa who might want to do Dr. Bradford harm?" Garcia said.

"No," Della said. "I can think of no one."

"Hell, Miss Della—pardon my language—why don't you just ask him?" Graham said.

"Ask who what?' the girl said.

"Ask your father if he hired killers to murder your doctor friend. Ask him straight out, and if he says no, which I expect Mr. Stark will, beg his help to track down the real culprits."

Graham was a top hand, but usually he didn't have enough horse sense to spit downwind and he'd just given advice to a woman without a lot of sense, either. Garcia, sharper than them both put together, was hesitant.

"Miss Della, right now I don't think you should tip your hand to anyone," he said. "If Dr. Bradford's killers are already here, then let's get him out of town. As soon as it shows dark, we can put him in the surrey and head for Austin, where there's a proper police force to protect him."

"No," Della said. "Will is right. I'll lay my cards on the table and see what Father has to say. I know in my heart of hearts he'll be horrified to learn that Ben is being stalked by killers. This is my chance to convince him that I really do love Ben and won't marry Don Miguel . . . ever . . . ever."

Garcia liked none of that speech. He knew he was

talking out of turn as he said, "Miss Della, I think you're making a big mistake. Gideon Stark is a harsh, severe man, and I don't think love enters into his thinking."

"He loves me, Manuel. There is no doubt of that," Della said, frowning.

Garcia was in deep, and now he dug himself deeper. "Before anything else, let's see to the doctor's safety. Me and Will can stay here in Fredericksburg and give him all the protection he needs."

"My father can give Ben all the protection he needs," Della said. "I'll see to it."

Reluctantly, Garcia played his hole card, knowing it could cost him his job. "Miss Della, your father wanted a son, and your mother died trying to give him one."

"And what's that supposed to tell me?" Della said, her face flushed as though her anger was on a slow burn.

"I can tell you what Gideon told me. This was a couple of years ago when we were up on the Llano chasing after horse thieves. We'd camped on the south bank of the river, and we'd both had too much to drink and . . . maybe I shouldn't tell you this."

"Tell me," Della said. "You started it, now finish it."

"Well, Gideon told me . . . he told me that he blamed you for his wife's death," Garcia said. "He said if you'd been a boy child, they would never have risked trying for another. But they did, and Annie Stark died giving birth to a stillborn baby. It was a boy, and Gideon had planned to call him Daniel." Garcia looked like a man about to slam a door behind him. "Miss Della, your father said that there were times when he hated you." He watched Della's stricken face and said, "Gideon was well in his cups. When a man is drunk, he's likely to say things he doesn't mean."

Della was silent.

Graham coughed and looked out the window into the street, suddenly seeing something of great interest.

Downstairs, dishes clattered in the kitchen.

Della spoke.

"I was four years old when my mother died, and I was never told about the dead baby. But you're so wrong about my father. The years have made him a kinder, gentler person, and when he speaks to me it's in the most tender terms. I have no doubt that after my mother died, he felt a dislike for me, but that is all gone. We had a disagreement about my marrying Don Miguel, and he did warn me that I'd be locked in my room until I relented, but that never happened." She touched her hair with her fingertips and said, almost dreamily, "You can't set store in the ravings of a drunk man. My father loves me. I know it, and everyone else knows it."

"Yes, Miss Della, I'm sure he does," Garcia said.

"Have you any doubts?" Della said. "If you have, say them now."

"None, no doubts at all," Garcia said, surrendering, the lies coming easy to him now that the girl's mind was made up.

"What about you, Will?" Della said.

The lanky cowboy grinned. "Mr. Stark is like a man with a spotted pup. Seen the boss lovin' on his daughter with my own two eyes."

Della nodded. "Good. Will, you'll take me back to the ranch just as soon as the surrey is ready. Manuel, you will remain in Fredericksburg and make sure that Ben stays alive until my father gets here. Do you need some money?"

"I can use a few dollars' advance on my wages to cover the hotel," Garcia said.

Della opened her purse, removed some notes, and handed them to the vaquero.

"Keep Ben alive," she said. "Kill anyone you have to, but make sure he's unharmed."

"I'll do my best, Miss Della," Garcia said.

"Do better than your best," Della said. "There's already a man being paid to guard Ben, but I don't have much faith in him. He's some kind of tramp."

"Then I'll put him out of a job," Garcia said, attempting a smile.

"And there's a woman, a Pinkerton agent staying here in the hotel," Della said. "Her name is Augusta Addington, and if you need help or advice, you can go to her. But above all, rely on your own judgment and skill with a gun."

"You can depend on me, Miss Della," Garcia said.

"I know I can," the girl said. "If I thought otherwise, as of just a few minutes ago you'd be no longer working for the Stark Cattle Company."

CHAPTER THIRTY-TWO

The search through the stack of wanted dodgers on Sheriff Herman Ritter's desk took Red Ryan all of fifteen minutes and produced no results. In recent years the breed Donny Bryson had tended to operate east of the Colorado, and it seemed his reward posters hadn't made it this far.

Disappointed, Red left the sheriff's office and headed back to the Alpenrose.

The young Fredericksburg belles he passed in the street, walking with stern, matronly mothers who hit the ground firmly with each step, were mostly blonde, pig-tailed, and robust, and more than a few fluttered their eyelashes as he walked by. Red later calculated that he'd smiled and touched the brim of his derby half a dozen times before he reached the inn's front porch. And there he paused as two events attracted his attention.

The first, and a sight to see, was four mounted monks . . . or were they assassins as Augusta feared? . . . as they trotted from the hotel corral onto Main Street and then headed out of town. All four had their hooded robes hiked up for riding, sandaled feet in the stirrups. Red put that out of his mind for the moment, his entire focus on the man who'd just sauntered onto the porch of a hardware store across the street. Tall, lean, with long hair spilling over the shoulders of a gray shirt, he leaned against one of the pillars and built a cigarette, his eyes fixed on the departing monks. He wore his holstered Colt fairly high, the handle between wrist and elbow, all of the cartridge loops on the belt filled. A breed by the dark, high-cheekboned look of him, there was an air of confident, self-assurance about the man, a bulletproof arrogance that Red had only seen in named shootists.

He studied the man more closely, and an alarm bell rang in his head.

A breed . . . hard-faced and significant . . . wearing a gun as though he was born to it . . . ignored by passersby and therefore a stranger . . . black eyes watchful, never at rest . . .

It slowly dawned on Red . . . this man could be Donny Bryson.

Then something happened that quickly threw his assumption in doubt.

The girl named Effie Bell that he'd met in the alley stepped out of a nearby baker's shop with a wedge of yellow cake in her hand. She walked quickly along the boardwalk, smiling, and threw herself into the man's arms. The two embraced briefly, and the girl offered the man a bite of the cake. The breed bit off a piece, chewed, and then asked the girl something. She nodded and produced from the pocket of her dress . . . a string of coral pink rosary beads. The breed took the beads, kissed the cross, grinned, and handed them back.

Red was stunned. Mortified. He'd misjudged the man

and blundered badly. The breed was obviously Effie's brother, or perhaps half-brother. Raised by a devout stepmother, Red Ryan knew that a rosary was much prized by Catholics and not something that a violent killer like Donny Bryson would revere. And they were eating cake together, for God's sake . . . how innocent was that?

Feeling slightly foolish, Red figured that the day was hot, the walk from the sheriff's office had been long and sweaty, and it was time for a stein of beer. But then Effie Bell crossed the street toward him. When she reached the Alpenrose porch, to make up for his earlier suspicions, he touched his hat brim and said, "Miss Bell." The girl gave him a perfunctory smile and walked into the lobby.

Red glanced across the street and saw Effie's brother watching him. He realized that with a killer on the loose he could be anxious about the safety of his sister. Determined to right his previous wrong, Red smiled, gave the man a reassuring wave and followed the girl inside.

". . . is one of the reverend monks, and I want to give this to him. It was our dead mother's rosary," she said.

"Your brother is one of the monks, you say," the desk clerk said.

"Yes, my oldest brother. His name is Friar Benedict."

"How did you know he was here, Miss . . . ah . . ."

"Bell. Effie Bell. He wired me in Austin, where my other brother and I live. It's been years, and my brother, he's a little older than Benedict and me, is much overcome at meeting him again and is waiting outside to obtain a firmer grasp on his emotions."

The clerk, middle-aged, baby-faced, thin brown hair parted in the middle of his small head and round glasses that gave him the look of an owl, said, "I'm so sorry,

Miss Bell, but you just missed your brother. He and the other monks rode out earlier to search for a site to build a mission." He shook his head. "I warned them about the Apache outbreak, but they wouldn't listen. They figure God will protect them, I guess."

Effie smiled. "My brother was always headstrong. I'll return later, but I'd like to leave the rosary in his room. He'll know where it came from."

"The monks are sharing one room, Miss Bell. We put in an extra cot, but they must be pretty crowded up there."

The girl's smile was a mix of pride and amusement. "Brother Benedict will offer up the discomfort as a penance. Now, may I leave my mother's rosary for him to find when he returns?"

The clerk smiled. "How sweet. Of course, you can. It's Room Twenty-two, upstairs and to your right. I'll get you the key."

"Thank you," Effie said. She took the key and said, "I'll just wave to my brother so he knows all is well."

Red stepped aside to let the girl pass. She returned a moment later and said to the clerk, "Brother Benedict will be so happy."

"Yes, I'm sure he will," the clerk said, looking pleased.

After the girl walked up the stairs, Red Ryan left the lobby, beer on his mind, and met Esau Pickles, who stood on the porch looking out into busy, dusty Main Street. Red glanced across the road, but Miss Bell's brother was gone.

"Howdy again, Red," Pickles said. "They caught that killer yet?"

"I don't think so," Red said, "Buttons got himself deputized and is with the sheriff trying to find him."

Pickles shook his head. "Any lowlife who'd gun a whiskey drummer would piss on a widder woman's kindlin'."

"You got that right," Red said. "All a whiskey drummer does is spread a little joy in the world."

"Him and a brewer," Pickles said. Then, "When are you boys hitting the road again?"

"Buttons is still trying to rustle up passengers."

"He ain't gonna rustle up passengers playing lawman with Herman Ritter."

"Seems like," Red said.

"You know what I reckon?" Pickles said. "I reckon the man who shot the whiskey drummer is one of them temperance rannies down on demon drink. One time I went to a meeting where one of them, a feller by the name of the Reverend Brown, was speechifying and he reads a poem to all us drunks in the audience that I still recollect. It went . . .

> *"Oh, thou demon drink, thou fell destroyer,*
> *Thou curse of society, and its greatest annoyer.*
> *What has thou done to society? Let me think . . .*
> *I answer thou has caused the most of ills, thou*
> *demon drink."*

Pickles stared hard at Red and said, "Now that's a fine poem, a great poem, but folks who think that way would put a bullet in a whiskey drummer fast as a duck on a june bug. If you see him before I do, you tell that to Deputy Sheriff Muldoon."

"I sure will, Esau," Red said. "And you're right, that is some powerful poetry. I once read in a newspaper that drinking leads to neglect of duty, moral degradation, and crime. And that's very true, but only for some folks. It don't apply to responsible imbibers like us."

"So, where are you headed, shotgun man?" Pickles said.

"I figured I'd have myself a few steins of beer. Want to join me?"

But before Pickles could answer, the desk clerk walked onto the porch and said to Red, "A touching scene, was it not, Mr. Ryan?"

"Huh?" Red said.

"Miss Bell leaving a token of love for her cloistered brother," the clerk said.

"Yeah, I guess it was," Red said. "I met her in the alley after the shooting. She talked about her brother, but she didn't mention a second brother being a monk."

"Perhaps she was afraid you'd think her boastful," the clerk said.

"Maybe so," Red said. "I guess she sets store by having kin in holy orders." He smiled. "Holy orders. My stepmother used to say that."

"Is she still alive, your stepmother?" the clerk said.

"No. She and my father were took by the cholera when I was just a younker," Red said. "I don't remember my real mother at all, and I barely remember my father, a big man with a beard and a silver watch chain. But I remember my stepmother. She was gentle, and she smelled good, and she sang all the time, Irish songs and hymns mostly."

"That's a crackerjack memory, Red, but my Pa was hung for a hoss thief," Esau Pickles said. "Lookin' back, it seems like a whole passel of us Pickles was hung, I mean everybody and the dog. Seems like my kin couldn't keep their mitts off other folks' plunder, and that habit done fer them." He shook his head. "Strange that. I mean how it all come about, them being thieves an' all. No watermelon patch was safe when a Pickle was around, an' that's a natural fact."

Red smiled. "Glad that you're such an upstanding citizen, Esau. A credit to Pickles everywhere, hung and as yet unhung."

The old man nodded. "Thankee, Red. Truth is I never wanted anything bad enough to steal it."

The desk clerk looked over his shoulder. "Seems Miss Bell should have returned by now," he said.

"She probably used the back door," Esau said. "Taking the alley home."

That familiar alarm ran in Red's head again.

"I think we should go look for her," he said.

"I don't wish to intrude," the clerk said.

"I do," Red said. "The alley isn't a safe place for a woman to be. Let's go."

The room smelled of men, was untidy, four opened carpetbags on the floor and razors and soap brushes on the dresser around the water pitcher. A monkish room that held no surprises. The pink coral rosary lay on the table by the bed and the only thing missing was the long case that held the staff of Moses. Red didn't remember seeing one of the monks carry it when they rode out of town but then he didn't really look at them closely. And after all, the staff was a holy relic and too precious to leave behind.

"It seems Miss Bell took the back door," the desk clerk said.

"Looks like," Red said.

But something about the girl and her brother troubled him.

"It's a rifle, a damn sharpshooter's rifle," Donny Bryson said. He swore under his breath, then, "It's worth about maybe fifty dollars." He glared at Effie Bell. "They took the golden staff with them."

"Why do monks need a rifle like that one?" Effie said. "What's that brass thing?"

"It's a telescopic sight," Donny said. "It brings the target closer up and sharp. Maybe the monks figure they'll need a rifle to shoot their chuck when they're building the mission."

"They'll be back, Donny," Effie said.

"Yeah, and we'll need to keep an eye on their comings and goings," Donny said. "The next time they ride out, I'm heading after them."

"Bet you never shot a monk afore," Effie said, grinning.

"I never did, but there's a first time for everything."

"I'm going with you."

"Of course, you are. I ain't leaving you here in Fredericksburg."

"Do you like me, Donny?" Effie said.

"Sure. I like you."

"Do you love me?"

"What's that? What's love?"

"It's when you feel that you more than just like a person."

"Nah, I don't feel that," Donny said. "I said I like you, and that's it. There's nothing more."

The girl smiled slightly. "That's enough for me."

"And so it should be," Donny said. He picked up the Marlin-Ballard. "Now shut your trap while I figure out this here fancy meat gitter."

CHAPTER THIRTY-THREE

Gideon Stark was mighty pleased. He'd pushed a herd onto Harold Fairfax's range and taken over the ranch house. It had all gone smoothly, and now the Englishman's land and cattle were his, adding to his already immense holdings.

Stark took a pull from his whiskey flask, studied the glowing end of his cigar, and then moved his cold gaze to the man swinging from the branch of a cottonwood. It was a pity about Jasper Stanton, Fairfax's foreman. He'd opened his big mouth just once too often, and Stark had closed it forever with a noose.

Gideon watched the Stark and Fairfax hands standing around the wagon with the beer barrel and whiskey jugs, getting loud. He thought that the hanging of Stanton might spoil the celebration, but the big foreman had been a hard-driving man, much given to reading the Bible, and not much liked. Stanton had mouthed off to Stark, told him to inform the belted earl in England that his son was dead and the ranch now belonged to the foreman, in the way of the West. Naturally Gideon had refused. He stated . . . both sets of hands thought reasonably . . . that before Harold

Fairfax blew his brains out, he'd bequeathed the ranch to his own good self. After that statement, the standoff with the foreman Stanton had gotten bitter. The man had called out Stark for a damned liar and threatened to write to the earl himself and tell him what had happened.

Gideon didn't argue any further. He'd called for a rope and hanged Jasper Stanton from a cottonwood that was conveniently located near the ranch house.

Full of whiskey and beer, the hands thought the hanging had gone well and that Stanton died game and had not embarrassed them. Indeed, the eight surviving Fairfax hands told Gideon that very thing and he rewarded them by increasing their pay to thirty-five dollars a month, top hand wages.

Now, as the afternoon wore on and the sun dropped lower in the sky, Stark gave the order for Stanton to be cut down and buried somewhere on the range. As for himself, he was returning home for a good supper and then bed.

"I can't keep up with you young whippersnappers any longer," he said. "Finish the whiskey and beer and bring the wagon back . . . if you're able."

This drew a cheer and a few wisecracks about old age and bed and nobody seemed in the least put out by the murder of Jasper Stanton. As for Gideon, well, he didn't give a damn if they did or did not.

Della's surrey was back.

Gideon Stark swung out of the saddle and stepped into the house.

"Pa, is that you?" Della Stark called out from the parlor.

"Who else would it be?" Stark said. He joined his daughter. No fatherly kiss. No hug. Just an angry question. "You stayed overnight in Fredericksburg . . . were you with Ben Bradford?"

"We met, but I wasn't with him," Della said. Then a small lie. "Manuel wouldn't let me out of his sight for two minutes."

"How much did your clothes shopping cost me?"

"Nothing. I didn't see anything I liked. Fredericksburg is not Paris."

Gideon poured himself a bourbon and then sat in his favorite chair. He studied his daughter closely and then said, "A bad thing happened here yesterday after you left."

Della smiled. "The sow hog get into the cook's herb garden again?"

"Almost as bad," Stark said. "Harold Fairfax blew his brains out just about where you're standing."

Della stepped away from the spot so fast it looked like she'd been pushed. "He what?"

"Standing right there, he punched his own ticket to Hell."

"But . . . but why?"

"Money problems, I guess. His wasn't making his payroll, and his ranch was about to go belly up. He said to me, 'Gideon, you can have it all . . . the whole sorry mess.' Then he drew his gun and shot himself."

"Oh, my God, that's so horrible," Della said. She looked down at the carpet as though expecting to see blood. "Where is . . . the body?"

"We buried him on his own range early this morning," Stark said. "Him and one of his hands."

"What happened to him, the puncher, I mean?" Della said.

"It was about me taking over the Fairfax spread. The foreman . . ."

"Jasper Stanton."

"Yeah, him. He gave me sass and backtalk, and I hung him."

Della looked like she'd been slapped. "Pa . . . how . . . how could you do that?"

"It was a disagreement between men, and I handled it the only way I know how," Stark said. "I couldn't show weakness to the Fairfax hands, not then, not when I'd just taken over the spread." He slapped his hand on the arm of his chair. "Damn it, I won't accept disrespect from any man."

Della looked behind her, backed to a chair, and sat. Her voice hollow, she said, "Pa, did you kill Harold Fairfax?"

Stark looked at his daughter for a long time. Then he said, "Does it matter?"

"Yes, Pa, it matters," Della said. "It matters to me."

"Marry Don Miguel de Serra and it won't matter. Nothing regarding me will matter. You'll have your own ranch to concern yourself with."

"He's a syphilitic pig, and I won't marry him," Della said. She was pale, her mouth tight.

"Seems like we've been on this merry-go-round before and got nowhere," Stark said. "All right, if you want to know the truth, I didn't kill Fairfax. He shot himself in the head, and there's an end to it."

"I so want to believe you, Pa," Della said.

"I didn't kill him. Now that's enough, girl. Let it go.

And do the same with Stanton. He asked for what he got, damn his impudence."

"I must go to my room and change," Della said.

"And change your attitude while you're at it, girl," Stark said.

As the day shaded into night, shadows deepened in the parlor. Stark rose and lit a lamp and an amber glow filled the room. He poured himself another drink and with a groan sank back into his chair. In that moment it dawned on Della that for all his vaulting ambitions, her father was old and tired. Decades of ranching in the West, its constant toil, dirt, and dust and battles with the elements, rustlers, and hostile Indians was a hard and dangerous business that killed women and took its toll on even the strongest men. Della realized that her father could be vulnerable.

She rose, poured herself a bourbon, and returned to her chair. The girl took a drink, then another, and finally said, "Pa, I think, in fact I know, that Ben's life is in danger."

Gideon Stark sat immobile for long moments, his face stiff. Then he instantly shed all appearance of age and weariness. He lurched forward in his chair and his voice breaking with anger yelled, "What the hell do you mean?"

Della was taken back and more than a little frightened, but she managed, "Somebody wants him dead."

"Who?

"I don't know."

Stark eased back in his chair. "Who told you this?"

Della hesitated.

"Tell me, girl," Stark said.

"I overheard one of the punchers say . . . please, Pa, I don't want to tell you."

"Tell me or I'll take a switch to you," Stark said.

"After one of our arguments over my marrying Don Miguel, I heard one of the hands say that Ben Bradford's life wasn't worth a plugged nickel."

"You foolish girl," Stark said. "Since when did a drover say anything that you should listen to? Who was he? I'll sack him right now."

"I can't remember," Della said. "But the Pinkerton says that Ben is in danger." Della stared into her father's wintry eyes. "Pa, she says . . ."

"A woman Pinkerton agent?"

"Yes, Pa."

"She says what? Out with it. A female posing as a detective is a damned abomination. It goes against nature."

Della let her words gush out in a torrent. "Her name is Augusta Addington, and she says the only one who has anything to gain by murdering Ben is you. She says your hired killers are already in Fredericksburg and are about to strike." The girl saw thunder gather in her father's face, and she said, "I didn't believe her, Pa. I don't think you're capable of such a terrible thing."

"Of course, I'm not," Stark said. "Has she told this to anyone else?"

"I don't believe so," Della said. "But I do think she confides in a man called Red Ryan. He's a shotgun messenger for the Patterson stage."

"Red Ryan," Stark repeated, as though he wished to remember the name. "Why the heck is there a Pinkerton in Fredericksburg in the first place?" Stark said.

Della shook her head so vehemently her curls bounced. "I don't know, Pa."

Gideon Stark liked none of this.

The Pinkerton agent was bad news . . . and she was smart. She had it all figured out. Why the heck hadn't the gunmen Ernest Walzer hired made their move? If the Pinkerton was right, they were already in Fredericksburg. Why the delay? He had questions without answers. When Bradford was finally out of the way, the Pinkerton . . . what was her name? . . . Augusta Addington . . . could tie him to the killing, something that Della must never know. Damn it all, killing begets killing, but Stark realized he was in this thing too deep to stop now. The Pinkerton would have to go and the shotgun messenger as well, a nonentity no one would miss.

"Did Manuel Garcia go to the bunkhouse?" Stark said. "I want to talk with him."

"No, Pa, I left him in Fredericksburg to keep an eye on Ben," Della said.

"No matter, I'll talk to him there," Stark said.

"You're going to Fredericksburg?" Della said, surprised.

"Yes. If someone really wants Bradford dead, I'll do my best to protect him," Stark said. "But, if I'm up against professional assassins and I fail, don't blame me."

"I won't blame you, Pa, and I knew you'd help," Della said. She rose from her chair and threw her arms around her father's neck. "I love you, Pa," she said.

Stark pushed her away, scowling. "Then stop that," he said. "You're no longer a child."

* * *

The hands, noisy and drunk, had ridden in about an hour before Gideon Stark went to bed. Now, his hands clasped behind his head, he stared at the ceiling . . . plotting.

He'd hired Manuel Garcia as a gun, and the man was a widow-maker who'd do his job. He could take care of the shotgun messenger. But Stark figured he'd attend to the Pinkerton personally. Della said the woman was staying at the Alpenrose Inn, and he wanted no slipups as far as she was concerned.

After Bradford was dead, Stark reckoned he'd return to the ranch, squeeze tears from his eyes, and tell Della how heartbroken he was that he'd failed to protect her doctor. She'd understand. Then they'd get on with the wedding plans. And Garcia would keep his mouth shut, and if he didn't . . . a rifle shot to the back can drop the fastest gun.

Stark closed his eyes and waited for sleep to take him.

He felt good, relaxed, and confident even. Everything was going to work out just fine . . . except for that tingling pain in his left arm and shoulder that he'd been experiencing for the past few days. That was a little worrisome. The rheumatisms probably.

CHAPTER THIRTY-FOUR

"Brother Benedict!" the Alpenrose desk clerk said.

The four monks, smelling of sweat and horses, stopped at the foot of the stairs and looked at one another. Finally, Sean O'Rourke said, "I'm Brother Benedict."

The clerk beamed. "Your sister was here. Miss Effie Bell. A little slip of a thing, but a charming lady. She left a little surprise for you in your room."

O'Rourke could not hide his scowl. "What sort of surprise?" he said.

"Oh, you'll find out," the clerk said, smiling. "But I can give you a little clue . . . it once belonged to your dear departed mother."

O'Rourke's mother had been a Dublin prostitute who'd died of consumption at an early age, leaving her son to be raised by Monto Maggie Mulgrew the infamous brothel keeper. The Irishman's mother had died penniless. She had no belongings. No legacy to leave.

Without another word, O'Rourke and the others hurried up the stairs and into their room. Helmut Klemm looked around, let out a string of snarling Teutonic curses and then said, "*Die Hure* stole my rifle."

"No, Helmut," O'Rourke said. "The whore stole the staff of Moses. Only by now, she realizes her mistake."

"I'll kill her," Klemm said. "And the dummkopf who allowed her up here."

Kirill Kuznetsov smiled and held up the coral rosary. The beads looked as though spots of blood covered his huge hand. "She left you these in trade, Klemm," he said.

"Yes, my sainted mother's rosary," O'Rourke said. "It's probably been blessed by the Pope." He took it from the Russian, stared at it for a moment, and then threw it into a corner. "This changes nothing," he said. "We go ahead and make the kill as planned. Klemm, tonight you will have a bellyache, and Kirill will take you to the doctor again. Tomorrow morning, once the horses are saddled, you'll have another bellyache, and that's when we kill the mark and ride out of town."

"What about my rifle?" Klemm said.

"When we get back to England, tell the Jew to buy you another," O'Rourke said.

"What does it matter?" Salman el Salim said. He was a small, slender man lost inside his monkish robe. "After the Bradford kill, you'll retire to your estate in Germany."

"Yes, where there's wild boar aplenty, and I'll have need of a fine rifle," Klemm said.

"Then do as the Irishman says," el Salim said, his smile as thin as a knife blade. "Force the Jew Ernest Walzer to buy you another." He shrugged. "Tell him it's a business expense. He'll understand."

Klemm said, "A slip of a girl, the clerk said. She won't be difficult to find in this town among the frauleins."

"*Da,* big and healthy, like Russian women," Kuznetsov said, grinning.

O'Rourke shook his head. "No, Helmut. The mark is why we're here. You've suffered a loss, but it's personal. Go after the thief and you could put all of us in danger."

"I understand," Klemm said. "But if I find her in a quiet place . . ."

"Then kill her," O'Rourke said. "But don't go hunting the woman. Save that for the wild boars."

Klemm looked hard at Kuznetsov. "Russian women are ugly. They have faces like sows."

"And German women are all hideous whores," Kuznetsov said.

"Enough!" O'Rourke said. He pulled the Adams revolver from the pocket of his robe. "I won't tolerate fighting among ourselves. The trouble is that we've been cramped together for too long. Tomorrow we make the kill, leave this damn town, and go our separate ways back to England. And I'll shoot any man who's not willing to abide by those terms." Then, "I've bedded German women and Russian women, and they all looked pretty enough to me." He smiled. "But none of them compare to Irish women."

"Or Arab women," el Salim said.

CHAPTER THIRTY-FIVE

"You're a beautiful woman, Augusta," Red Ryan said. "How many men have told you that?"

"Not enough," Augusta Addington said. She smiled. "You know how to talk pretties, Red. I suppose you've had a lot of practice."

"No, not a lot," Red lied. "Only them as really deserved it."

"And I deserve it," Augusta said.

"Yes. You deserve it *mucho*, as the Mexicans say."

"Then I'm flattered," Augusta said.

The candlelight of the Golden Horn restaurant was more than kind to Augusta Addington . . . it adored her. Its soft glow tangled in her shoulder-length hair, shimmered in her eyes, and transformed a woman in a plain white dress into a fairytale princess.

Or so Red Ryan thought.

The waiter brought platters of spring lamb with mint sauce, new potatoes, and peas and refilled their wineglasses with Bordeaux.

As they ate, Augusta said she was worried that Della

Stark had returned to her father's ranch. "She's gone back into the lion's den with her pretty eyes wide open," she said.

Red speared a small, round potato, chewed, and then said, "This isn't the conversation I had in mind for tonight."

"I know, and I'm sorry," Augusta said. She smiled. "Red, you can try to seduce me later. But as of now I'm a Pinkerton agent, and there are lives at stake."

"I still don't think Gideon Stark wants the doctor feller dead. Well, maybe he does, but I don't think he'll be the one to pull the trigger."

"No, he won't, because he's hired professional assassins to do that."

"The holy monks."

"The unholy monks. Remember what they did in San Angelo."

"We don't know it was them killed Stover Timms and Len Harlan," Red said. "It could have been Apaches."

"Red, it wasn't Apaches." Augusta's strong fingers tore a bread roll apart. "You know it and I know it."

"So what do you intend to do about it?" Red said.

"Tomorrow morning I'll order Sheriff Ritter to do his duty and arrest the four assassins on a charge of conspiracy to commit a felony murder as stated in the Texas Penal Code," Augusta said.

"Ritter isn't going to arrest four monks in robes and hold them in the juzgado on your say-so, Pinkerton or no," Red said. "Heck, there would be a Catholic uprising in Fredericksburg."

"Then I'll arrest them myself," Augusta said. "The lamb is excellent; don't you think?"

Red's fork stopped midway between his plate and mouth. "You can't arrest them. If they are hired gunmen, then they'll kill you for sure."

"It's my duty as a Pinkerton agent," Augusta said. "Allan Pinkerton took a chance on me and the other women he hired as detectives. I can't let him down."

"Getting shot is letting him down in a big way. And yes, the lamb is good."

Augusta smiled. "Red, meet me tomorrow morning at sunup in the hotel lobby. Maybe you can talk me out of it, but as of right now, my mind is made up and my revolver is loaded."

"I thought you gave your revolver to the chicken thief," Red said.

"A Pinkerton detective always has a spare," Augusta said.

"Bavarian chocolate cake for dessert?" the waiter said.

After dinner, Red suggested a stroll in the moonlight, but Augusta Addington said, "Yes, but only as far as Dr. Bradford's place. I need to see how my hired man is holding up."

"You mean, if Mercer is holding up," Red said. "He is probably out raiding a chicken coop."

"That was petty and not worthy of you, Red," Augusta said. She took his arm. "We had a very pleasant dinner. Please don't ruin it."

"Sorry," Red said, smiling. "I guess I am a bit testy at that."

"The Dr. Bradford business is getting you down, perhaps."

"When you boil it down, the Dr. Bradford business is none of my concern," Red said. "At least I don't think it is. I don't know what the Abe Patterson and Son Stage and Express Company would say about me getting involved."

"Involved? Of course, you are since I'm a likely future passenger," Augusta said.

"Yeah, there is always that," Red said. He placed his hand over Augusta's. "And there's always you."

The woman smiled, her teeth white in the gloom. "What a nice thing to say, Red. I always knew you were a romantic at heart. Ah, here's Dr. Bradford's house, and there's a lamp burning in the parlor."

Red Ryan and Augusta Addington were greeted at the door by Chris Mercer and his .450 revolver. But he smiled instantly as he recognized them and said, "Come to visit?"

"No, we don't want to set a spell," Red said. "Miss Addington is here to see that all is well."

"So far, so good," Mercer said. "The doc is studying up on medical stuff from a book so big it would break your toes if you dropped it on your foot. When he has his nose buried in a book, he ignores everything else. Did you know that human stomach acid can dissolve iron? And if you dropped some on your hand it would burn right through it."

"Is that a natural fact?" Red said. "I can't believe I've lived my entire life without knowing that."

"Well, it's all in Dr. Bradford's book," Mercer said. "He told me about it, the many wonders of stomach acid."

"Then if the doctor is at study, we won't disturb him," Augusta said. "Tell him we stopped by."

"I sure will, Miss Addington," Mercer said.

"There is one thing you should know, Mr. Mercer," Augusta said. "I'm confident that after tomorrow your services will no longer be needed as bodyguard for Dr. Bradford. I plan to tell Sheriff Ritter to make several arrests in the case."

"Anybody I know?" Mercer said.

"I don't want to say anymore tonight, but you will find out tomorrow," Augusta said.

"I'll tell the doc," Mercer said. "That's good news."

"No, don't say a word about this to Dr. Bradford," Augusta said. "Until the culprits are locked up, I don't want him to let his guard down, or you."

Then Red let the cat out of the bag.

"Miss Addington believes the four holy monks that came in on the stage are the assassins who've been paid to kill Doc Bradford," he said.

Chris Mercer didn't blink. "One of them has already been here with a bellyache," he said. "A bad case of that stomach acid I was telling you about. He and another with him. They both had the hands of gentlemen. I made a judgment that night, but I could be wrong. It could be that some monks do all the hard work and others pray."

"The four monks in question don't pray, and they don't

work, either," Augusta said. "And, Red, I so wish you'd kept your mouth shut."

"Mercer should know," Red said. "If four monks descend on him, he'd better be ready to shoot."

"Beware of monks with bellyaches, huh?" Mercer said.

"Yeah, that's about how it stacks up," Red said. He read something in the other man's eyes, how they glittered in the darkness. Mercer had just made his mind up about something. To get the heck out of town, Red guessed.

"Call it woman's intuition, but I don't think the assassins will strike before tomorrow," Augusta said. "They'll want daylight to make a clean escape, especially with Apaches around and a posse on their back trail. So be on guard come sunup, Mr. Mercer, though I'll be pounding on Sheriff Ritter's door well before then."

"I'll keep good watch," Mercer said. "I'd rather trust a woman's intuition than a man's reason."

"Just make sure you remain at your post, Mercer," Red said. "If the doc dies because you lit out, I'll come looking for you."

"Ryan, your threat doesn't scare me," Mercer said. "But I'll stick. I've took a liking to Doc Bradford, and I have a lot of respect for him and what he does. Never in my life felt that before."

"I never doubted that you would do otherwise, Mr. Mercer," Augusta said. "That's why I hired you. Just be careful until the arrests are made." She smiled. "Now I'll bid you a good night."

As they walked back to the hotel, August said, "Red, you're very hard on that little man."

"I don't trust him," Red said. "He was somebody once, but now he's just a drunk."

"He seemed to me that he was sober enough," Augusta said. She pulled Red's arm closer and smiled. "Now, between here and the Alpenrose, talk some more pretties to me."

CHAPTER THIRTY-SIX

A man's finger pulls the trigger, but instinct tells him when to load the gun.

Late as it was, Chris Mercer fully expected that something prophetic, something fraught with danger, would occur that night. And he was ready.

The British Bulldog .450 was not a Colt, but he was confident enough of his shooting skills that he was sure he'd acquit himself well with the unfamiliar weapon if and when a gunfight came down.

He sat in the doctor's office, its open door giving him a good view of the entryway corridor. Gunslinging monks. He could drop all four before they reached him . . . of course, they'd be shooting back, and that was a great unknown. How good were they? If they were professionals, they'd be good enough.

Dr. Bradford stepped out of his office, looked down the shadowed hallway, and said, "Mr. Mercer, you're still awake? What time is it?" He consulted his watch. "Twelve midnight. The witching hour. Good heavens, have I been studying this long?"

"Since sundown, Doc," Mercer said.

"Have I dined?"

"Not as far as I know," Mercer said.

"Have you?" Bradford said.

"No."

"Then I'll make us a sandwich," the doctor said. "I have a loaf of good sourdough bread and some Bavarian ham. Do you like ham?"

"Sounds good to me," Mercer said.

"Coming right up, my faithful Heimdall," Bradford said, smiling.

"Heimdall? What is that?" Mercer said.

"You mean, who is that?" the doctor said. "Heimdall is the watchman who guards the halls of the Norse gods. It is said that he can see for a hundred leagues, night and day, and can hear the grass growing. He also keeps his horn handy to announce the end of the world."

"Well, let's hope he doesn't sound it tonight before I eat my sandwich," Mercer said. "I'm sharp set."

Heimdall's horn didn't sound that night, but as Ben Bradford walked into the kitchen, knuckles rapping on the front door did.

The doctor stepped back into the hallway. "Oh dear, sounds like an emergency." He addressed himself to Mercer, but when he looked down the hallway toward his office the man was not in sight.

More knocking. Urgent. Demanding.

"All right, all right, I'm coming," Bradford said.

He opened the door.

Two robed monks stood in the gloom, one supporting the other. "Our brother is very sick, Doctor," Kirill Kuznetsov said. "It's his belly again."

"Bring him inside," Bradford said. "I'll examine him in my surgery."

The big Russian was pleased. The doctor asked no questions and that bode well for tomorrow morning. Then, a flash of inspiration. Why wait that long? Kill him now and hide the body where no one would find it? He and the others could still ride out of town at dawn as planned. Then he suddenly heard the Irishman's buts . . . *But* what if the body is found early? Then anyone trying to ride out of town would be suspect, even monks. *But* suppose the doctor has a gun, decides to fight for his life and cuts loose. The sound of shots would bring just about everybody in the rudely awakened town running to his house. *But* why not follow our agreed-upon plan so we don't bungle things and face a hangman's noose?

Kuznetsov was not an imaginative man, and his thoughts were jumbled enough that he decided to wait until morning and do the thing quickly and silently with a knife. The Irishman was clever and had it all figured out, so his way was the right way.

And then, if the Russian had any lingering doubt, his mind was made up for him.

As Helmut Klemm groaned in pretend pain and Kuznetsov tried his hardest to look concerned, Chris Mercer stood in the doorway of the surgery, the British Bulldog in his waistband. He leaned a shoulder on the frame, his eyes on the Russian.

Dr. Bradford looked up and said, "Oh, there you are, Mr. Mercer. I wondered where you'd gotten to." He glanced at Mercer's revolver but said nothing more.

"How is the reverend monk?" Mercer said. "Nothing too serious, I hope."

Kuznetsov lowered his head and stared at Mercer from under his shaggy eyebrows. The Russian's blue eyes were narrowed, full of murder.

"I still suspect an ulcer," Bradford said. And then to Klemm. "We'll try something a little stronger to reduce the acid. But if you don't feel better by tomorrow, I may have to consider surgery as a last resort. Dr. Theodore Billroth is a brilliant pioneer in that field, and he's had good results. I have studied his methods and . . ."

Bradford talked on and on as Klemm tried his best to look like a man in pain who was interested in what the doctor told him. But not Kuznetsov. He and Mercer locked eyes, each fully aware of what the other would bring to a gunfight and liking none of it.

In 1903 it was left to historian Bernard Loss to sum up that confrontation as "a clash of killers, made all the more peculiar by the frail appearance of the gunfighter Chris Mercer who was small and slender, his mild brown eyes revealing not the slightest tendency to malice or hostility. The Russian Kuznetsov on the other hand was tall and burly and much given to violent episodes. He was also a gunman of considerable skill. Mismatched as they were physically, each considered the other a man to be reckoned with, and the result of their suppositions would all too soon be fatal for a number of parties in Fredericksburg."

Dr. Bradford mixed a powder in water and then filled it into a brown bottle. "Take this as soon as you return to your hotel," he said to Klemm. "Drink the whole bottle."

The German nodded, groaned convincingly, and Kuznetsov helped him from his chair.

"Nothing more pathetic than a monk with the croup, is there?" Mercer said to the Russian.

"Maybe it's fatal," Kuznetsov said, his eyes hard. "Like lead poisoning."

"No, that's not the case," Dr. Bradford said, shaking his head. "If it was lead poisoning, I'd expect headache and joint and muscle pain. Your brother monk does not have those symptoms. No, it's undoubtedly an ulcer, and that's quite serious enough."

Kuznetsov smiled and said to Mercer. "Heed what the doctor said. Lead poisoning is a serious business."

"Indeed, it is," Bradford said. "Now, remember, drink the whole bottle. Come back tomorrow if you still have pain."

"How much do we owe you, Doctor?" the Russian said.

"At the moment, still nothing," Bradford said, "Seeing as how you're members of the clergy and all that. We'll see how the patient is feeling tomorrow."

"Seems like we're all waiting for tomorrow," Mercer said.

Kuznetsov nodded. "Maybe we should start praying now," he said.

"As a physician, I don't discount the power of prayer," Bradford said.

"Listen to the doctor," the Russian said to Mercer. "Start saying your prayers, little man."

For a moment Bradford seemed puzzled by that statement, but when Klemm groaned horribly, he forgot all about it as he helped the doubled-over German to the door.

* * *

"Yes, I agree with the Russian," Helmut Klemm said. "The little man is a problem. The doctor called him Mr. Mercer."

"Why the bloody hell is he there?" Sean O'Rourke said.

"I think someone knows the doctor's life is in danger and supplied him with a bodyguard," Klemm said.

"Can he be dealt with?" O'Rourke said.

"Of course, he can be dealt with," Kuznetsov said. "But he's a gunman. He'll get work in with his revolver."

"Bang! Bang!" O'Rourke said. "Too noisy. As soon as the door is opened, can you rush him and the doctor, take them both down at the same time before a shot can be fired?"

"Perhaps," Klemm said. "It depends where Mercer is standing. He'll draw and shoot in a split second." The German shrugged. "And hit what he's aiming at."

"I don't like this," O'Rourke said. "I don't like this at all. And I especially don't want to think that someone knows the reason we're here. Any ideas? I need ideas."

"Yes, I have an idea," Kuznetsov said. "And we should have done it days ago."

"Then speak, my Russian friend," Klemm said.

Kuznetsov said, "I'm not your friend, German. I'm nobody's friend. A professional assassin is what I am, and I'm paid to take chances and risk my life if need be to get the job done."

"So, Kirill, your idea is dangerous?" O'Rourke said.

"An idea that's not dangerous is unworthy of the name idea," Kuznetsov said.

"Then let's hear it," O'Rourke said.

"Let me say first that the four of us are more than a match for any serfs this town might assemble to stop us," the Russian said.

"This is true," O'Rourke said. "Go ahead. Let's hear you."

"Then I say at first light tomorrow we ride to the doctor's office and shoot him as soon as he opens the door," Kuznetsov said. "The man called Mercer will be careful and won't rush out of the house, giving us time to gallop out of town."

"They might come after us," O'Rourke said. "With what the Americans call a posse."

"Yes, and as I said, we can take care of any . . . posse," the Russian said. "Come after us and the peasants of this town ride into a nightmare they can't imagine."

There was a silence after Kuznetsov spoke, then finally O'Rourke said, "Right. I say we do it. What about you, Klemm?"

"We do as the Russian says."

"Salman el Salim?"

The Arab nodded, but then said, "We have knives and pistols." He looked at Klemm. "We've lost our expert rifleman."

O'Rourke smiled. "Pistols are all we need for a bunch of bumpkins. Kirill, how do you say peasants in Russian?"

"*Krest'yane* is the Russian word for peasants," Kuznetsov said.

"That's it . . . pistols for a bunch of *krest'yane*." O'Rourke said.

And the others laughed.

CHAPTER THIRTY-SEVEN

Red Ryan kissed Augusta Addington at the door to her room.

"I'm not inviting you inside, Red," she said as she gently pushed him away. "It's too soon. I've got a lot to think about."

Husky-voiced, Red said, "I understand."

"You do?"

"Not really."

"I'm a Pinkerton. Do I want to remain a Pinkerton, or would a love affair end my career?"

"A baby," Red said. "A baby would end it."

"Probably. Or if I got shot."

"Let's not think of either of those things," Red said.

"Oh, but I must," Augusta said. "I must think of those things and a lot of others."

"I'm only a shotgun messenger. I could be something else. If that's what you wanted."

"And if you wanted me to stop being a Pinkerton, what else could I be?"

"My wife," Red said.

"This is sudden," Augusta said.

"I know."

"Now I need even more time to think things through."

"Take all the time you need," Red said. "I'll wait."

Augusta kissed him again, a light brush of her lips. "I'll see you in the morning."

"You still plan to arrest the monks?" Red said.

"Yes, early. After I wake up Sheriff Ritter."

"I'll come with you," Red said.

Augusta shook her head. "No, Red. This is a matter for the law."

"Buttons Muldoon is a deputy," Red said.

Augusta smiled. "Of a sort. Now I must leave you, Red. Thank you for a wonderful evening."

After the door closed on him, Red stood where he was for a while. Had he really proposed marriage? To Augusta Addington? To a beautiful woman so high above his station? The answer was obvious . . . yes, he had. And she hadn't said no!

Red was too worked up to sleep just yet. He walked downstairs, through the darkened lobby, and onto the porch. Fredericksburg was in bed, the buildings silvered by moonlight, coyotes yipping out in the hill country. The air smelled clean, of the blue night, the dust of day long settled.

Red built a cigarette and enjoyed the quiet. He smoked for a few minutes and then turned to his right as he heard the slow thud of boots on the boardwalk, the footsteps of a weary man. Buttons Muldoon emerged from the heart of the night, his round face gloomy. A shiny new deputy's star glinted on his chest.

Red grinned and said, "Good evening, thou sorrowful apparition."

"That ain't funny," Buttons said.

"You catch the killer?"

"Not a sign of him."

"Any new people arrive in town?"

"Only that little Bell gal and her brother, and he's sick in bed and she says she's worried that it might be something catching. Me and Ritter didn't stay around to find out."

"Walk with me, Buttons," Red said.

"The heck I will. My feet hurt. It's roosting time, and I'm for my bed."

"Buttons, there's something tugging at me," Red said.

"Oh, no, don't tell me. Not the Irish an dara sealladh again?"

"Yes. I have two sights, and it is the sight of the seer that's troubling me."

"Your mother told you that, didn't she? That you have the gift?"

"My Irish stepmother told me that. She saw it in me. But she said it's not a gift but a curse."

Buttons grabbed the makings from Red's shirt pocket, looked down at the tobacco and papers, and said, "What do you see in your crystal ball this time?"

"It's not what I see, Buttons, it's what I feel."

The driver made an untidy cigarette, lit it, and said, talking out smoke, "So what do you feel then?"

"It's tugging at me, Buttons."

"Then tell me, damnit."

"I think Dr. Ben Bradford's life is now in the greatest danger," Red said.

"Heck, we already know that," Buttons said, weariness making him snappy. "That's why Archibald is with him."

"Chris Mercer is a useless drunk," Red said. "He can't protect anybody."

"So your second sight is telling you that we should. Is that it?"

"Yes, but only tonight," Red said. "Augusta plans to get Sheriff Ritter to arrest the assassins tomorrow morning."

Buttons made a face. "You know that Ritter doesn't drink? I mean, not even a beer. I've been so thirsty all day I've been spitting cotton." He drew deeply on his cigarette, and the tip glowed bright red in the darkness. "Miss Augusta still think it's them four holy monks?"

"Yes. She thinks they're gunmen in disguise," Red said.

"Heck, Red, a false beard is a disguise," Buttons said. "Not a heavy, itchy brown robe."

"I reckon they must be careful men," Red said. Then, "Buttons, I need you with me tonight."

"Count off the reasons why."

"You're steady, determined, handy with the iron, and the bravest man I know," Red said.

"And good-looking," Buttons said. "You forgot that."

"Yeah, and good-looking too," Red said.

"All right, I'll do it," Buttons said. "The sawbones has got to have a comfortable couch where I can stretch out. You can wake me up when we get attacked by a bloodthirsty band of holy monks."

CHAPTER THIRTY-EIGHT

As they walked the shadowed streets, it seemed to Red Ryan that he and Buttons Muldoon were the only people awake in Fredericksburg in the early morning hour, not yet one o'clock. The night sky was ablaze with stars, and a rising breeze set the chains of the shop signs chinking and sent a page of newspaper bounding along the street like a ghostly jackrabbit.

Dr. Bradford's house was in darkness except for a rectangle of pale orange light that was the parlor window.

"Seems peaceful enough," Buttons said. "Maybe Archibald is doing his job."

"Could be," Red said with some reluctance.

They walked closer, the only sound the soft footfall of their boots on the dirt road. A pair of coyotes hunted close and exchanged yips, and from somewhere farther off a screen door slammed open and shut in the wind. The night air was warm and smelled sweet of prairie grass and night-blooming wildflowers.

"Going somewhere, caballeros?"

A man's voice behind them made Buttons and Red stop dead in their tracks.

"On your way to visit the doctor, perhaps?" the man said. "You are sick, maybe so."

Buttons turned slowly, his hand well away from his gun. He immediately saw that the elegant and beautifully dressed vaquero who faced him also had his Colt holstered. That spoke of confidence. Buttons carefully raised his gun hand to the star on his chest and pointed to it. "Deputy Sheriff Muldoon," he said. "I'm a driver for the Abe Patterson and Son Stage and Express Company and the law around these parts." Then, out of the corner of his mouth, "Turn around, Red, damnit."

Red did as he was told and the vaquero said, "I am Manuel Alejandro Carlos Garcia. I ride for the Stark Cattle Company."

"Right pleased to make your acquaintance, I'm sure," Buttons said. "This feller here is Red Ryan, a well-armed and determined stage messenger and a man who's helping out the law."

"Why are you here?" Garcia said.

Red said, "I suspect for the same reason you are."

"And that is?" Garcia said.

"I think Della Stark told you to protect Dr. Ben Bradford from harm. Why else would you be here at this time of night?"

The vaquero visibly relaxed. "Miss Stark and the doctor are enamorado . . . much in love."

"But her father disapproves," Red said.

An expressive shrug, then, "But Mr. Stark is not here, and so I take my orders from Miss Della," Garcia said.

"Red Ryan here says the assassins could strike tonight," Buttons said. "He says they're disguised as holy monks."

Garcia shrugged a second time. "Some monks are holy, some are not. A monk is a man like any other."

"I believe they are gunmen in the guise of monks," Red said. Then, frowning. "Manuel Garcia . . . Manuel Garcia . . . hey, were you the Manuel Garcia in Bandera that time?"

"What time?" Garcia said, smiling. "I have been in Bandera on many occasions."

"Yeah, now I remember," Buttons said. "As I recollect you went after Pug Sutton and his Rocking-T drovers in the Golden Garter saloon up on the Medina."

"I went after the reward," Garcia said. "Ten thousand dollars for all five, dead or alive."

"Them boys played hob in some Mexican village, didn't they?" Buttons said.

Garcia said, "Yes, in the village of Majadillas. If rape and murder is playing hob."

"You shot all five," Buttons said. "They say you had five cartridges in that there fancy Colt you're packing and didn't have to reload."

Garcia smiled. "They say many things. It wasn't this Colt, but another, and I had a round in all six chambers. It took two shots to drop Sutton. He was a big man, heavy in the belly."

"They fired back?" Red said.

"Yes, they did, and they got their work in quite well. I was hit twice, but I lived and they died."

"And you got the ten thousand, huh?" Buttons said.

"No, I did not. The bodies lay out in the sun for so long, they were unrecognizable by the time the Texas Rangers got there. They said they would not pay me for rotted corpses that could be anybody. And, of course, by then the traps of the dead men had been stolen and no one could identify them."

"Too bad," Buttons said. "You were shot twice for nothing."

"I avenged the village of Majadillas," Garcia said. "That was reward enough."

Lightning shimmered in the sky to the north followed by the sound of distant thunder.

"A storm coming up," Red said. "Buttons, maybe we should go impose on Doc Bradford's hospitality."

"Red, I can't take this seriously," Buttons said, shaking his head. "Nobody starts a gunfight in a thunderstorm, even holy monks. I'm plum tuckered, and I'm headed back to the hotel."

"How about you, Garcia?" Red said.

"Miss Della ordered me to guard the doctor, and that's what I'll do," the vaquero said.

Lightning flashed, and the thunder rolled louder.

"Then we'll guard him indoors where there's shelter and hot coffee," Red said.

"You expect trouble?" Garcia said.

"Yeah, I do, and it could come soon."

"Then I'll go with you," Garcia said.

"You two suit yourselves," Buttons said. "But I think it's a godawful waste of time."

He turned and headed toward the Alpenrose, looked back, grinned, shook his head, and walked into glimmering darkness.

CHAPTER THIRTY-NINE

Rain pattered on Red Ryan's plug hat as he knocked on Dr. Bradford's door.

Then Chris Mercer's authoritative voice came from within. "Who is it? State your intentions."

"It's me, Ryan, and one other seeking refuge from the storm."

"Ryan, when I open this door if it ain't you, I'll drill you square," Mercer said.

"It's me. Who the heck else would be out this time of night on what could turn out to be a wild-goose chase?"

"Who's with you?"

"A feller by the name of Manuel Garcia."

"Bandera Manuel Garcia?"

"None other."

"All right, then if I see any fancy moves, Ryan, I'll shoot Garcia first and then you."

"Right neighborly of you, Mercer," Red said. "Now open the damn door."

Mercer opened the door and ushered in Red and Garcia,

and with them a sizzling flash and a banging bellow of thunder.

"That's the way to make an entrance," Mercer said after the din had passed.

"Where's the doc?" Red said.

"Asleep, or at least he was until you brought the thunderstorm," Mercer said. "Into the parlor with you. This way."

He led Red and Garcia into the lamplit room and then Mercer backed off several steps and said, "No offense, Garcia, but unbuckle that pistol belt and lay it on the table over there by the window. Real slow now. We got all night. Nothing quick and nothing fancy."

Garcia glanced at the British Bulldog in Mercer's waistband, smiled and said. "No offense taken." He shucked the gunbelt with its holstered Colt and laid it on the table.

"I got nothing against you, Garcia," Mercer said. "But you made a name for yourself in Bandera, and I get uncomfortable around pistoleros."

"Heck, Mercer, you're one yourself," Red said.

"I was one, you mean," the little man said. "I haven't fired a pistol in years. Pistoleros are only pistoleros because they keep on shooting."

A blinking, sleepy-eyed figure filled the parlor doorway. Dr. Ben Bradford wore a long white nightgown and a sleeping cap and Red figured he must be the most square-toed man in a square-toed town. What did Della Stark see in him?

"Mr. Mercer, I heard voices," he said. "And I see we have patients . . . or guests."

"Doc, the ranny with the red hair and plug hat is Red Ryan, a shotgun messenger and friend of Miss Augusta Addington," Mercer said. "The other is Manuel Garcia . . ."

"A vaquero for the Stark Cattle Company," Garcia said.

"Gideon Stark's spread?" Bradford said.

"Yes. That's the one." Garcia said.

"Are you here to kill me?" the doctor said.

"No, I'm here under orders from Miss Della," Garcia said. "I am to ride herd on you and protect you from harm."

"And Mr. Ryan, you're here for the same reason?" Bradford said.

"I think an attempt may be made on your life tonight by men disguised as monks," Red said. "Yes, that's why I'm with you."

The doctor managed a weak smile. "Then I seem to be well-protected. But monks? One of them is a patient. He has an ulcer."

"Doctor, Augusta Addington is a Pinkerton, and she plans to get Sheriff Ritter to arrest the four killers this morning. I don't think that's gonna happen. They're professionals, and they came here to test your defenses. I think they'll return in force, and I think it will be tonight."

"Monks . . . I can scarcely believe it," Bradford said.

"Well, it's happened," Red said.

The doctor looked at Red and said, "Thank you for being here. If I was alone, they'd kill me for sure."

Red nodded. "You got me and Garcia." He nodded in Mercer's direction. "I don't put any store in the drunk. He's a grasshopper, liable to jump one way as another."

It was a measure of Bradford's agitated state of mind

that he let that go and said, "Should I join you in this all-night vigil? I have a revolver."

"No, go back to bed, Doctor," Red said. "If we need you, we'll get you up."

"I am somewhat tired," Bradford said. "It's been a long day."

"Then go catch some shut-eye," Red said.

"There's coffee in the kitchen and bread and ham for sandwiches," Bradford said. "If you get hungry, help yourselves."

Buttons Muldoon saw the dim outline of a woman sitting in the swing that hung from the rear rafters of the Alpenrose porch, the unmistakable tall, elegant shape of Augusta Addington.

"Good evening Mr. Muldoon," she said. "Or should I say Deputy Muldoon?"

"I won't be a deputy much longer," Buttons said. "Me and Ritter are nowhere near catching the killer of the whiskey drummer." He shook his head. "Whiskey drummer murdered. What a damned waste."

"You're up late," Augusta said.

Buttons said, "I could say the same thing about you."

"I don't want to oversleep," Augusta said. "Early in the morning, I'll demand that Sheriff Ritter make an arrest."

"The holy monks," Buttons said, smiling.

"Yes, the holy monks." Augusta said. Then, after a silence, "Red asked me to marry him. That's also keeping me awake."

Buttons kept his surprise to a minimum. "And did you accept?"

"No. I'm thinking about it," Augusta said. "Have you known Red for a long time?"

"Time enough."

"What can you tell me about him?"

"What do you want to know?" Buttons said.

Augusta smiled. "I guess I want to know if he'll make a good husband."

"Red has frequented bawdy houses and is fond of fancy women."

"Go on."

"He sometimes drinks rye whiskey to excess."

"Go on."

"He's foolish with money. If he has a dollar in his pocket, he can't wait to spend it. You sure you want to hear more?"

"Go on."

"He can cuss like a drunken sailor."

"Go on," Augusta said.

"He's never in his life lived within the sound of church bells."

"Go on."

"Sometimes he don't bathe near enough."

"Go on."

Buttons sat beside Augusta and said, "Red Ryan comes out of the Western lands, and nothing and no one can ever change that. He's a man forged by hardship and danger, and he's often been alone, and all that has made him as strong and unbending as fine steel. He's kind to women, children, and animals and will go out of his way to help a body in need. He's one of the bravest men I know, and he will not be stampeded. I would trust him with my life and have done so too many times to count. He's loyal to a fault and will never let you down. He lives on the wild side and needs a special kind of woman, a woman who can match his own honor, honesty, and courage . . . and before you ask . . . yes, Miss Addington, you are that kind of woman."

Augusta took Buttons's big calloused hand in her own. "Thank you. You've told me all I needed to know."

"Will you marry him?"

"Yes, I think I will. But the bawdy houses, rye whiskey, and cussing will have to stop and the bathing will become much more frequent."

"Miss Addington, I'm happy for you, but a word of advice. Don't try to turn Red into something he ain't. You can't make a farmer out of him or a bank clerk or the manager of a mercantile. If you did, like a prairie cactus flower he'd wither away and die."

"Why would I marry him for all the reasons you have stated and then try to change him?" Augusta said.

"Well, the drinking and the cussing . . ."

"He'll do that on his own," Augusta said. "And only he will decide what he wants to do with his life. If I'm to be the wife of a shotgun messenger, then so be it."

"And what about them Philadelphia and New Orleans Addingtons?" Buttons said.

"My family will be shocked, as though I haven't already shocked them enough."

"Well, let 'em be shocked," Buttons said. "That's what I say."

"And that's what I say, too," Augusta said. She rose from the swing. "I'm going to rest now. Mr. Muldoon."

"Call me Buttons, since we're soon gonna be kissin' kin."

"Then Buttons it is." Augusta yawned. "I have a feeling that tomorrow will be a busy day."

CHAPTER FORTY

"Not too busy, are we?" Chris Mercer said.

"What time is it?" Red Ryan said.

"Ten minutes later than the last time you asked that question. It's now nearly three."

"It's early yet," Red said. "Heck, they may wait until sunup."

"Or not come at all," Manuel Garcia said.

"They'll be here," Red said. "I can feel it."

"In my water," Mercer said. "I once knew a feller who used to say when something bad was about to happen, 'I can feel it in my water.'"

"I've never heard of that," Red said.

"Me neither until I heard the Scottish feller say it," Mercer said.

"He had the gift," Red said.

"Maybe so, but it didn't save him from the Cheyenne up on the Cimarron in Kansas. They shot him full of arrows and then scalped him. He was a trader. They took all his stuff and ate his mule."

After some contemplation, Red said, bored, "Mule meat's all right, if you've got nothing else."

"So is horse," Mercer said.

"Cougar is good, or so I'm told," Garcia said.

Everyone fell silent, thinking about eating cougar, until Mercer said, "My God, will this night never end?"

Red rose from his chair and stepped to the window. He pulled the curtain back a couple of inches and peered outside. "Dark as the inside of a coffin," he said. "I can't see a thing."

"Criminals are the bastard children of darkness," Mercer said. "If your assassins attack us, it is the coming of the light that will drive them here."

"An attack at dawn could make sense," Red said. "After the killing it would be easier for them to ride out into the flat in the morning light and put a load of git between them and Fredericksburg." He stared at Mercer. "You're pretty smart when you ain't drunk."

"Aren't we all," Mercer said.

With agonizing slowness, the endless night dragged on . . . and on . . .

Around five, Manuel Garcia retrieved his gunbelt and buckled it around his hips. No one objected.

"Best to be ready," Red said.

"Like you, I feel something," Garcia said. "I feel the night and I taste my own fear."

"No need for that, vaquero," Mercer said. "It may never happen."

"So let me be concerned a little," Garcia said. He reached inside his frilled shirt and produced a small horseshoe-shaped medal on a silver chain. He kissed the medal, crossed himself, and then held it between his thumb and forefinger.

"What have you got there?" Red said.

"It is the medal of San Martin Caballero, the patron saint of cowboys," Garcia said. "He is a very powerful saint who protects those who venerate him."

"Was he a cowboy?" Mercer said.

"No, he was a Roman cavalryman who became a monk and did many good works," Garcia said. He smiled. "A real monk."

"Send his worship a howdy from me," Red said. "We need all the help we can get."

Mercer pulled the British Bulldog from his waistband and checked the loads. He hefted the revolver in his gun hand, getting familiar with its weight and balance, and then shoved it back, ready for a cross draw.

"Mercer, on account of how the Gypsy woman told you that your next gunfight will be your last, are you gonna shoot that thing or just wave it around and try to scare folks?" Red said.

"I don't know," Mercer said.

"What do you mean, you don't know?"

"Whose life has more value, Ryan, mine or Doctor Bradford's?" Mercer said.

"The doc's, I guess. He heals sick people and you steal chickens and get drunk,"

"And that's why I don't know."

"Every man thinks his own life is the most valuable," Garcia said. "Only the Lord Jesus laid down his own life for others."

Red said, "If the monks come this morning, my advice

to you, Mercer, is to haul out that pistol and get your work in the best you can. Let fate decide if you live or die."

"That also applies to you and the vaquero," Mercer said.

"Damn right it does," Red said. "I hope that when the smoke clears all three of us will be standing and none of us leaking blood."

"Look on the bright side, Ryan, we got a doctor nice and handy," Mercer said.

"Depends on how he is with bullet wounds," Red said. "As a general rule, not too many folks get shot in Fredericksburg. What time is it?"

"Around five," Mercer said.

"When is sunup in this town?" Red said.

"Around seven."

"Two hours to stay awake," Red said. "Who wants to make the coffee?"

At five-thirty, Chris Mercer brought steaming cups of coffee into the parlor on a tray. "Black as midnight and sweet as mortal sin," he said.

At six o'clock, Red Ryan pulled back the curtain and checked outside. "Still pitch black," he said.

At six-thirty, Manuel Garcia said a prayer to the Madonna of Guadalupe. "For good luck," he said.

At seven, the endless night shaded into a thin dawn. "Thank God," Chris Mercer said.

At two minutes after seven, Kirill Kuznetsov crashed through the front door.

CHAPTER FORTY-ONE

Chris Mercer was nearest the parlor door. He stepped into the hallway and immediately took to a .44 to the chest from Kirill Kuznetsov's Smith & Wesson Russian revolver. Instinct took over, and Mercer triggered the .450 Bulldog. A hit. A shot to the belly that stopped Kuznetsov in his tracks, his face suddenly stricken. Beside him, Salman el Salim threw a knife that embedded itself to the hilt in Mercer's left shoulder. Red Ryan fired. He fired again and Salman went down. Sean O'Rourke and Helmut Klemm, shocked by their violent reception, backed away from the door. El Salim had drawn his Colt and tried to get to his feet, but Manuel Garcia got his work in and fired at the Arab, who went down again. Hit smack in the middle of his forehead, he would not rise a second time. Red prepared to shoot at O'Rourke . . . but then disaster.

Ben Bradford burst out of his bedroom, still in night-gown and sleeping cap, threw up his hands and yelled, "No! Stop! Stop this at once."

The doctor had stepped in front of Red's gun and before he could adjust his position, O'Rourke's .450 Adams barked twice and Bradford staggered as he took both shots in the chest. Kuznetsov, in shock from the bullet in his belly, was nonetheless a hard man to kill. But he made a bad mistake that no professional gun handler should ever make. Instead of engaging the two men who were still on their feet and shooting, he sought revenge on Mercer and fired into the dying man. Mercer had propped himself against the wall, but now he slid down to the floor, leaving a streak of blood on the floral wallpaper. Red and Garcia fired at the same time. Hit twice, the big Russian fell to his knees and then collapsed forward, hitting the ground with a thud that rattled the crockery in the kitchen.

When Red looked along the smoke-filled hallway, O'Rourke and Klemm had vanished, then the sound of running horses told him that they'd fled in the direction of the open prairie. When Red stepped outside, all he saw was dust as the two riders galloped into the maw of the misty gray morning. He fired a couple of shots at the fugitives and then went back inside to give his attention to the living and the dead.

Garcia had taken a knee beside the still form of Dr. Bradford. When he saw Red Ryan, he shook his head, unable to do anything for a dead man. Ignoring the fallen Kuznetsov and el Salim, Red went to Chris Mercer, who sat with his back against the wall. The death shadows had already gathered in his eyes and cheeks and despite his wounds he appeared to be in no pain.

"How is the doctor?" Mercer said. "I can't . . . I can't see him."

"He's going to be just fine," Red said. "You saved his life."

Mercer nodded. "I'm glad." He managed a weak smile. "At the last moment I decided his life was worth more than mine."

"You done good, Chris," Red said. "You stood your ground and played the man's part."

Praise indeed from Red Ryan . . . but his words fell unheard on dead ears.

"I swear, every time the Patterson stage visits Fredericksburg it leaves behind a heap of dead men," Sheriff Herman Ritter said. "How do you explain that, Ryan?"

"I guess we just bring trouble with us, Sheriff," Red said. "Did you try to arrest the monks?"

"All we found were four empty monk robes," Ritter said. "Then the shooting started."

"I'm so relieved you were not hurt, Red," Augusta Addington said.

Red took the woman in his arms and said, "You were right about the monks. I'll never doubt your word again."

Ritter said, "Yes, she was right, and I'll let the Pinkertons know that they hired a great detective." He frowned. "But she isn't right about Gideon Stark. He's not the one that hired those four gunmen to kill Dr. Bradford. I can assure you of that. But don't worry, I'll find the guilty party."

Red and Manuel Garcia stood outside the doctor's house with Augusta and Ritter, while Buttons Muldoon in his capacity as deputy sheriff kept the ogling crowd away from the door.

"And I can assure you that Stark is the culprit," Augusta said. "He had Dr. Bradford murdered so that his daughter couldn't marry him."

"Where's your proof, Miss Addington?" Ritter said. He looked beyond Augusta to Buttons and said, "Deputy Muldoon, is the posse mounted yet? Or are they still drinking coffee in the Alpenrose restaurant?"

"I see them, Sheriff," Buttons said. He pointed. "Look, they're headed this way."

A dozen horsemen made up of three of the town's wealthy merchants, the rest young clerks and apprentices, rode into view.

"Get mounted yourself, Deputy Muldoon. I'll handle the crowd," Ritter said. "Lead the posse to victory and bring back those killers."

"Sure thing, Sheriff," Buttons said. He looked like a suffering martyr in a Renaissance painting. "But after that I'm turning in my badge."

"No, Deputy Muldoon, not yet. There's too much to be done," Ritter said. "We still have to find the killer of Nathaniel Foxworthy."

Buttons ignored that, and Ritter said to Augusta, "Gideon Stark is one of the richest and most influential men in Texas. You accuse him at your peril. Even if you could bring such a wild accusation to court, have you any idea of the battery of expensive lawyers you'd face? Miss Addington, you are the one that could end up in jail."

"Why don't you ask his daughter if her father is behind

Dr. Bradford's murder, Sheriff?" Augusta said, her pink cheekbones betraying her anger.

"I will. Depend on it, I will, but it won't get me anywhere. I expect Miss Della will laugh in my face." Ritter watched Benny Bone and his men take away the bodies of Kuznetsov and el Salim, and then he turned and addressed the onlookers. "Return to your homes," he said. "It's all over here."

"It's a damn shame that a fine young doctor was murdered in his own home," a plump matron in the crowd said. "And there's still another killer loose in the streets."

"I'll find the killer, and I assure you the two men who helped murder Dr. Bradford will be arrested and brought to justice," Ritter said. "Fear not, dear lady. And remember at election time, a vote for Ritter is a vote for reason."

Years after these events, the matronly woman would say to a reporter, "Little did I know that day that a killer stood just a hoot and a holler away from me."

Like moths drawn to a flame, Donny Bryson and Effie Bell showed up outside the doctor's house soon after the shooting ended. Donny gathered from the conversations around him that four men who had earlier disguised themselves as monks had murdered the doctor. Two had been killed in the attack and all four had worn regular clothes. A search of the carpetbags tied to the saddles of the dead men revealed only a change of shirts and some food supplies. Both carried large sums of money in their wallets, but there was no mention of the golden staff of Moses. Donny could only assume that one of the two fugitives had it.

As the crowd drifted away, Donny said to the girl, "Time to saddle up."

"Where are we going, Donny?" Effie said.

"The two that escaped have the golden staff. We're going after them."

The girl said, "But the posse . . ."

"Those rubes ain't got a prayer of finding them boys," Donny said. "They'll raise a dust cloud that will be seen for miles."

"But so will we, Donny," Effie said.

"No, we won't. I'm half Apache, and I've lived at my ease in deserts and plains where a white man would starve . . . and if I need to, I can track such a man to the gates of Hell and never be seen."

Effie smiled. "Oh, Donny, we're about to get rich."

"Yeah, we are, but let's find them monk men and kill them before we count our money," Donny said.

Chapter Forty-two

"Red, I know you wanted to go with the posse," Augusta Addington said. "Thank you for staying close to me."

"I don't think you're out of danger yet," Red Ryan said.

"You mean Gideon Stark?"

"More likely one of his boys," Red said. "And Manuel Garcia is still in town."

"After what I told Sheriff Ritter, I don't think Stark would dare make an attempt on my life," Augusta said.

"Ritter didn't believe you," Red said.

"He might believe Della."

"If he even talks with her."

Augusta watched a teamster try to right a shifted load of lumber on a flat wagon and then step back and scratch his head, puzzling over his next move.

Then she said, "I'm not sure that Della really believes her father hired the killers. And who could blame her?"

"So where do we go from here?" Red said.

"I send Della my bill, and then resign from the Pinkertons."

"Resign because of me?" Red said. "Because I asked you to marry me."

"That is part of the reason, but it's mainly because I failed my assignment," Augusta said. "I was sent here to save Ben Bradford's life, and now he's dead. I'm hardly a credit to the Pinkertons and their other female detectives."

"We all failed him, Augusta," Red said. "Me, Buttons, and Ritter, and on top of that I failed Chris Mercer. He'd changed, and I didn't see it. I didn't want to see it. I didn't want him to change. I wanted him to stay a drunk, remain someone I could look down on and make fun of."

"We're flogging ourselves because of a combination of self-love and self-loathing," Augusta said. "In the end, it will get us nowhere. Ah, here we are at the Alpenrose."

Red stopped and took the woman's hand. "Listen to me, Augusta, you did everything you could and you did it better than most. If Ritter had gotten here to the inn earlier, he could've caught those four gunmen in the act of changing from monks to murderers, and Bradford would still be alive."

"Or Ritter and me would be dead along with the doctor," Augusta said. "Red, let me have a while alone. I have much to think about."

"Will you marry me, Augusta?" Red said.

"Yes, I will, Red. And I say that with all my heart. But I don't want to talk about it right now. Wait until we're out from under this cloud and all the muddy waters run clear."

"Hey, Ryan, where's Muldoon?"

Esau Pickles stood in the road, his face concerned.

"Out with the posse," Red said.

"After them two monks?"

"Yeah," Red said.

"I knew them fellers was up to no good," Pickles said.

"You got a problem, Esau?" Red said.

"I reckon one of them swings of yours has the colic. He's sweated up some and breathing hard. I'd call in Doc Anderson the vet, but Buttons Muldoon has to sign off on the bill."

"I'll come see the horse," Red said. And then to Augusta, "Supper tonight?"

The woman smiled. "I look forward to it."

Gideon Stark led his horse into the livery stable and said to the towheaded kid who greeted him, "Unsaddle him for me." He flexed his left arm. "Damn arm is paining me, and I got a headache to beat the band."

"Too much sun, maybe," the kid said. "You ride far?"

"A fair piece," Stark said. "Brush the roan down good and give him oats with his hay."

"You missed all the excitement, mister," the kid said as he threw Stark's heavy silver saddle onto a rack.

"What kind of excitement?" Stark said. Sudden unease spiked at his belly. Had his hired assassins been discovered? He spotted Manuel Garcia's flashy palomino in a stall. What did that portend?

"Four fellers burst into Doc Bradford's house and killed him," the kid said. "The doc shot two of them but the other pair escaped. There's a posse out looking for them right now. They say once they're brung in, Sheriff Ritter is gonna hang them." The kid smiled. "That'll be a sight to see. There ain't been a hanging in this town in a coon's age."

Stark hesitated, afraid to ask the question, but he steeled himself and said, "Why did they kill the doctor?"

Busy with a brush, the kid turned his head and said, "The way I heard it from Tom McCabe over to the hardware store, the four men were the brothers of some feller who died under Doc Bradford's knife at a hospital back east. They wanted revenge for their brother's death and they sure got it."

Stark felt a flood of relief. No one had tried to connect him with the shooting . . . and the only one who could was the damned, interfering Pinkerton woman. She had to die . . . and soon. A careful man, Stark knew he couldn't risk a gunshot. But his homemade garrote, a thin length of buckthorn barbed wire attached to a pair of wooden handles, would cut deep and silently strangle the life out of her.

Stark untied a small canvas sack from his saddle, stepped around his horse, and walked toward the livery door. He turned his head and said to the yellow-haired kid, "Do a good job, and I'll give you a dollar when I get back."

It would prove to be an empty promise . . . because Gideon Stark would never come back.

CHAPTER FORTY-THREE

Her doctor was dead, and all Manuel Garcia could do was return to the ranch and break it to Della Stark as gently as possible.

He stepped into the livery and told the kid in charge to bring his horse. "I'll get my saddle," he said.

"There's a beauty on the rack there," the kid said. "See it? I didn't know there was that much silver in all Texas."

Garcia recognized his boss's saddle immediately. "Where did the man who owns that rig go?" he said.

The kid shook his head. "I don't know, but he told me he'd be back, so he ain't intending to go far. I reckon he's feeling right poorly, so he might be seeing a doctor, if we have any left after this morning."

Garcia discounted a doctor visit. Gideon Stark had never been sick a day in his life, and he always said that doctors kill a man quicker than any disease.

"Did you tell the man with the silver saddle about the murder of Dr. Bradford?"

"I sure did," the kid said.

"How did he take it?"

"Take it?"

"Yes, how did he seem?"

"He was a bit shaken, but who wouldn't be? Doc Bradford was a well-liked man in this town."

"Leave my horse for now," Garcia said. "I'll get it later."

He walked from the gloom of the stable toward the door's rectangle of bright sunlight and then into the street. Where was Gideon Stark? And why was he here? It had something to do with Miss Della's love for Ben Bradford, he was sure. But now the doctor was dead, the boss's problem was over. So why stay in Fredericksburg? He'd want to tell Della right away that her lover was dead.

Then Garcia smiled. Of course . . . it was a long ride from the ranch so Mr. Stark was probably getting a bite of lunch. A quick search of the restaurants in town and he'd find him.

Manuel Garcia failed to find Gideon Stark at any of the beer halls and eating places in town, and he finally headed to the Alpenrose Inn, where there was a small restaurant.

Red Ryan stood in the street outside the hotel talking with a bearded old-timer. Red saw Garcia and nodded. "I thought you'd have left town already."

"I was about to when I saw Mr. Stark's roan and saddle at the livery," Garcia said. "Have you seen him? I've been looking all over town."

"Can't say as I have, but I've been out back for a spell with a sick horse," Red said.

"Maybe he's eating in the hotel," Garcia said.

Suddenly Red was appalled. Oh my God, was Gideon Stark in the Alpenrose . . . within a few steps of Augusta?

CHAPTER FORTY-FOUR

After leaving the livery, Gideon Stark walked toward the Alpenrose Inn. His headache had worsened, and he was in considerable pain, but that only strengthened his resolve to deal with the Addington woman. He'd let Garcia take care of Ryan, the shotgun messenger.

Stark had it all planned. He'd tell the desk clerk that he wanted to talk with Miss Addington. "It's a private business matter, you understand." A five-dollar gold piece would make the man more cooperative. Then, when the deed was done. "Miss Addington is indisposed and doesn't wish to be disturbed." By the time the woman's body was found he'd be well on his way back to the ranch and he'd be the last man on earth anyone would suspect. He'd say, "Oh my God, when I last saw her, she was so happy that she was coming to work for me as a bookkeeper."

Despite his headache and the throbbing in his left arm, Stark smiled. Keep it simple. That was the ticket.

Five dollars made the desk clerk smile, and he quickly provided Mr. Stark with Augusta's room number, adding his hope that their business dealings would be successful "for both parties."

"I'm sure it will," Stark said. He wore black broadcloth and hand-tooled boots, the very picture of a prosperous cattle rancher.

Gideon Stark tapped on Augusta's door.

"Who is it?" A woman's voice from within.

"Gideon Stark, Miss Addington. Please, it's a matter of the greatest moment that I speak to you about Della. She's been badly hurt."

Against her better judgment, Augusta opened the door. "Come in," she said, admitting a stocky man of average height with hard, weather-beaten features who looked to have great strength in his arms and shoulders, the result of decades of hard, physical work.

"What can I do for you?" Augusta said, her hardened eyes signaling her dislike of this man.

As to what happened next . . . that has proven to be controversial over the years.

The newspapers of the day would have us believe that for a solid hour Augusta Addington berated Stark for a scoundrel and low down. She blamed him for the death of Dr. Bradford and promised that she would see him hang . . . adding, as a postscript to her tirade, "And be damned to ye." On hearing that last, realizing that he was undone, an enraged Stark then viciously attacked the helpless woman.

Only the final part of that account is true. Stark didn't go to the Alpenrose to talk that day . . . he went there to kill.

Bear in mind that the rancher planned to keep things simple, and indeed he did.

He closed the door behind him, turned quickly and savagely backhanded Augusta across the face, a powerful blow that staggered her and sent her reeling to the floor. She fell onto her hands and knees, blood and saliva stringing from her mouth.

Stark took the garrote from the sack and instantly darted behind the woman. Augusta had no time to scream before the wire bit into her throat and the man crossed his arms at the wrist and used both hands to push violently on the handles, tightening the wire, driving the cruel barbs deeper into her throat and neck, drawing thin rivulets of blood.

"Die," Stark said though gritted teeth. "Die, you damned whore . . ."

Then a terrible cry of a man in mortal agony.

The pressure on Augusta's neck ceased, and Gideon Stark thumped to the floor beside her. His eyes were terrified, and the left side of his face and body seemed paralyzed. Stark had just suffered a massive stroke and already his brain cells started to die at a rate of two million a minute, robbing him of speech. He reached out to Augusta with his right hand, making unintelligible, gurgling noises that were desperate pleas for help.

Augusta removed the garrote from her throat, dropped it on the floor, and staggered to her feet. Her voice tattered by the ravages of the wire, she managed, "There is no help, you sorry piece of trash."

Stark dragged himself across the floor, his hand still raised, eyes frightened, gasping, choking, beseeching, begging . . . appealing for his life. He grabbed onto the hem of Augusta's dress, and she jerked it away from him.

"What would you give up for Dr. Bradford to be here to save you, Stark?" she said. "All your dreams, all your yearnings . . . what else?"

Stark was fast losing his sight, his eyes searching, seeing only a blur.

"All you can do now is die," Augusta said. "And let your greed, avarice, and ambitions die with you."

All the life that was in Gideon Stark left him a few moments later. There is one thing historians are agreed upon . . . he had neither a painless nor a peaceful death.

The hotel room door burst open, and Red Ryan rushed inside. He took in the scene at a glance and ran to Augusta. She bled from her throat, and the front of her dress was streaked with scarlet. Red took her in his arms and she spoke into his shoulder.

"Stark tried to kill me, Red," she said, forcing the blood-clogged words. She turned her head and nodded to the garrote. "With . . . with that monstrosity."

Esau Pickles stepped into the room. He'd taken the stairs as fast as his gamy leg would allow, and he panted for breath. "Red, what the heck?" he said, looking around him. "What's happened here?"

"Later, Esau," Red said. "Go bring a doctor."

"Old Dr. Monroe is close," Pickles said. "One time he helped me with the croup and . . ."

"Bring him," Red yelled. "And hurry."

As Pickles scuttled out of the room, Red helped Augusta onto the bed. She seemed to be in shock, her eyes were glazed, her torn throat was a bloody mess, and he knew with awful certainty she'd be scarred for life.

* * *

"Hey, amigo," Manuel Garcia said to Esau Pickles as the old man rushed out of the inn. "You see Gideon Stark, the rancher in there? Maybe lunching in the dining room?"

"Gideon Stark?" Pickles said. "Yeah, I seen him. He's upstairs in Miss Addington's room, stone-cold dead. And now I got to go. Miss Addington is hurt bad."

Garcia didn't wait to hear that last. He ran into the hotel, past the startled desk clerk, and took the stairs two at a time. The door to Augusta's room was open, and Garcia slowed to a walk and stepped inside.

He saw Stark lying on the floor, then Augusta on the bed with a bloody towel around her neck. Garcia took a knee beside Stark and pushed the man over on his back. He crossed himself hurriedly and said, "What happened?"

Red Ryan booted the garrote in the vaquero's direction. It skittered across the floor and hit the man's boot. "Stark tried to strangle Augusta using that," he said. "He almost succeeded. Look at the blood on his hands."

Garcia's eyes were cold, his voice flat, menacing. "How did my patron die?" he said.

The vaquero's loyalty to the brand drove him, an emotion Red Ryan had seen many times before among cowboys and understood.

"As he tried to murder Augusta, his heart stopped," Red said. "He had an apoplexy that paralyzed him down one side. That's why half his face is twisted."

"Mr. Stark was never sick," Garcia said, disbelief in his tone. "He was a strong man."

"Yeah, well it seems his ticker was sick," Red said. "And in the end, it killed him and saved Augusta Addington's life." Red took a step away from the bed, his gun hand out from his right side and ready. "Garcia, are you here to give me a problem?" he said.

Augusta coughed and then whimpered and arched her back in pain.

The vaquero shook his head. "I want no trouble with you, Ryan. You told me the how of it, now tell me the why."

"You know the story, Garcia. Stark wanted his daughter to marry a rich rancher, but Della threatened to ruin his plans when she fell in love with Dr. Bradford. Those gunmen that attacked us this morning were bought and paid for by Gideon Stark. Your boss wanted the doctor dead."

"It's hard to believe," Garcia said. "Mr. Stark . . . my boss . . ."

"It was Della who sent for a Pinkerton to investigate her father," Red said. "Maybe she believed it. Or at least, half-believed it. I don't know."

"I will take the patron's body back to the ranch for burial," Garcia said, talking to no one but himself.

"No, you won't. Not yet. What's going on here?" Sheriff Herman Ritter stepped into the room. He had his gun drawn. "I met Esau Pickles in the street, and he said there had been a murder."

"Attempted murder," Red said. "Gideon Stark tried to kill Augusta Addington." He picked up the garrote from the floor. "With this."

Ritter backed away from the bloody wire as though he was afraid to touch it. "Why?" he said.

And Red told him.

Echoing Garcia, Ritter said, "It's hard to believe." He looked at the body on the floor. "Gideon Stark of all people. Mein Gott."

"He was an ambitious man," Red said. Then, after adjusting the bloodstained towel around Augusta's neck, "Where is that damned doctor?"

"The damned doctor is here," John Monroe said, a stocky, white-haired man who wore pince-nez glasses at the end of his snub nose. He looked unflustered and competent. "All of you out," he said. "Leave the patient some air to breathe."

"Doc, is she going to be all right?" Red said.

"Son, how would I know?" Monroe said. "I haven't examined her yet. Now out. All of you."

"The man on the floor is dead," Ritter said, "Apoplexy."

"It doesn't take a doctor to see that," Monroe said. "A massive stroke, for sure. He's been dead for at least fifteen minutes."

"Aren't you going to examine him?" Ritter said.

Monroe bent over Stark, felt the man's neck, straightened and said, "There, I've examined him, Sheriff. He's dead."

"One more thing," Red said. He held up the thick, viciously spiked wire. "This is what he used to try and strangle Miss Addington."

Monroe looked at the garrote and nodded. "Yes, I see. Now get out of here."

Red and the others stepped out of the room and stood in the hallway. Red built a cigarette, as did Garcia, and they both smoked. Sheriff Ritter, looking worried, seemed as though he was trying to say something helpful, intelligent, or at least official, but gave up the attempt and stood with his back to the wall, his face empty.

Red smoked three cigarettes before the door opened

and Dr. Monroe stepped into the hallway. "How is she, Doctor?" Ritter said.

"She's still in shock, but she'll be fine," Monroe said. "I treated the wounds on her throat and the sides of her neck and then I bandaged her. I'll come see her again tomorrow to make sure that there's no sign of infection." The doctor looked at Red and said, "My female patients tell me the fashion trend is for dresses with high collars. That is good, because she'll need them . . . at least for a while until the scars fade." Then to Ritter. "Did you send for Benny Bone to take care of the dead man?"

Garcia answered that question. "He was my patron. I will take him back to his ranch."

Monroe nodded and then said, "Any progress in finding the killer of that poor whiskey salesman, Sheriff Ritter?"

"Not yet, but my investigation is proceeding apace," Ritter said.

"I hope you find him soon," Monroe said. "First the drummer and then Dr. Bradford. It's getting to be that a man can't sleep safe in his bed at night."

"I have a posse out now on the trail of two of the men connected with the doctor's slaying," Ritter said.

Monroe shook his head. "A bad business, Ritter," he said. "You'd better stay on top of things around here. You know that Bill Summers is considering a run for sheriff?"

"Yes, I've heard," Ritter said.

"A good man, Bill," Monroe said. "Fought in Tennessee under General Patrick Cleburne in the war." He tipped his hat. "Well, good day to you gentlemen. I have impatient patients waiting." He smiled. "Just a little doctor's joke."

* * *

Red Ryan sat on the bed and took Augusta Addington's hand. "How are you feeling?" he said. He shook his head. "Stupid question. I think I have a good idea about how you feel."

Augusta tried to smile, failed, and said, "The doctor gave me something for the pain. I feel all right."

"You'll be up and about in no time," Red said. "I see the roses coming back to your cheeks already."

"Dr. Monroe says the scars will go away when I'm an old lady," Augusta said.

Red kissed her pale mouth. "Then we'll celebrate that day, you and me," he said.

"Yes, we will," Augusta said. She squeezed Red's hand. "Just the two of us."

CHAPTER FORTY-FIVE

To say that Buttons Muldoon was as frustrated as a woodpecker in a petrified forest is an understatement. He'd found the trail of the two fleeing killers and then lost it again. Found it a second time and again lost it. Red Ryan could follow tracks like an Indian, but Buttons could not. Give him a wagon road stretching into infinity and he was in his element. But trying to spot a bent-over blade of grass or a partial hoof print in a rolling wilderness of pastureland was beyond him. And none of the dozen rubes riding with him were any better.

And to make matters worse there was . . . Sniffles.

His name was Elijah Blake, a small, frail, insignificant man who worked as a part-time bookkeeper and was quite a celebrity in Fredericksburg because of his wife, who tipped the scales at three hundred and fifty pounds. Unfortunately, Blake suffered from hay fever and was horribly allergic to ragweed and grass, and he sneezed and sniffed incessantly and drove Buttons Muldoon crazy.

"If grass makes you sneeze, why the heck are you out here on the damned prairie?" Buttons asked, irritated.

Blake, riding a pony-sized, mouse-colored mustang he'd rented for the day, wiped his nose with a large blue bandana, sniffed, and said, "It was my lady wife's idea. She said I must ride out and capture the fugitives and cover myself in glory." He sneezed several times, then added, "Oh, dear." The tip of his nose was wet and red.

"We ain't gonna cover ourselves in glory on this hunt," Hans Schmidt the blacksmith said. "Those boys are long gone."

"We'll find them," Buttons said, without much conviction.

"When?" Schmidt, a surly man, said.

"Soon," Buttons said. His horse shook its head at a fly, and its bridle chimed.

Blake sneezed.

"Seems to me we'll run out of daylight soon," Anton Bauer, the baker said.

"At least six hours left," Buttons said.

Blake sniffed.

Annoyed, Buttons said, "This damned posse wasn't my idea, you know."

"You're the deputy sheriff," a man toward the rear of the column said. "You're in charge."

"Acting, unpaid," Buttons said. Blake sniffed again, and Buttons called out, "Can any of you square-heads pick up a trail?"

"No," Bauer said. "Can you?"

"I'm trying," Buttons said,

"Then try harder," Bauer said.

"Well, we ain't making much dust," Buttons said. Again, an attempt at being optimistic.

"And neither are the men we're chasing," somebody said.

"We're not chasing anybody," Schmidt said, his joyless face grim. "I think we're going around in circles. See that lightning-struck oak over there by the gulch? I think this is the third time we passed it."

"The two murderers are headed east and so are we," Buttons said. "I may not be Dan'l Boone, but I know in what direction we're going. Blake! Stop that damned sniffing!"

"I can't help it," the little man said, his whiny voice plaintive and penitent. "I'll have some harsh words to say to my lady wife when I get home."

"She'll sit on you, Blake," Bauer said. "Squash you like a bug."

The men laughed, and Buttons Muldoon took that as a good sign. They were still in fairly good spirits and not quite ready to give up the chase . . . at least for the time being.

The sun was high, and the day was hot and sultry. Men and horses sweated, and out in a nearby grove of wild oak a quail called. Buttons, as used to heat as he was to snow and rain, held up well, but some of the posse members showed signs of suffering, using their canteens often, especially those that worked indoors.

Buttons had the advantage of numbers, but he worried over how his men would perform against a couple of professional gunmen. Experience told him that the outcome of this pursuit was far from certain. The only even half-capable gun handler was himself, but he didn't rate very highly in the shootist hierarchy . . . he figured somewhere near the bottom where mediocrity reigned. But this would probably end up as a long-range rifle duel anyway, and most of the men with him had cut their teeth on squirrel rifles. That gave him hope.

An hour passed. The land held a solemn silence, the only sounds the steady plodding of the horses and the creak of saddle leather. Blake sneezed and sniffled constantly, and the bandana he used had become a damp rag. Buttons considered shooting him.

Ahead of them stretched an endless sea of rolling hills, mile after mile falling away until blue sky met green grass where the horizon shimmered.

The biggest and the strongest of them was the first to give up.

The blacksmith Hans Schmidt, a morose, unpleasant man, said. "That's it, I quit." He pulled his horse out of the column. "Anybody else tired of this wild-goose chase?"

"Schmidt, get back in line." Buttons said. "I'll tell you when it's time to quit."

"You tell me nothing, stagecoach driver," Schmidt said. He looked around at the others. "So, who's coming with me?"

Buttons knew he had to save the situation or lose the posse. The men were listening to Schmidt, thinking things through. The big blacksmith was heavily muscled, enormous in the shoulders and arms, and he'd be a handful. But right then Buttons had no alternative, aside from shooting the man . . . and that would cause too many complications, a whole lot of questions asked.

"These men are going nowhere, and neither are you, Schmidt," Buttons said.

Schmidt's gaze measured Buttons from the toes of his

boots to the top of his hat, seeing a solidly built man with some fat on him, especially around the middle. "And you're going to stop me, I suppose?"

"If I have to," Buttons said.

"Schmidt, get back in line," Anton Bauer said, coming to Buttons's rescue. "Deputy Muldoon is in charge here."

"The hell he is," the big man said. Menacing, with a reputation as a dangerous fighter, he swung out of the saddle and stepped toward Buttons. "I don't like you, driving man, never did," Schmidt said. "And I plan to ride out of here and take the posse with me. So try and stop me." His fists hung at his side, as big and as hard as anvils. "I'm waiting," he said.

Hans Schmidt didn't have to wait long. Buttons was not a man to be intimidated.

He threw a straight left that Schmidt knocked aside with his right, but, as Buttons, a wily old street and saloon fighter, had anticipated, the block left his chin open. Buttons followed up instantly with a wicked right hook that slammed into the blacksmith's chin and sounded like a sledgehammer striking a tree trunk. The punch staggered Schmidt, and Buttons went after him. The man's hands were hanging loose by his sides when Buttons hit with a left hook and followed up with a smashing right to the jaw. The right dropped the blacksmith, and, stunned, he went down on all fours, spitting blood. Now, under normal circumstances Buttons would have followed up with a boot to the man's ribs, but since the entire posse was watching with fascinated interest, he decided to do the decent thing. Very much against his better judgment, he took a step back and let the man get to his feet.

Schmidt, aware that he was getting pounded by

someone who knew how to scrap, came off the ground snarling, his massive arms spread wide for a backbreaking bearhug. As the man lunged at him, for an instant Buttons let him come. Then he quickly stepped inside and cut loose with a mighty right uppercut that snapped Schmidt's head back and sent the man reeling, his arms and legs cartwheeling. Buttons had enough of playing nice since it very much went against his nature. Riled now, he went after the blacksmith and slammed a left and then a right to his mouth, splitting the man's lip. Schmidt, his fists flailing ineffectively, stumbled toward Buttons and ran into a straight right for his trouble. This time the blow felled the blacksmith, and he went down, gasping for breath, his face a bloody mess.

"My advice is for you not to get up again," Buttons said, head bent as he looked at Schmidt. "I can take you apart piece by piece, and I can keep it up all day." He shook his head. "What a slaughter that would be. Now state your intentions. Will you quit the chase or soldier on?"

But Schmidt was through.

He got slowly to his feet, picked up his hat, and lurched to his horse. One of the other riders had to help him mount. Without a word, the battered blacksmith headed west at a walk, toward Fredericksburg, and Buttons let him go. The man was all used up, and it would be quite a spell before he felt like himself again.

Buttons swung into the saddle and said, "Blake, you should go with him."

The little man looked frightened. "I'll stick, if you don't mind," he said.

"Suit yourself," Buttons said. "Anyone else want to leave with Schmidt?"

A few men muttered under their breath, but one man with a loud voice yelled, "No, sir," and none disagreed with him.

"I'm proud of you boys," Buttons said, smiling. "And from now on we'll keep it civil, huh?"

"Anything you say, boss," the loud man said.

"Good," Buttons said. "Now let's go find those two murdering scoundrels and bring them in to face justice."

Caught up in the moment, Elijah Blake yelled, "Huzzah!" And Buttons gave the little man a mental pat on the back.

Fifteen minutes later, the posse heard the sound of gunshots.

"Where away?" Buttons said, one of the nautical terms he used from time to time.

A babble of voices and eleven fingers pointing in eleven different directions.

"Keep quiet, everybody," Buttons said. He stood in the stirrups and held himself very still, listening.

There it was again, a flurry of shots and then silence. But this time Buttons got a fix on the direction.

"The firing is to the southeast of us," he said. "Forward, men, at the gallop. We've got them now."

CHAPTER FORTY-SIX

Helmut Klemm was hurt bad. Real bad. During the gunfight at the doctor's house, he'd taken a stray round that had entered just above his cartridge belt on the left side and exited at the small of his back. He'd lost a lot of blood and rode bent over in the saddle, groaning in pain with every hoof fall of his horse.

"I'll take you to a doctor in Austin," Sean O'Rourke said. "He'll fix you up in no time."

"How far to Austin?" Klemm said, through gritted teeth.

"Not far. We'll make camp tonight and be there tomorrow afternoon."

"I'll be dead by then," Klemm said.

"No, you won't," O'Rourke said. "You're too tough to die from a bullet wound."

"Two wounds," Klemm said. "One going in, one going out. Eins plus eins ist zwei."

Heat waves danced in the distance and high up, buzzards traced lazy loops in the sky. Nothing stirred in the grass, and around the riders lay a vast, ancient silence, as though they rode along the nave of a ruined cathedral.

Then Klemm said, "Irishman, find me a shady place to die. Under trees. My estate in Bavaria has many trees where the wild boars live, a spruce, pine, and beech forest. Dappled it is. It's not sunlight that makes a forest beautiful, it's shadow." The German gasped as an iron fist of pain hit him. "I'll never see my beautiful *Eingehurn* again."

O'Rourke said, "What does that mean, Klemm? Keep talking. When you're talking, you're not dying, so tell me."

"*Eingehurn* means unicorn, because hundreds of years ago unicorns lived in my forest. But they're all gone now and only the boar and the red deer are left." Then, "Irishman, we fulfilled the contract, didn't we?"

"Yes, the doctor is dead," O'Rourke said.

"When you reach England and meet the Jew Ernest Walzer, tell him my share of the payment is yours."

"You'll be with me," O'Rourke said. "With your hand out."

"I'm in terrible pain," Klemm said. "Find me a restful spot to lie down."

"I think I see trees in the distance," O'Rourke said. "We'll linger there for a while."

"They'll be after us," Klemm said.

O'Rourke turned in the saddle and checked his back trail. The brassy sunlight was blinding and he raised his hat against the glare. "No one is behind us. I can't see any dust."

"It's getting dark," Klemm said. The hand he held at waist level was scarlet with glistening blood. "Darkness is falling fast, and it's our friend, Irishman."

"Yes, it's getting dark," O'Rourke said. He realized that the death shadows were gathering around Klemm, and he was dying. He'd never particularly liked the man, but they were in the same profession, and in O'Rourke's eyes shared experiences forged a bond. He'd stay with Klemm until his soul departed and then give him a blessing. It was the Irish way.

O'Rourke picked up the reins of Klemm's horse and took a narrow game trail that led to a clearing in the middle of a grove of mixed wild oak and mesquite. He helped the German from the saddle and sat him in the shade of an oak, his back against the trunk.

"Drink," O'Rourke said, holding his canteen to Klemm's mouth. The man drank a little and then coughed it up again, the water now streaked with blood. A quail called out in the long grass, but O'Rourke paid it no heed. He used a shirtsleeve to mop sweat from his face and he was aware that he smelled rank of sweat and his eyes were red and sore from the pitiless glare of the sun.

Klemm saw the Irishman's obvious discomfort and said in a whisper, "It won't be long now." He tried a smile. "Strange to think that in all the wide world, only the boar and the red deer will grieve for me."

"Even though you hunt them," O'Rourke said.

"There is a spiritual covenant between hunter and hunted. They will know when I die, and they'll rise from sleep and mourn." Klemm grabbed O'Rourke by the front of his shirt. "Maybe, if there is an afterlife, I will be the hunted and all the men I killed will be the hunters."

O'Rourke smiled and shook his head. "There is no hunting in heaven."

"No?" Klemm said. "Then what a boring place it must be."

"But I don't know that for sure," O'Rourke said.

"Don't know what?" Klemm said. He was ashen, as though all the blood had fled his face. His skin had a candlewax sheen.

"I don't know that there is no hunting in heaven," O'Rourke said.

"I think in heaven a deer you kill one day will be alive again the next," Klemm said.

O'Rourke nodded. "A good arrangement."

"What is that?" Klemm said.

"What?"

"The bird call."

"It's a quail, I think. There seems to be a lot of them around."

Klemm's fading eyes moved beyond O'Rourke to the edge of the clearing.

"Irishman," he said, "I think we have a problem."

"Stand up slowly and turn," Donny Bryson said, his Colt leveled and ready. "Keep your hand away from your pistol."

Sean O'Rourke did as he was told. His Adams revolver was fastened in a British army flapped holster, never intended for a fast draw.

"You too, mister," Donny said to Klemm. "On your feet, handsomely now."

"He's dying," O'Rourke said. "He can't get on his feet. You have no call to get stirred up, mister. We were traveling east toward Austin and just stopped for the night."

"Effie," Donny said, "take care of the dying one. I'll do my talking to this ranny here."

The girl smiled. "I'll do it, Donny," she said.

She carried the Sharps and had made a chaplet of white and pink prairie flowers for her hair. Effie Bell did a sort of faery dance, knees high, toes pointed down, until she stopped in front of Klemm, shoved the muzzle of the rifle against his forehead, and pulled the trigger. The man's head jerked under the bullet's impact and when it exited at the back of his skull it splashed the trunk of the oak with blood, bone, and brain matter.

The girl squealed in surprised laughter and ran back to Donny's side. "Did you see that?" she said. "Boom!"

Donny grinned. "Yeah, I saw it. The big fifty can put a hurtin' on a man for sure."

"Damn you," O'Rourke said. "You damned filth."

"You keep your trap shut until I tell you to open it," Donny said. He looked around him. "Where's the golden staff of Moses?"

"There is no staff of Moses, you idiot," O'Rourke said.

"Where have you stashed it?" Donny said. "Mister, if you make me mad enough, I'll shoot you in the belly where it hurts and you'll scream for days and then you'll thank God for letting you die."

"There is no staff," O'Rourke said. "That was just a lie I made up to convince folks that me and the others were monks."

Donny looked doubtful and spoke out of the corner of his mouth. "Effie, look around. Start over there near the dead man. Find it."

"I'll find it, Donny," the girl said. "And if I don't, we can make that one talk."

"We sure can," Donny said. "I know some Apache tricks with a knife that will open his trap in a hurry."

Effie searched the entire clearing and found nothing.

"There's grub in the carpetbags," she said.

"Good. We'll need that," Donny said. He stared at O'Rourke. "You planned to shake the posse and you stashed the golden staff somewhere between here and Fredericksburg, figuring to go back for it. So where is it? Take me there or I'll shoot you where you stand."

"I can't take you there, because there is no golden staff and there never was," O'Rourke said. "You're a damned fool if you believe otherwise."

Donny Bryson dropped his gun. He grimaced, stretched his mouth wide in mortal agony and sudden blood spilled over his chin. He made a strange, strangling "arg . . . arg . . . arg" sound as his throat worked around the strap iron arrowhead lodged deep in his gullet. The arrow had come from Donny's right and had hit an inch under his ear and penetrated deep. It was a killing wound, and Donny dropped to his knees as a mounted Apache cantered past and threw a lance into his back. He fell forward, skewered like a pinned butterfly in a case, dying a more honorable death than he deserved.

Half a dozen Apaches dismounted and surrounded Sean O'Rourke, eager for a living prisoner who would provide endless hours of fun. But he thwarted them. At close range O'Rourke fired the double-action Adams with speed and accuracy. He killed three Apaches and wounded another but kept his last round for himself . . . a shot to his right temple. The Irishman fell, dead before he hit the ground.

Angry at losing so many warriors and frustrated, the Apaches turned their attention to Effie Bell. Eight of them formed a semicircle around the terrified girl. She tossed away the Sharps and forced a smile. Then, in a moment of both inspiration and desperation, she pulled open the front of her dress and showed the leering Indians what lay beneath. Her ploy worked. Effie exchanged certain death for a living death. Since she disappears from history at this point, it is not recorded what she later thought of her bargain.

"Heck, I thought the Apaches were gone from this part of Texas," Anton Bauer said.

"So did I," Buttons Muldoon said. "Looks like we were both wrong."

"Three dead," another man said, stating the obvious. "Deputy, you said two of them were the sham monks, so who is the third?"

Buttons pulled the lance from the dead man's back, then turned him over with his boot. "This ranny has long hair and looks like a breed," he said. "Since he's supposed to be hanging around this neck of the woods, I'd say that there could well be Donny Bryson."

"The notorious killer?" a man said.

"None other," Buttons said.

Bauer said, "Well, don't that beat all. Obviously, he was in cahoots with the other four."

"Until the Apaches punched his ticket," Buttons said.

"O dear," Elijah Blake said. He sniffed. "My lady wife will be so surprised. I wonder if there is a reward?"

"I'm sure there is," Buttons said. "We'll split it among us. Except for Schmidt, that is. He ran out on his share." He glanced at the sky. "We got some daylight left. Get the bodies up on your horses. He pointed at Bauer, Blake, and another man. "You, you, and you."

"Oh no, Mr. Muldoon. Remember my hay fever. I can't travel with a dead man hanging behind me."

"Then hang him in front of you," Buttons said.

CHAPTER FORTY-SEVEN

Three days had passed since the deaths of Dr. Ben Bradford, Chris Mercer, Donny Bryson, and the four assassins. Benny Bone had been busy. Bradford's burial had been well-attended, most of the town turning out along with Red Ryan, Buttons Muldoon, and Augusta Addington, but Della Stark had been noticeably absent.

Red and Buttons sat in the Alpenrose Inn's front porch drinking afternoon beers with Augusta who still had her throat bandaged.

Red let a brewer's dray rumble past, then said to Buttons, "How many passengers does the Crawford couple make?"

"Four. The Crawfords, a ladies' corsets drummer by the name of Jenkins, and a man called Peter Cream that I know nothing about except that he's in the plants and seed trade," Buttons said. "But I'm not real sure about the Crawfords. They're a mite nervous about the Apaches. Maybe they won't show tomorrow."

"Five passengers, Buttons. There's me, remember?"

Buttons smiled. "You're not a passenger, Miss Augusta. Since you're Red's bride-to-be I count you as a special guest of the Abe Patterson and Son Stage and Express Company. That's why I'll only charge you half-fare."

"You're so kind," Augusta said, smiling.

After he gave Buttons a scorching glare, Red said, "What does Sheriff Ritter say about Hans Schmidt?"

"What about him?" Buttons said.

"I thought he was pressing charges against you for assault."

"Oh that. No, Ritter says it was a fair fight and no charges are forthcoming. Besides, he made me promise him that me and you would leave Fredericksburg and never come back. He says we ride into town like the Four Horsemen of the Apocalypse and leave death and destruction in our wake."

"I thought the holy monks were the four horsemen," Red said.

"Yeah, well, now Ritter doesn't see it that way, if he ever did."

"What about the reward for Donny Bryson?" Red said.

"He says he ain't a hundred percent sure that it was Donny we brought in. But he said he'll contact the Mexican authorities and let me know."

"When will that be?"

"Ritter says he has no idea," Buttons said. "Then he fired me from my deputy sheriff position, as if I gave a damn."

Red set his beer mug on the table and said, "Well, well . . . lookee here."

Della Stark pulled up in her surrey, a cowboy at the reins, the gun vaquero Manuel Garcia as an outrider. She wore a plain black day dress without a bustle and a poke bonnet of the same color that tied under the chin.

The cowboy helped Della from the carriage, and as she mounted the steps to the porch, Augusta noticed a gesture that perhaps betrayed the young woman's state of mind. The custom dictated that a lady used only one hand to lift her skirt high enough to take the steps. Della used two hands . . . the mark of a whore.

The girl was very pale, no trace of paint or powder, and she looked tired, as though she hadn't slept in days. "Pardon my intrusion," she said.

"You're not intruding," Buttons said, standing. "Take a seat, Miss Stark."

"No, what I have to say won't take long," Della said. "I really want to talk with you, Augusta, but I don't mind if the others hear."

"I don't mind, either," Augusta said. She sounded cool, distant. "Please, go ahead."

"First I want to apologize for my father's actions," Della said. "He hadn't been himself recently and was prone to sudden outbursts."

"Ma'am," Red said, "it wasn't an outburst. He tried to strangle Augusta with a length of barbed wire."

"Yes, I know. Manuel told me," Della said. "That was unfortunate."

Augusta's fingers moved to her bandaged throat. "Yes, wasn't it?' she said.

"I'm sure that if my father had time to reconsider his actions, it would never have happened," Della said.

"He rode here from your ranch," Augusta said. "He had hours to reconsider his proposed actions."

Feeling a niggle of annoyance in his belly, Red said, "Dr. Bradford's funeral was well attended. Just about the whole town turned out."

"Did they?" Della said. Her face showed little emotion. "I'm so glad." Then, perhaps realizing how cold that sounded, she said distantly, "Ben was a good man and a fine doctor. What a pity my father could never accept him."

"Yes, it was a pity," Augusta said. "A lot of men died because of Gideon Stark's lack of acceptance."

"Are you still blaming him?" Della said.

Augusta said, "For Ben Bradford's death? Yes, I am. For trying to kill me? Yes, again."

"Father was disturbed," Della said. "As I said, he wasn't himself and didn't know what he was doing. I know because I was the cause of it."

"Your father's own ambition was the cause of it," Augusta said.

Manuel Garcia stirred, his web between his thumb and trigger finger rested on the hammer of his holstered Colt. Suddenly he seemed uncomfortable, and Red watched him closely.

"As a tribute to my father's memory I've decided to marry Don Miguel de Serra," Della said. "Our lands will be joined as father always wanted."

Augusta realized she was dealing with someone

mentally unbalanced and said, "I hope you and Don Miguel will be very happy."

"We won't be happy, that's too much to ask. But I do hope I can drive him into an early grave," Della said. "He is an old man and sick. When he dies all the land will be mine."

Buttons could always be depended on to say the wrong thing at the wrong time. "From Monterrey to San Antone . . . that's a whole heap of range, Miss Della."

"Enough to found a dynasty in my father's name," Della said.

"Boss, it's time to leave," Garcia said. "Best we get back to the ranch before dark."

Della nodded and opened her drawstring bag. "Augusta, Miss Addington, how much do I owe you?" she said.

Augusta shook her head. "You don't owe me a thing, Della."

"I insist."

"You hired me to save Dr. Ben Bradford's life and I failed. You owe me nothing."

"Not even expenses?"

"No. Not even expenses."

Della drew the bag closed again. "Then I'll be on my way," she said. She hesitated and then said, "I'm sorry about what happened."

"So am I," Augusta said.

Della Stark returned to the surrey, and Manuel Garcia said to Augusta, "Black clouds ahead for Miss Della, I think."

"I'm sorry," Augusta said. "I had hoped for something better."

The vaquero nodded. "After she weds Don Miguel, I will ride on."

"I suspect Della will be very much alone," Augusta said.

"She will not be alone," Garcia said. "Her father will never leave her."

CHAPTER FORTY-EIGHT

"I'm sorry to do this," Sheriff Herman Ritter said, "but it's a lifetime plus a year ban from the city limits, both you and Red Ryan."

"You ain't sorry," Buttons Muldoon said. "I can see it in your face that you ain't sorry."

Ritter sought to soften the blow. "Of course, the Patterson stage will always be welcome, so long as it has a different driver and messenger."

The passengers, including the old Crawford couple who had decided to brave the Apaches, had already boarded the stage, and Red and Buttons along with Augusta Addington stood on the Alpenrose porch, facing Ritter and five of the city fathers, stern-looking gents in black or gray broadcloth with aggressive, Teutonic faces.

The sheriff reached into his shirt pocket and produced a piece of paper that he opened and then read from. "It has also been decided by those present, that this ban does not apply to future Patterson passengers, with the exception of one Miss Hannah Huckabee and her associate, the Chinaman known as Mr. Chang. In the future, any stage bearing the aforementioned will be stopped at the city limits. It has also been determined that Miss Augusta Addington, due to the ordeal she suffered in our fair city, can return to Fredericksburg, *zu jeder Zeit* . . . in English, anytime."

"Hear, hear," the grayest of the city fathers said. "It will always be our pleasure to welcome you, dear lady."

Augusta smiled. "You are very kind. I look forward to my next visit."

Under her riding outfit, she wore a blue and white pin-stripe blouse with a high collar that covered the bandage around her throat. She'd left off the top hat, preferring to let her unbound hair fall over her shoulders in soft waves.

Red thought her a flawless beauty that morning and a fine lady.

Buttons glared at Ritter and said, "Have you finished?"

"Let me see," Ritter said. "Patrick Muldoon . . . Red Ryan . . . banned for life . . . don't ever come back . . ." He smiled. "Yes, I think I've covered it."

One of the city fathers—he wore pince-nez glasses on a thin black ribbon and had a protruding round belly that spoke of a love for beer—said, "We are sorry to be so harsh, Mr. Muldoon, but every time you visit our city sundry disasters befall us. In short, sir, you are a Jonah."

"Well, you needn't worry about that, because I've no intention of coming back," Buttons said. "And I will let it be known to the Abe Patterson and Son Stage and Express Company that we are as welcome in Fredericksburg as a rattlesnake in a prairie dog town."

"I'm glad to hear that, ex-Deputy Muldoon," Ritter said. "I think the per capita life expectancy of our city just went up by about twenty years."

Buttons gathered his dignity around him like a cloak,

ignored that last, and said, "Please, Miss Addington, enter the coach and let us shake the dust of this town off our feet."

As a mark of his displeasure, Buttons didn't showboat out of town but left at a sedate pace, the stage creaking its way toward the city limits.

The reins in his hands, eyes on the street ahead, Buttons said, "You think them square-heads meant all that."

"About us being banned?" Red said. "Yeah, they did. Every word. We're banned for life plus a year. That means we can't come back even if we're dead."

"Well, I won't miss the place," Buttons said.

"How about the beer and the frauleins?" Red said.

"Yeah, that's right, Red, go ahead and spoil things for me."

"Spoil what?"

"My determination to never set foot in that burg again."

"Maybe you'll be able to go back one day," Red said. "You could go in disguise like the holy monks."

"Wear a robe?"

"Heck, no, just grow a beard."

Buttons slapped the reins, smiling, his good humor restored. "Now you're talking sense," he said.

CHAPTER FORTY-NINE

Buttons Muldoon had changed horses three times by the time the dusty stage reached Kickapoo Springs station under a clear morning sky. San Angelo lay about twenty miles of good road ahead of him, hilly grasslands on either side of the track with scattered groves of trees and wide prairie basins many miles in extent.

As Jim Moore and his sons helped Buttons change the team, the manager said, "I hear tell Smiler Thurmond and Jonah Halton are back in this neck of the woods."

"Damn that man," Buttons said. "He keeps turning up like a bad penny."

"The word is he and Halton held up a Wells Fargo stage and robbed twenty thousand dollars from the strongbox," Moore said. "That's the story a Ranger told me no later than the day before yesterday, and I got no reason to doubt his word."

"Seems to me Smiler will head for the nearest big town to spend his ill-gotten gains," Buttons said. "But there ain't anything like that in this part of the country."

"San Angelo," Moore said.

"Heck, it would take a man his whole lifetime to spend

twenty thousand dollars in San Angelo," Buttons said. "My guess is that he'll head for a burg with snap, maybe El Paso or Fort Worth."

"Well, be on the lookout for him, Buttons," Moore said. "I figure you and Smiler get along, but he's still bad news."

"He knows the Patterson stage doesn't carry a strong-box, so he pretty much leaves us alone," Buttons said. "But I don't trust him. Outlaws can be mighty notional."

After the fresh team was hitched, Buttons stepped into the cabin to roust his passengers. Edgar and Fanny Craw-ford were all worked up as only a pair of old, timid folks can get. It seemed that Mrs. Moore had casually men-tioned that the gunslinging outlaw Smiler Thurmond was in the area.

"I said, maybe he's in the area," Gertrude Moore ex-plained to Buttons. "I didn't say he was here fer sure."

"Oh, Mr. Muldoon, are we in great danger?" Fanny Crawford said.

She was a small, gray-haired, lumpy woman, dressed all in black like Queen Victoria, with a small, nervous mouth surrounded by wrinkles. Edgar Crawford, equally small and just as agitated, had a bristly beard, a few sparse hairs in place of eyebrows and blue, slightly protruding eyes that were quick and darting.

"Will the outlaw rob us of our money and my snuffbox and then shoot us?" Edgar said.

"Buttons smiled. "Put your minds at rest, Mr. and Mrs. Crawford, Smiler Thurmond is far from here. Why, I do believe that right now he's in El Paso or maybe Fort Worth probably disporting himself with fancy women."

"We are not without protection, Fanny and me," Edgar

said. His right hand suddenly dived under the front of his pants and he pulled out a revolver of the largest proportions and waved it in the air. "We have this, by God."

Taken aback, Buttons said, "Where in blue blazes did you hide that cannon?"

"Down my drawers," Edgar said.

"Give me the damned thing before you do yourself or someone else an injury," Buttons said. He grabbed the gun, a rusty Colt Dragoon, capped and ready to go, and said, "I'll return this to you when we reach San Angelo."

"Then you leave us defenseless," Edgar said.

"You were just as defenseless with the Dragoon," Buttons said. "That's too much gun for a nubbin' like you to handle."

"The man at the hardware store in Fredericksburg told me . . ."

"That it's a sweet-shooting gun just so long as you rest it in the fork of a tree before you cut loose."

"Yes, or a fencepost," Edgar said.

"He saw you coming," Buttons said. "When we reach San Angelo, trade it in on a squirrel rifle." He turned to the others. "Now, all aboard for San Angelo."

Red escorted Augusta to the stage, where she sat and immediately reassured the Crawfords that Smiler Thurmond was not the ogre some made him out to be.

"In fact, he can be quite the gentleman," she said.

"I do hope so, dear," Fanny said. She didn't look at all reassured.

Peter Cream the seeds salesman, a gaunt, brown-eyed man with a full beard and bad haircut, said, "There have been many gentleman bandits in history. I can name two off the top of my head, Robin Hood and Jesse James."

"And now you can add Smiler Thurmond to your list," Robert Jenkins, the women's corsets drummer said.

"That remains to be seen," Cream said. "Not that I want to meet the gentleman in person."

Up top, Buttons Muldoon hoorawed the team, and the Patterson stage jolted into movement. Side lamps lit, it reached San Angelo in a dark blue dusk without incident.

Chapter Fifty

Red Ryan and Augusta Addington were married in the Church of the Immaculate Conception in San Angelo. Buttons Muldoon was best man, and Abe Patterson gave the bride away.

Abe insisted on holding a wedding reception at the stage depot where cake and ice cream was served, and the refreshments for the drivers, messengers, and horse handlers in attendance came in gallon jugs. A half-drunk fiddler provided the music, and every booted gent present insisted on dancing with the bride . . . and a few with the groom.

The merriment was well underway and the crowd, with the lone exception of Augusta herself, was feeling no pain, when a shadow fell over the dancers on the floor and the fiddler screaked to a stop.

Red Ryan left Augusta's side and stepped forward to meet the baleful threat, but Abe Patterson, feisty and aggressive, pushed him aside and confronted Smiler Thurmond almost as soon as he stepped through the door.

"Smiler Thurmond, you know me. We go back a ways,"

Patterson said. "This is a wedding here, so do you come in peace or in war? State your intentions."

"I'm here to congratulate the bride and groom," Thurmond said. He raised the burlap sack in his hand that looked as though it held something quite heavy. "And I brought them a present to bring joy to their wedded life."

Abe was suspicious. To mutters of approval, he said, "Why would someone like you, an outlaw and low down, bring a present to anybody?"

"Not just to anybody," Thurmond said. "It's for the bride. Miss Augusta saved the life of one of my men. I may be low down, but that was a favor I won't forget."

"She's now Mrs. Ryan to you, Smiler," Abe said.

"She was Miss Augusta then," Thurmond said.

"Yes, I was, and you are most welcome to our wedding celebration," Augusta said, beaming. "And my, don't you look very elegant, Mr. Thurmond."

The outlaw wore a gray broadcloth suit and a collared shirt without a tie, and he sported a red wildflower in his buttonhole. He leaned on a gnarled walking stick, favoring his left leg that had stopped a bullet during the recent Wells Fargo robbery.

Thurmond bowed. "Thank'ee Mrs. Ryan," he said. "And I brought you this." His eyebrows rose, as though he'd just remembered something and added quickly, "I didn't steal it. I bought it."

"I'm sure you did," Augusta said, smiling. She wore a pale blue gauze scarf around her scarred neck, but Thurmond would later say that she was the prettiest bride he'd ever seen in the state of Texas. He put his hand in the sack and said, almost shyly, "Well, here it is."

Thurmond produced a metal box about the size and

shape of a Texas lawbook that seemed to be gold-plated. The box was also decorated with enameled panels of colorful woodland scenes, and Augusta smiled and exclaimed, "How pretty!"

"Now watch," Thurmond said.

He pressed something at the back of the box and part of the lid popped open and a little silver bird appeared. The bird's wings flapped up and down, its beak open and closed and its tail fluttered . . . and it trilled a birdsong for about twenty seconds before the lid closed and it vanished into the box.

Augusta laughed and clapped her hands. "It's beautiful," she said. She kissed Thurmond on his lean cheek. "A wonderful wedding present."

"I'll show you the key and how it works," Thurmond said. He actually grinned.

Buttons Muldoon was sufficiently moved by this scene to say, "Smiler, you're a credit to your profession. Not only because you don't rob the Patterson stage, but because you played the gentleman's part today and brought the happy couple a musical box."

Red Ryan agreed and ordered whiskey and cigars all round.

"Happy?" he said to Augusta.

"Perfectly happy," his bride said. "And you?"

"The happiest day of my life," Red said.

Now there are some revisionist historians who say the marriage between Red Ryan and Augusta Addington was one of convenience between an emotionally and physically scarred woman and a wild, womanizing shotgun messenger who knew the spread of the railroads would soon put the stage lines out of business. They say Red realized that it was time to settle down and find a new occupation and that Augusta, whom he'd only known for a short time, was merely a convenience, a stepping-stone to the future he envisioned for himself. Of course, that means their love was a lie. But if this is true, then it should be said here that the lie grew less of a lie with every passing year of the long, happy, and productive life they were destined to spend together.

EPILOGUE

Red Ryan rode shotgun messenger for a year after he married Augusta Addington, who resigned from the Pinkerton Detective Agency on her wedding day. They later opened a bar and restaurant in San Angelo and prospered. Their descendants live in the area to this day.

Patrick "Buttons" Muldoon continued working as a stage driver until Abe Patterson sold the business in 1899. Buttons later worked as a laborer on the Panama Canal and died there of yellow fever in 1908 on his fifty-third birthday.

Della Stark married Don Miquel de Serra in 1884 and within a year he died from the accidental discharge of a shotgun he was cleaning. Della never remarried, sold her land in the early 1900s, and later became active in the Suffragette movement. She died in 1940 in New York.

Herman Ritter was not reelected as sheriff and entered politics and no more of him is known.

Smiler Thurmond was lynched for a horse thief in the Oklahoma Territory in 1896. He committed one crime too many.

In 1928 a woman claiming to be Effie Bell tried to sell

her memoir, *I Wed an Apache War Chief*, to Adolph Zukor, the head of Paramount Pictures. But nothing ever became of it, and the woman claiming to be Effie soon vanished from history.

Nothing is known of gun vaquero Manuel Garcia.

During World War 1, Ernest Walzer, the Englishman who hired the four assassins to kill Dr. Ben Bradford, became a multimillionaire selling arms to both sides. He lived to the ripe old age of 103, and his career proves that sometimes crime does pay.

And now a word about Honeysuckle Cairns. In 1889 she joined a traveling circus as the Fat Lady and after five years on the road retired and married strongman Louis St. Cyr, the French Hercules. The pair later explored central Africa, then known as the Dark Continent, where St. Cyr allegedly overawed the natives with his amazing feats of strength. Honeysuckle and the French Hercules then tried to repeat their triumph in South America and were last seen in the city of Puerto Maldonado in Peru in 1910 as they prepared to enter the Amazon rain forest. They were never seen again.

*Keep reading for a special excerpt of the next
Western adventure!*

NATIONAL BESTSELLING AUTHORS
WILLIAM W. JOHNSTONE *and* J. A. JOHNSTONE

BY THE NECK
A Stoneface Finnegan Western

Brand new series!

**Introducing a new Western hero in the grand
Johnstone tradition:
a mining town saloonkeeper who serves up justice
like a shot of liquor—150 proof.**

**JOHNSTONE COUNTRY.
BOOMTOWN JUSTICE.**

*Rollie Finnegan is a man of few words. As a Pinkerton
agent with two decades of experience under his belt, he
uses his stony silence to break down suspects and
squeeze out confessions. Hence the nickname
Stoneface. Over the years he's locked up plenty of
killers. Now he's ready to make a killing—for himself . . .*

There's gold in the mountains of Idaho Territory. And
the town of Boar Gulch is a golden opportunity for a
tough guy like Finnegan. But when he arrives, the local
saloon owner is gunned down in cold blood—and
Finnegan makes a cold calculation of his own. Instead
of working in a mine, he'll buy the saloon. Instead of
gold, he'll mine the miners. And instead of getting dirty,
he'll clean up this grimy little boomtown once and for
all—with his own brand of Stoneface justice . . .

Look for **BY THE NECK** *on sale now!*

CHAPTER ONE

Rollie Finnegan, two-decade veteran of the Pinkerton Detective Agency, almost chuckled as he descended the broad stone steps of the county courthouse. Not an hour before, he'd taken no small pleasure in seeing the arched eyebrows of the jury men when he'd been called to the stand.

He suspected it would be a long time before the defendant's city-bred whelp of a lawyer would drag him up on the stand again. Finnegan had seen even more surprise on the pocked face of the inbred mess that was Chance Filbert, defendant and self-proclaimed "Lord of the Rails."

Trouble was, "Lord" Filbert was gifted with bravado and little else. He also liked to swill tanglefoot, and at Corkins' Bar he'd yammered about his impending robbery of the short-run mail train from Mason's Bluff to Randolph. It hadn't worked out that way.

Chance had managed to clamber aboard the train with the help of a fat cohort named Kahlil, who'd somehow mounted the rumbling car's fore platform first. Not receiving any response to their rapping on the door of the mail car—the train was by then cranking along on a flat, the grinding steel pounding for all it was worth and the men inside didn't hear the ruckus—Chance sent two shots at the door handle.

One bullet managed to free up the lock. The second found its way into the right temple of little Sue-Sue Campbell, who had been obeying her harried father, Arvin, one of the two workers sorting mail. He'd had no choice but to take her along on the run that morning, because her mother was deep in the agonies of pushing out a little brother for sweet Sue-Sue, who until then had been an only child. And so would her brother, Arvin Jr., be thanks to Chance Filbert and his eagerness to avoid a legal occupation.

Filbert's greasy, snaky head had entered the car before the rest of him, and though he didn't see the slumped girl to his left, he did see two men in the midst of sorting the mail. With hands full of letters, their jaws dropped, and they stared at the appearance of the homely man and the fat, long-haired one behind him, both with guns leveled.

In court, Rollie wore his twenty-dollar pinstriped, storm-gray boiled-wool suit, and capped it with a matching gray topper, what he referred to as his city hat. He recalled when the salesman had set it on his head while standing before the tall looking glass how much like his long-dead father he looked. He also had to admit that the salesman had been correct—the hat made the suit, and the entire affair looked damn good on him.

Though he'd rather tug on his old fawn Boss of the Plains, like he did most every day, Stoneface Finnegan did not ever miss a court date. He had vowed long ago to always see a case through, from top to bottom, front to back, and inside out. He knew, not unlike his old man once more, if he didn't do everything in his ability to nail shut the door on each and every lawbreaker and miscreant he nabbed, he'd be setting himself up for a month's worth of sleepless nights, all the while grinding down his molars and enduring his ticked-off-with-himself attitude. And at fifty-four, he didn't need that crap in his life anymore.

If wearing a fancy suit and shaving himself close and pink and oiling his hair and waxing his mustache (which he did each morning anyway) helped the prosecuting attorneys send the devils to the prison or the gallows, then he'd tug on the suit and do the job.

There had been ample and irrefutable damning evidence and painful, tearful testimony from the dead girl's parents. There had also been the precise recounting of events by Agent Rollie Finnegan. Despite this, in a last-minute courtroom effort, Moe Chesterton, attorney-at-law for Chance Filbert (and closet dice roller, much to the detriment of his anemic bank balance), had stood before the assemblage, red-faced and thumbing his lapels in an effort to draw attention to what he hoped were persuasive words.

He'd told the crowd stinking of sweat and the weary jury that Stoneface Finnegan had once more put his charge, in this instance Chance Filbert, in a most dire situation. Most dire, indeed. Yes, it was true, Chesterton nodded. And he could prove it. The lawyer's pink jowls quivered and drooped suitably. "Hold up your hands, Mr. Filbert . . . if you are able."

With much effort, the smirking killer had managed to raise his palsied hands aloft. Soon, they dropped to the mahogany tabletop before him and his head bowed, exhausted from the strain.

Rollie had rolled his eyes then, from his seat in the first aisle behind the prosecution. Not for the first time in the proceedings did he wish he had let his Schofield have its way with Chance when he'd finally caught up with him in that creekside cave in Dibney Flats. All that nonsense could have been avoided. Waste of time, waste of money.

But the law was the law, and Rollie told himself if he had wanted to break it, he should have taken the owlhoot trail instead of tracking scofflaws after the war. Or gone into politicking, making laws to suit his base whims like those oily rascals in capitol towns everywhere.

Instead, on that thundering, wet morning in the cave two months before, after tracking the outlaws for a day and a night, the snout of Rollie's Schofield parted the desiccated viny roots draping the entrance. It was then he'd seen Chance Filbert seated inside on a low boulder. He'd watched the oily man a moment, uncertain of Kahlil's whereabouts in the dim hole. The close air, scented of warm muck, had forced thoughts of thick, slow snakes and crawling things.

Rollie had seen Chance and fat Kahlil ride there with intent, then dismount, tie their horses, and enter the cave. They'd lugged in what they made off with from the train, a small arch-top wooden trunk and a squat strongbox wrapped in riveted strap steel. They'd left their horses lashed to a low, jutting branch, saddled and without reach of water. The poor beasts swished and nipped and stamped at a plague of biting flies.

For minutes, Rollie had wondered if Chance was the

only man alive in the cave. Of the two, Rollie had seen only Chance venture out with increasing frequency as the hours dragged by. He'd poked his malformed face between the mossy vines, then satisfied he was not surrounded, would saunter out more loosely each time, limbered, no doubt, by drink. Of Kahlil, there had been no sight or sound.

Unless the man had a steel bladder or there was a back entrance to the cave, which from Rollie's reconnoiter of the region didn't seem likely, he bet himself a bottle of Kentucky's finest that Chance had knifed his slop-gutted partner.

Rollie had won the bet when he'd looked inside and saw a massive, unmoving dark form off to the left. Not even snoring. To his right and babbling in a whiskey stupor, Chance sat atop that boulder before the flop-topped trunk, torn papers all about the muck-rock floor—intimate letters unlikely to make it to their destinations, orders for goods long saved for by some lonely bachelor dirt farmer or farmwife helpmate, or perhaps awaited countersigned deeds to land and goods—all pillaged for cash by the stunted, drunken Chance Filbert.

The strongbox had fared better and appeared to be intact. Rollie hadn't heard shots, Chance's favored means of opening locked things. Maybe he had been afraid of a bullet whanging back at him, though Rollie had not credited the man with such forethought. Likely he was saving the strongbox for dessert and pilfering the easiest pickings first.

Subduing the killer had been a simple matter of pushing his way through the clingy green vines and thumbing back the Schofield's hammer. The hard, solid clicks would make a dead man rise. Except for Kahlil. Rollie had quickly inspected the dark shape enough to note it had indeed been slit open. He'd smelled the rank tang of blood mixed with the dank earth stink of the cave. He was glad he'd decided to keep his hat on his head, tugged low though it was, mashing his ears in an undignified manner. Beat having something with too many legs, or too few, squirming on his head and down the back of his shirt.

"Who you?" said Chance when his vision and his head had together in a wobble.

For a moment Rollie had considered replying, but he was not fond of excessive chatter. *Why speak when you could act?* The unspoken motto had served him well for years. He reckoned it was proven enough to keep on with. He stepped forward quick—one, two strides—while Chance made a sloppy grab for his own gun. His fingertips barely touched the nicked walnut grips as the butt of a Schofield mashed his hat into his head above the left ear.

Chance knew no more until he found himself lashed over the saddle of Kahlil's horse. The saddle and the horse under it smelled bad. Why was he on his dead pard's horse? He could see his own, perfectly good horse, walking along, tied, behind this one. But hold on there. Fat Kahlil was tied to it, dripping all manner of black-looking goo and cultivating a cloud of bluebottles that rose and dipped together as if they were training for a stage presentation.

But even that was the least of Chance Filbert's concerns.

He'd known for certain his head had somehow been cleaved in half and was leaking out what he was certain were the last of his precious brains onto the heat-puckered earth. Nothing less could account for the volleys of cannon fire thundering inside his skull.

The pain doubled as the day had ground on, one pounding hoof step after another. He'd tried several times to speak to the vicious brute who'd ambushed him, but his strangled pleas, which came out as little more than gasps and coughs, brought new washes of agony that ended in his throbbing hands lashed behind his back.

The man on the horse ahead showed him only his back, tree-trunk stiff and wide-shouldered. Who was he, and why did he think it was acceptable to bust in on a man when he'd been tucked away in a cave, tending his own business?

The farther they walked, the angrier Chance became. He'd regained more control of his throat, but the lack of water, a desperate need at that point, rendered his usually loud voice to little more than a hoary whisper.

Several yards ahead of Chance, Rollie had struck a match and set fire to the bowl of his briar pipe, packed full of his least favorite tobacco, a rank, black blend of what tasted like the leavings of an angry baby and a gut-sick drunkard. The thick clouds of smoke would drift back into Chance Filbert's face and gag him. With hours to go yet, Rollie had two pouches of this special blend. He had smiled then, for a brief moment.

In the courtroom two months later, Moe Chesterton had asked Rollie what he thought about the fact that Chance Filbert's hands had been rendered all but useless by the too-tight restraints Rollie favored—smooth fence wire.

"It's a shame," said Rollie.

"A shame," repeated the lawyer. "And, Mr. Finnegan,

would you care to enlighten us as to why you feel this . . . this avoidable affront . . . is a shame?"

"A man without hands is near useless."

"Near useless, but not wholly useless? Hmm. I wonder what you could mean by that."

Rollie looked at Chance. "I assume he has his pecker. I guess he could be of use to somebody. Likely will in prison."

That had caused a stir and Rollie had nearly smiled, but not quite. He knew that Judge Wahpeton, indulgent though he may be, was not inclined to tolerate uproar in his courtroom. His gavel rapped hard and his bushy eyebrows arched like the wings of some great, riled eagle. The courtroom hushed.

"Any talk of prison will be of my own making, Agent Finnegan." The judge surprised everyone by stepping down from his dais and walking across the front of the room. Without warning, he pivoted and lobbed a palm-size brass ashtray toward the sneering defendant. The man snatched it from the air with ease.

Too late, Chance realized his mistake. He dropped the ashtray to the tabletop and fluttered his hands before him like two agitated sparrows.

"I think not, Mr. Filbert," said the judge as he mounted the steps to his dais and cleared his throat before proceeding to pass his commandments to the jury.

CHAPTER TWO

The jury took shy of five minutes to render its verdict.

And so, with Judge Wahpeton's final words, and then the mallet-strike echoing in his head and warming his heart, Rollie "Stoneface" Finnegan stood outside, waiting for a fringe topped surrey to pass by. It ferried a fetching woman wearing a long-feathered hat that looked to be more feather than hat, with a veil that didn't hide the pretty smile he imagined was meant for him. He was tempted to wave her down, strike up a conversation perhaps.

He crossed the street and recalled the reason he was walking west—yes, he could almost smell the heady aromas from Hazel's Hash House. The eatery was two streets over and one lane back behind the courthouse. His nostrils twitched in anticipation of hot coffee and the singular pleasures of Hazel's sticky, sweet pecan pie, a slice as wide as it was tall and deeper than the tines of a fork. He'd earned it, after all, helping cinch tight the legal noose on Chance Filbert's pimpled neck.

The bum's death wouldn't bring back the seven-year-old girl or even Kahlil, but it damn sure made Rollie's day a good one. Then came the pretty lady in the surrey, and he was about to indulge in a slice of heavenly pie and a couple cups of hot coffee before tucking into his next assignment. Yes, the day was turning out to be one of the best Rollie Finnegan had had in years.

He warbled a low, tuneless whistle as he angled down the alleyway that would cut off an extra block's worth of walking.

He never heard the quick figure catfoot up behind him, never felt the long, thin blade slide in. It pierced the new wool coat, the satin lining, the wool vest, the crisp white shirt, the undershirt, the pink skin. The blade was out, then in again for a second quick plunge into his back, high up, caroming off a rib and puncturing the left lung, before retreating for a third slide in.

Instinct drove Rollie to spin, to face the source of this sudden flowering of pain as his left hand shoved away the hanging coat, then grabbed at the holstered Schofield. But he was already addled enough that his gun never cleared the stiff leather sheath. He made it halfway around as the knife slipped free of his back a third time and plunged in a fourth, into the meat of his left thigh.

The spin lacked strength. Hot pain bloomed inside him with eye-blink speed. As Rollie's slow dervish spin gave way to collapse, he saw a dim specter—a thin, dark, wavering flame drawn upward. Red, not from rage but from spattering blood, washed before him, over him, becoming a choking black curtain.

Rollie "Stoneface" Finnegan would not get to taste his sweet pecan pie and hot coffee.